M000198052

THE BAKERY AT CLAMSHELL BAY

SARA JANE BAILEY

Storm

PUBLISHING

This is a work of fiction. Names, characters, business, events and incidents are the products of the author's imagination. Any resemblance to actual persons, living or dead, or actual events is purely coincidental.

Copyright © Sara Jane Bailey, 2023

The moral right of the author has been asserted.

All rights reserved. No part of this book may be reproduced or used in any manner without the prior written permission of the copyright owner.

To request permissions, contact the publisher at rights@stormpublishing.co

Ebook ISBN: 978-1-80508-118-0
Paperback ISBN: 978-1-80508-120-3

Cover design: Leah Jacobs-Gordon
Cover images: Shutterstock, Depositphotos

Published by Storm Publishing.
For further information, visit:
www.stormpublishing.co

ALSO BY SARA JANE BAILEY

The Cottage at Clamshell Bay

ONE

How simple you are, bread, and how profound.

PABLO NERUDA, ODE TO BREAD

The man walked in the way new customers usually did their first time at the Clamshell Bakery and Café, somewhat tentative. Cleo Duvall watched him take in the mismatched tables and chairs, sparsely occupied at this time of day, the local paintings she displayed (all for sale, prices on handwritten tags below), the shelves of coffee, and the mugs handmade by local potters (also for sale), and then he looked over to where she was standing behind the bakery display case, giving her a nod as though he approved.

She gave him a minute to read the chalkboard of possibilities above her head. She wasn't positive he'd never been here before, but there were a lot fewer tourists at this time of year, and while she didn't know everybody, she knew most people around town.

And yet he was oddly familiar. Maybe he had been in before. He was tall and on the lean side. His hair was salt and pepper and shaggy, badly in need of a cut, and his beard could use a trim. His jeans were well-worn, his boots even more so, and the flannel shirt he wore over a gray T-shirt looked like it spent a lot of time there, as did the ball cap on his head. Having made his decision, he stepped forward to stand in front of her counter.

Maybe Cleo wasn't in charge of the tourist board at Clamshell Bay, but she figured it was up to every one of the shopkeepers and innkeepers and restaurateurs to do their bit to make everybody feel welcome. Tourism was their lifeblood, after all. "Hi," she said, with her welcoming smile. "What can I get you?"

She had a rule about these things. When somebody first came in, she acted like she was in New York City or someplace where everybody was a stranger. Once a person had been in two or three times then she got more friendly. Maybe asked where they were from and how long they planned to stay in Clamshell Bay. In her experience, not everybody wanted that friendly, small-town chit-chat. Sometimes they were passing through and all they wanted was a coffee. Sometimes they craved the connection of a small-town café. She wasn't sure yet which he was. Not that many people passed through Clamshell Bay. It was off the highway, tucked in a crescent of Washington State oceanfront. Nobody came here unless they meant to.

They might be staying in a holiday home, docked at the marina and looking for fresh bread, or, and this never ceased to thrill her, they'd read about Clamshell Bakery and Café in a blog somewhere or seen it on an Instagram post and they'd driven out of their way to pick up some of her famous cinnamon buns.

Social media definitely had its dark side, but chatty people who liked to share everything from their vacation photos to restaurant reviews on their Facebook, Twitter, and TikTok accounts, had been a boon to her business.

"Just coffee," he said. Even his voice was familiar. She looked into gray-green eyes and smiled in recognition. He smiled back, but it was wary.

And then it hit her. She didn't *know him*, know him. She recognized him from TV. She'd been in love with Ethan Crisp twenty-five years ago, as had pretty much every female who owned a TV.

She turned to get the coffee to cover her sudden embarrassment. Clamshell Bay wasn't a famous outpost for celebrities who needed to hide away, but they got a few. One of the reasons people came here was nobody in town ever ratted them out. You could walk down the main street and not be bothered, asked for an autograph, or have to listen to some idiot spout about how much they loved your last picture.

Nick Badminton. That was the character he'd played. *Badminton Run* had been a wildly successful comic mystery television show in the nineties. And the lean guy with the shaggy hair had been its star. Heartthrob gorgeous, chosen sexiest man of the year and adored by female fans. Had she seen him in anything since the show ended? She didn't think so.

She turned with the coffee and found him inspecting the muffins inside the case.

"Those sure look good," he said. How far had his star fallen? She didn't know much about the entertainment business, but if someone hadn't worked in twenty-five years, could he be flat broke?

"There's a free muffin with every coffee for first time visitors," she said. He glanced up, obviously surprised.

"Thanks, but just the coffee."

He pushed a five-dollar bill at her and she gave him his change, pleased when he dropped all of it into the tip jar. Not broke then.

"Do you know where I'd find the marine store?" he asked.

So, he was a boater docked in Clamshell Bay's marina. "Motor trouble?" she asked with sympathy.

His smile had lost the cockiness that she remembered from that long-ago TV show. It was self-effacing, wry. "My sailboat needs a new water pump."

Was he planning to install the pump himself? So not her business. "Filbert Marine's not far at all." She pulled one of the local tourist maps from the display case at the end of the counter and quickly drew a ring around Filbert and, in case he didn't own a smartphone with GPS, drew his route from her coffee shop to the store. No one could get lost. It was only a few blocks away.

"Appreciate it," he said. And he took his coffee and left.

Cleo used her few minutes before the next customer came in to bus tables and do some general tidying up. As she walked by a small table by the window, two locals and good friends, Skylar and Annie, were gossiping over coffee and the remains of a cinnamon bun they had split. Skylar motioned her over.

She said, "Was that Ethan Crisp?"

Cleo kept her voice low, not wanting anyone else in the coffee shop to overhear them. "I think it was."

Annie shook her head. "I don't believe it. I used to have such a crush on him in that mystery show. Remember? Where he was the hot detective, or was he a thief? And he was part-nered with that gorgeous redhead who was a psychiatrist. Or was she his CIA handler? It's all kind of fuzzy now. But I remember how much I loved that show."

Skylar nodded, looking blissed out. "Every Thursday night I would tune in to *Badminton Run*."

"He still looks good. Has he been in anything in the last couple of decades? Besides reruns?" Annie asked.

Skylar shrugged. "I thought he was dead."

Cleo gazed out the window where the man they were discussing was walking on the other side of the street in the direction of the marine store. His walk was slow and languid, not a guy with places to be or deadlines to meet. "I guess maybe his career is, anyway."

She headed over to freshen up the station where she kept the milk and the cream, the different sweeteners for all the finicky coffee drinkers who came through her café.

When she'd finished and walked back, Annie called her over once again. Said, "Skylar and I are driving to Seattle tomorrow. We'll do some shopping, make a day of it. Why don't you come?"

She shook her head. "Can't. It's one of my baking school weekends."

Skylar shook her head at her. "You should take it easy. You work too hard. You must work seven days a week."

"And I get here before dawn, every day but Sunday and Monday."

"Honey, you're no spring chicken. I know, 'cause we're the same age."

And they were. Both fifty-two years old. They'd gone to high school together, which they both referred to as the dark ages. Annie was a few years older and had moved to Clamshell Bay two decades earlier to take over the local school. Now they were both retired and, in Cleo's opinion, didn't have enough to do. She liked working, she loved the bakery, and thought if she was going to spend half her day in the café anyway, like these two did, gossiping over their coffee and muffins, she might as well be behind the counter making money.

"Don't say that," Annie jumped in. "What will we do if Cleo ever closes the bakery? It's the heart of this town. How do you think I find out what's going on?"

"Good point. Never mind, Cleo. You are never allowed to retire and that's official."

She picked up the empty cinnamon bun plate. "Now we have that settled, I'd better get back to work."

Annie called out, "What was that line he used to say in every show?"

It came to her right away, as though she were young again, watching the hero of her TV dreams solve another crime with style and corny humor. "It's a sticky situation," she said, half smiling as she heard Ethan Crisp saying the words in her head in that trademark way he'd had. Head cocked, wearing a deadpan expression that made it seem like he and the audience shared an inside joke.

"It's a sticky situation, that's right," Skylar said. "Sounds like one of your cinnamon buns. Maybe you two were made for each other."

The two women were laughing too hard to hear her if she'd bothered to reply. Even if Ethan Crisp had strolled into Clamshell Bay with the express desire of sweeping the middle-aged baker off her feet, like some mid-life Cinderella, she would have to decline. She was done with good-looking charmers. Done and done.

TWO

Ethan took his time getting to Filbert Marine. He wasn't in a hurry. He was never in a hurry. He paused to look about him and take in the latest small seaside town that he would temporarily call home. Clamshell Bay was shaped like a clamshell, depending on what variety of clam you were thinking of. It had the depth and roundness of a littleneck with some nice deep-water moorage for his sailboat, maybe more like a Manila clam. He wondered if the name wasn't from the shape of the bay but because there were clam beds around here. He bet there were. The place had everything he needed for the few days to a week that he would drop anchor here while he fixed the water pump.

He could also stock up on supplies, including bread and coffee from the bakery.

Clamshell Bakery and Café was the kind of place he would once have avoided the way he'd avoid a mob of overeager fans. It was small, with only one door in and the same narrow door to get out again. But, fortunately, time had lessened his fame, so year after year, fewer people remembered the famous detective show as more hits arrived, more new celebrities were made and then they, in their turn, sank into obscurity as he had. He was content for the memories of Nick Badminton PI to fade to a dull, weathered gray like an old boat bleached by time and weather. Better that they faded away altogether.

The woman in the bakery had recognized him. He could always tell. She was the right age, and female, so he hadn't been surprised. There'd been that moment that he was used to now where she'd looked at him with a puzzled expression. Did she know him? And then he saw the second that the knowledge clicked in and she put together his aged, beaten up, middle-aged guy face and the shaggy hair that he usually cut himself when he got irritated with its length. Mentally, she must have compared it with the airbrushed, tuxedo-wearing, seven hefty workouts a week, version of himself as he'd appeared twenty-five years ago.

He'd been pretty, even he could admit that, but nobody was that pretty. A staff of makeup and hair and wardrobe people had made sure he looked his best on camera. Then, no doubt, they did some sort of airbrushing or other magic to buff him up even more for the TV public. Still, those few crazed years had both made him rich and showed him that the life of a celebrity wasn't for him. He'd got out when the hit show ended and resolutely refused the offers that had initially come pouring in and then petered out. Now that *Badminton Run* was on a streaming service it was getting a newer, younger viewership, but he was a lot older and scruffier than Nick Badminton so it took them a moment to place him.

He wondered which would die first, their ability to recognize him, or him. He kind of hoped it was the former so he'd at least have a few years of complete anonymity.

And that was enough thinking about his death for one morning. He looked around and enjoyed the feel of the sun on his shoulders, solid ground under his feet, and the admittedly excellent taste of coffee in his mouth. He could make a perfectly adequate pot of coffee aboard *Vagabond*, but his brew was never going to compare to that of a fancy barista machine. It was one of the few things he really longed for when he was at sea.

He'd liked that the bakery woman hadn't made a big deal about it when she recognized him. He'd liked her eyes. Green with little streaks of blue and a fan of wrinkles around the edges when she smiled that she didn't bother to hide. Long red hair streaked with gray tied back off her face. She seemed like a woman who knew who she was and quite liked it. And she obviously wasn't going to ask for his autograph or blab around town that a once famous guy was hanging around. She got extra marks for that.

Of course, she might at this very moment be on the phone to all her middle-aged friends, but instinct told him she wasn't. After that startled moment of recognition, she'd treated him like he suspected she'd treat any other customer. There had been that odd moment when she'd offered him a free muffin though. He didn't think it was because he was a celebrity. He had a sneaking suspicion she thought he couldn't afford it.

This was clearly a town that made most of its money during the summer months. There was an old-fashioned candy store that advertised ice cream. A toy store. Three casual restaurants, one claiming to have the best fish and chips in the Pacific Northwest, a claim he would test out for himself while he was here. Gift shops, a pub, a small grocery store of the organic and vegetables with the dirt still clinging to them variety, and then the usual banks and financial planners that would look after the older folks who'd probably retired here. He knew this kind of town. He'd been in dozens of them.

But each had a slightly different character. That was the fun of his lifestyle, he'd sail all the way up the coast and nose into whatever bay seemed to call his name. Though, in this case, he'd deliberately chosen Clamshell Bay because of the marine store.

Following the directions from the woman in the bakery wasn't difficult. He turned exactly as she told him to and then made another turn. He could see the marine store sign at the end of the block. Off the main drag were stores and services that catered more to residents. He passed a knitting and craft store, a dentist, and a pet store. Activity in the front of the pet store made him stop and peer inside the window.

Pushed up against the glass was a cage containing six kittens. They weren't the kind of kittens he normally saw in pet shop windows. They weren't purebred anything, and the sign in the window said, "free to a good home", which made him think these were strays that had been born in somebody's garage or barn or an alley somewhere. There didn't seem to be a mother, just these six bundles of multi-colored fur. Tortoiseshell, he thought they were called. Five of them were playing with each other or poking their tiny paws through the squares of wire that made up the cage. A sixth sat in a corner eyeing its brothers and sisters warily. Poor thing had runt written all over it. It was a little smaller than the others, its fur was a little patchier, and on closer inspection he noticed it only had one ear.

A teenage boy opened the door at that moment and came out holding a plastic bag with three fish in it, which reminded him he had to get to the marine store. He took one last look at the sad little cat in the corner and wished it a good home and then headed on his way. The teenage boy had sent him a cursory glance, and the flicker of interest he was certain was because he was a stranger in town, not because the kid recognized him.

He kept walking. It felt good to stride along. Since he'd probably be here for a few days, he'd have to find out about the local hiking trails. Maybe find a gym. He did his best, but living aboard a 45-foot sailboat wasn't conducive to a regular workout schedule.

Filbert Marine was exactly the kind of marine store he

liked. The sign was an old, white glass one that probably lit up at night, with *Filbert Marine* in faded green letters. There was nothing cute or kitschy about it, not an anchor or mermaid in sight. In the window he saw crab traps, lengths of rope, floats and life preservers.

He walked in and even the sound of the bell above the door made him feel like he was stepping back in time.

It was dim inside and smelled like engine grease, dust and fish. Perfect.

He made his way further inside and saw rows of goods. Fishing gear, engine parts, floats, clothing, and the fittings for a galley kitchen. He looked around for somebody to help him. Standing behind a glass counter that contained all manner of boating accessories and parts was a balding guy who looked to be in his sixties in a gray overall fiddling with a depth sounder.

Ethan went up and said, "Morning."

The guy looked up. "Morning." He didn't stop working, but since he was the only one who seemed to be here, Ethan stated his request anyway. "I need a new water pump, mine's gone south, for a Jeanneau 45."

The guy paused in his activities and looked up at him. "Nice boat. Don't have a water pump in stock, though."

Ethan was not surprised. This was a pretty small marine store, and it looked like it catered to locals and weekend fishermen. "No problem. Can you get one?"

The guy rubbed his hands on a rag and went to a computer. Banged away for a little bit and said, "I can order you one. It'll be here in three days. Maybe four."

"Great. Thanks."

The guy looked up at him. "Name?"

"Ethan Crisp."

Not by a flicker of an eyelash did the guy show any recognition. He wasn't sure if this man had never seen his famous cop show or just didn't care. Either way Ethan was relieved.

He was starting to like this place. It was pretty, they had enough services but not too many, and so far they left a man alone. Not to mention the coffee at that bakery was excellent and so, from the look of it, was the bread.

He wouldn't mind spending four days here at all. While he was there, he stocked up on batteries, got some extra sunscreen and a marine chart. After leaving his cell phone number for when the part was in, he walked back out into the sunshine.

There was a small flurry of activity now outside the pet shop. A couple of little girls with a harried looking mother. Each girl held one of the kittens. The girls looked too young for school. One was taller than the other so they weren't twins. Each of them was cooing away to a little bundle of fur. The mother said, "We'll get them settled for a couple of days, but then we'll have to take them to the vet. They'll need shots and things."

"Can mine sleep on my bed?"

"We'll see."

"Can mine too?" asked the littler one.

"We'll see."

The mom carried a bag that no doubt contained whatever kittens ate, and he could see the furred edge of a cat bed peeking out from a second bag.

When he reached the pet shop, he couldn't help looking in the window. Neither of those girls had chosen the cat that only had one ear. It looked even more forlorn now that two of its siblings were gone. The other three seemed to have all fallen asleep in a furry heap, but the runt sat up watching as though it didn't dare close its eyes.

He really hoped someone adopted that poor little thing soon.

A glance at his watch showed him it was nearly one p.m. so he decided that now was the perfect time to try out the restaurant and see if indeed they did serve the best fish and chips in the Pacific Northwest.

Then, this afternoon he'd change the oil and filter on his boat engine as part of his regular maintenance and do a few repairs he'd been putting off until he was anchored for a while.

The fish and chip place was fine. He probably wouldn't have called it the best fish and chips in the world, or even the best fish and chips in the Pacific Northwest. That was a very tall order. But these were good. Nice, crunchy batter. The halibut was obviously frozen, but that was okay. The place had a nice view of Clamshell Bay, and he could even see his boat from here. The *Vagabond* bobbed serenely in the water, patiently waiting for him.

They'd both be waiting a few days until the water pump came, but he'd manage. Get more maintenance work done, get some exercise.

A group of ladies came in to have lunch at a table near him. He felt the moment one of them recognized him. It was like a flurry inside a chicken coop when a new bird is introduced to the flock. A lot of rustling of feathers and shifting to peer at him while pretending they weren't.

He was used to it. Sometimes people would come and ask him for his autograph and he would try to be a good sport about it. Even though he thought they should get a life if they were still stuck on a TV show that hadn't even been in rerun for nearly a decade, though streaming services had given the old show another run. Now, even younger people were starting to recognize him. He'd sign his name, chat for a few minutes, and then always find an excuse to leave.

However, the women soon got to chatting amongst themselves and nobody came to bother him. He dipped a fry in ketchup and popped it into his mouth. He was liking this town more and more.

After lunch he really felt like a coffee. He could order one here, but there was no barista machine and that pot had been sitting on the warmer since he'd arrived. He could go back to the boat and make himself a fresh pot.

He paid his bill, thanked the young server, and made his way back out into the sunshine. For some reason, he retraced his steps to the pet store and checked on the kittens. One more had gone since he'd last walked by. The forlorn kitten with only one ear almost seemed to feel his presence and turned to look at him out of big, hopeless eyes.

He walked into the pet store. He had no idea why. Some instinct compelled him. Besides, he didn't have a lot to do this afternoon. Why shouldn't he walk into a pet store if he felt like it? So, what if he didn't have a pet. They didn't have to know that.

"Hi there, can I help you?"

A cheerful woman was cleaning a row of fish tanks with a long-handled tool.

"I was just browsing."

Who browsed in a pet store? Didn't people come in a place like this for dog food? Or cuttlefish for their pet bird?

If she thought it was an odd thing to say she didn't call him on it. But she did put down the tool and walk over to where he was standing looking at a wall of flea collars.

"You have a cat?"

He shook his head. "No."

"Dog?"

This could go on a very long time as she listed every pet he didn't own. In order to cut off the flow of conversation he motioned with his head to the cage of kittens. He'd resolutely not looked, but he felt them there. Felt those big, beseeching eyes staring at his back. "Cute kittens."

The woman made a sad face. "Strays. Normally the vet would take them, but she's out of town."

"Yeah. I guess you don't make a lot of money off free kittens."

"Well, the owners do need to buy food and things like flea collars," she motioned to the collars he'd been staring at only a moment ago. "But, yeah. Normally I stock purebreds, and not many of those. This isn't that big a town."

"What happened to their mother?"

He had no idea why he was so interested in a bunch of homeless kittens. He clearly needed to find something to do.

"Who knows? It was probably a raccoon. Maybe a cougar. She could have got run over by a car. One of my neighbors found the litter in his garage, poor things. I thought at least I'd give them a chance."

"What happens if they don't get adopted?"

"I'll drive them up to the animal shelter," she said in a clipped tone.

"Will they find homes there?" He was getting a bad feeling about this.

She looked over at the cage. His gaze followed hers. The poor cat with one ear was looking at him again.

"Maybe."

What did maybe mean? He decided not to ask.

He had to buy something. He was her only customer and he'd feel like a fool if he walked out again empty handed. He said, "I live on a sailboat, but I like to keep some dog and cat treats on board. It's amazing how many people travel with pets." It made sense. And it was a good idea. So, the woman helped him choose a packet of dog biscuits and a bag of liver treats for cats and he headed outside once more, avoiding so much as a glance at the cage of kittens.

He ambled back to the marina and *Vagabond*, which put him once more on the road with the bakery. Instead of making his own coffee, he'd have another cup of the excellent brew at the café. He walked in and found nobody at all in there, just the woman who obviously ran the place.

"Hello again," he said.

"Hi."

He walked up to the case. "I'll have another cup of your excellent coffee, please."

"Sure thing. To go?"

It was nice in here. Cheerful and it smelled of coffee and baking. He'd spent enough time with only his own company. Besides, there was no one in here but the woman behind the case and him. "No. I'll have it in here."

She turned and got down a big, bright yellow ceramic mug that reminded him of something he'd find in Italy. Her body was long and lean, surprising him. Wouldn't someone who worked with bread and cakes all day be rounder?

She turned. "Anything to go with that?"

"Yes. I'll take a loaf of—" He looked up at the racks and realized there was almost nothing left.

She followed his gaze to the nearly empty racks and then back at him. "There's not too much left this time of day. Most people get here pretty early."

He felt like an idiot. He should have thought of that. "I'll take whatever that one is."

"Raisin walnut?"

"Done." He was certain if he toasted it, raisin walnut would taste just fine.

She bagged the loaf and he paid and then sat at the closest table. "You make excellent coffee."

She laughed. "Thanks. But you know what I'm best known for?"

"I sure do. Your world-famous cinnamon buns."

"Somebody read the slogan on my front window."

"Hard to miss. This is quite the town you have here. World-famous fish and chips, world-famous cinnamon buns. I can't believe what I've been missing all these years."

"If you look again, you'll see my sign doesn't say world-famous cinnamon buns. Just famous. And that wasn't my idea. It was the mayor's. It's part of our push to bring more tourists here."

"Hey, I didn't mean to make fun. I think it's great. People should be proud of what they do. Anyway, maybe they are the best cinnamon buns in the world." He gazed carefully at the display cases. There were no cinnamon buns there. He looked up at her and found her green-blue eyes regarding him with amusement.

"Right. You sell out of cinnamon buns early too, don't you?"

"We do. But I'll be sure to save one for you tomorrow." And then she looked all embarrassed, like she was hitting on him or something. "I'm sorry. That is, if you decide to come back tomorrow, and you'd—"

"I'd love for you to save me one. Thanks."

She went back to cleaning the glass on the display cases. He took another sip of coffee. He could get out his phone and check his emails or scroll social media or something, but he didn't feel like it. He felt like chatting. He liked people, liked hearing their stories. Especially when he was traveling on his own. Wherever he went in the world, he found that everybody had a story.

He also made friends easily. Always had. Sometimes it had been a bit of a problem how many women wanted to be his friend, but that had changed as he'd got older.

He started by saying, "This seems like an interesting town."

"Clamshell Bay?" She gazed out her own front window as though she'd never seen the place before. "I suppose so. There's not a lot to it. But we're mostly nice people who live here. The population increases about tenfold in the summer. But off-season, I actually prefer it."

"What do people do around here for fun?"

"Fun?" She stopped cleaning the counter and paused, a white cloth in her hand that was perched on her hip. "There's a movie theater. Our amateur theater troupe may not be the greatest actors you've ever seen, but they're very enthusiastic. That's always worth a ticket. Though they don't have anything on right now, they do most of their productions in the summer when there are more people around. The restaurants are pretty good." She seemed to think harder. "Oh, there's bingo every Friday."

He blew out a breath. "I'm not sure I could stand all that excitement."

She laughed. "People don't come here for excitement. They come for the fishing, beach vacations. Or just to be in a pretty place by the water."

"Plus, there's a marine store."

"Right. You were asking about Filbert Marine. Did you get your water pump?" She glanced at the bag he'd set on the other chair. He didn't share with her that it contained dog and cat treats.

"Nope. It will be four days before I get my new water pump. So it looks like you're stuck with me. At least for a few days. You'll be seeing a lot of me."

"I'll look forward to it."

She suddenly looked down and got busy with the cloth again, as though she'd been too forward.

And yet, here he was, a man all alone. He'd chosen to sit right by her display case and start a conversation. He looked at her again. Asking her out wasn't a terrible idea. He was single. He didn't see a ring on her hand but that didn't mean anything these days. Oh, what the heck, he'd ask her.

"Are you married?"

Now she did blush. Which was kind of sweet on a middle-aged woman. "No."

"In a relationship?"

"You ask a lot of questions for someone who's only been in town a few hours."

"Don't mean to be nosy, just don't want to get beaten up by a jealous boyfriend."

She scrubbed at a spot. "You won't. There isn't one."

"I'm single too." He grinned at her. "If you're interested."

Her lips twitched but that was all the answer he got.

"I'll be back tomorrow. I always like to start a relationship with a woman with a coffee date."

She raised her head at that and her eyes opened wide. "You're asking me on a date?"

"Thinking about it."

She looked like she was trying not to laugh. Maybe not the most flattering response he'd ever had. "Most men wouldn't ask a woman for a date at her own coffee shop."

His lady-killing grin might be out of practice, but he pulled it out anyway. "I'm not most men."

And he'd been in the TV business long enough to know a perfect exit line when he delivered one. He took his bread, his cat and dog treats, and with a casual wave, sauntered out.

THREE

Cleo watched Ethan Crisp all the way out of her bakery, glad he didn't turn around as he'd have caught her looking stunned. A celebrity had asked her out. Okay, he was a washed-up former celebrity but still. She admitted to a small thrill. No doubt he'd forget he'd ever asked her and their "date" would never materialize, but that was okay.

She'd enjoyed the moment.

And then the moment was swept away as two women walked in. One she knew, and one she knew by sight.

Megan Alexander wore her usual uniform of coveralls with a short-sleeved T-shirt underneath. The white canvas coveralls were liberally spattered with paint, wood stain, and what looked like rust. Her dark, curly hair was pulled back in a ponytail tucked through the back of her baseball cap. On her feet she wore steel-toed boots, also liberally splattered with paint. She was in her early thirties and the best painter and decorator in town. She looked down-to-earth and solid.

Beside her was an ethereal creature of delicate beauty. Brooke Mattson was a former supermodel and part-time resident of Clamshell Bay with her husband, billionaire entrepreneur Kyle Donovan.

Brooke wore a simple green sweater over jeans and still looked like a million bucks. On her feet were heels so high they made Cleo's back hurt to look at them. Her makeup was flawless and her blond hair gleamed in a perfect fall to her shoulders, as though it were a magazine image. Even though Cleo had seen Brooke Mattson around town, she was almost certain this was the woman's first time inside her bakery. This seemed to be the day for celebrities.

"Megan," she said warmly, "Good to see you. Are you still coming to the baking class tomorrow?"

"You bet. I'm painting a couple of rooms at Brooke's house and I told her about your class. She's interested in joining too."

Cleo tried not to look shocked. Brooke Mattson did not look like the bread-baking type. She was over six feet and so slender she looked like she kept in shape by punching carbs in the face. Brooke took a step closer and said, in a cool, clear voice, "If there's room." And Cleo immediately felt judgey for making assumptions. Brooke couldn't be forty and her career seemed to be over. Why shouldn't she take up baking?

"Yes, it's going to be a small class, anyway. I've definitely got room." She didn't know how much Megan had already told Brooke, so she said, "Saturday mornings are busy, but it's slow in the afternoon, so we start at noon and go until four. Sunday I'm closed, so I teach from nine until four. We'll make several kinds of bread and cinnamon buns."

"Which is basically what everybody signs up to learn," Megan added.

While Brooke filled out the simple form and paid, Megan walked around the bakery with a critical eye. "Paint job's holding up pretty well," she said, scrutinizing her work. When Cleo had called her in to repaint the bakery, she'd talked her into a redesign that she loved. Megan had painted the walls a buttery cream, reclaimed and varnished the original wood floors, left the brick wall at the back alone, and painted the old tables and chairs in pale green. Now it looked as though the mismatched tables and chairs were intentional.

Megan had even sourced the shelves, made of local cedar, to display coffee mugs, teapots, and teas and coffees for sale. The same rustic wood now framed the community bulletin board that was always crowded with goods and services for sale.

"Is the class held here?" Brooke asked, looking around.

"No. In the back. Come on, I'll show you."

She led the two women into the big kitchen. Pepper, her assistant, was busy preparing dough for the Saturday morning rush. They baked everything fresh each day but saved a lot of time by making the dough the night before and refrigerating it.

"It's bigger than I'd imagined," Brooke said, looking around at the organized chaos. Shelves of everything from different flours to colored sprinkles, racks of pans, the walk-in fridge, the ovens, and the dishwasher. "Do you do all the baking with only two of you?"

"I hire extra people in the summer, but off-season it's mostly Pepper and me."

"She's a slave-driver," Pepper offered, glancing up from the big Hobart mixer. "I do the work of at least three people and only get paid for one."

Brooke looked as though she might call the sheriff but the other two laughed. "Tough gig," Megan said. "I'm always looking for help if you don't mind painting ceilings, stripping floors, and sanding."

Pepper shook her head, looking horrified. "No. I'm good."

"I thought you came in to learn to bake, not steal my assistant," Cleo said.

Megan grinned at her. "I'm good at multitasking."

Ethan returned to his boat with a smile on his face. He didn't know what had possessed him to ask the woman from the bakery for a date but he was glad he had. As he unloaded his purchases, he realized he didn't even know her name. Shook his head for a fool.

Also, he'd forgotten to buy caulking to fix a leaking window. Not sure if the marine store was open over the weekend, he headed back out.

Naturally his journey took him past the pet store one more time. He glanced in the front window. There was only one kitten left now. The runt of the litter. Its one ear twitched as it looked up at him through round, golden eyes that seemed huge in the tiny face.

While he was standing there the woman who owned the shop came up and opened the cage. Oh good. Little one ear was getting adopted after all. He looked around to see who the new owner was but there was nobody else in the store.

She put the cat into a carrier. It didn't protest. It seemed to accept its fate, whatever that might be. The woman came out and then closed and locked her shop.

"Hi," he said.

She looked up at him. "Hi." She glanced at her watch. "I close at five. Did you need something?"

"No. Did the kitten find a new home?" Even he could hear the doubt in his tone.

She shook her head. "I'm taking it to the shelter." She looked sad. "I tried my best, but no one wants the poor thing."

She might as well have said, "I'm going to tie it in a bag with rocks and throw it in the river and drown it."

"At the shelter, will they...?"

"Put it down? Probably they'll have to. It's still a better end than starving to death."

The tiny face looked at him through the mesh and made a sound like a sigh.

"I'll take it." He couldn't believe the words had come out of his mouth.

"Really?" Her face lit up with a relieved smile. "She's perfectly healthy, you know. Only missing an ear. But she could live a perfectly normal, happy life."

"Yeah. I'll probably try to find it a home myself." Because one thing he knew, he did not have room in his life for a helpless kitten. He didn't do obligation. And he most certainly didn't do broken females. Not anymore.

"Do you have cat food?"

He shook his head. "Well, I've got some cat liver treats that I bought from you."

Her keys rattled as she opened the door once more. "Come on in. I'll get you set up." She let him in and snapped the lights on in the store. As she put the carrier down, he asked, "How old is she?"

"About seven weeks. A little early to leave their mother, but they're weaned and eating solid food." She glanced at him. "She'll need lots of attention."

A hundred bucks later, he had food appropriate for a kitten, the name of a local vet, and his very own cat carrier.

And a feeling that he'd done something very foolish.

Before he left, he asked, "Do you know the woman who runs Clamshell Bakery?"

Her eyebrows rose as though it was a strange question. Which it was. "You mean Cleo Duvall?"

"Long red hair? Slim build?"

"Yes, that's Cleo. What about her?"

"Nothing. I wondered what her name was, that's all."

"You have to try her cinnamon buns. They're world-famous."

"So I hear. Thanks. And have a nice evening."

"It'll be better now that I don't have to worry about that kitten."

Better for her, maybe, but as he maneuvered himself, the kitten, and the bags of supplies out of the pet store, he already regretted his impulsive decision.

"Do not get any ideas," Ethan said, as he opened the door of the animal carrier and watched the kitten pop its head out of the opening and gaze around the interior of his boat as though it were about to check into a hotel.

How such a bedraggled little thing could be so hoity-toity immediately amused him. He'd worried that the kitten might freak out when he stepped off the dock and climbed up onto his boat, but no noise at all had issued from the cat carrier.

He'd made his way across the foredeck and climbed awkwardly down into the cabin with the carrier held away from his body so it wouldn't bang into anything. Now he settled it onto the upholstered bench that sat in front of the table. He could see his little friend was shy, so he popped a beer and settled himself at the table with his laptop.

Then smacked himself lightly on the forehead. "And because of you, I didn't get the caulking for the windows." But he did have the name of the woman he'd all but asked out. Cleo Duvall. *Cleo.* Had a nice ring to it.

There was an email from Neil, his contractor in Denver, who wanted to touch base about the construction project. He agreed and within seconds they were talking online on Zoom.

He'd worked with Neil on enough projects now that they trusted each other. Neil didn't try to screw him over, and he'd proven that he didn't keep changing his mind all the time, and he paid his bills on time. It was like dating a lot of flaky women and finally discovering a sensible one. Having that thought made him think of Cleo, the baker. She looked like a sensible woman. She had the look about her that life hadn't always been kind. She'd been kicked around a little and survived. Not many people got to middle age without getting taken into a back alley and dealt with by fate until they were left crumpled in a heap, but she'd hauled herself up again. She looked like someone who faced each day not just with grim determination to get through it, but with something he didn't see very often. It might have been joy.

"I sent you the new budget figures to fix the dry rot. Did you get them?"

"Yeah. Got them right here." He dragged his mind away from the bakery and back to the project at hand.

They chatted on for a few more minutes about progress and building permits.

He was so engrossed in the conversation he didn't even notice that the kitten had dared its way out of the cage and, with the usual curiosity of a cat, had climbed up onto his lap. He nearly jumped when he felt as though tiny needles were digging into his thighs. He looked down and there was the cat staring up at him as though he needed an intense session of acupuncture.

He stroked the kitten behind its one ear, and then went back to supply lists and wage sheets.

"They're wondering about a grand opening. What do you think?"

Even though he knew Neil would love the extra publicity, the resigned tone in his contractor's voice indicated he already knew what Ethan's answer would be.

"That's a hard no."

Neil cracked a grin. "A guy can ask. And keep asking."

"You're never going to get a different answer."

Neil was about to come back with no doubt another sarcastic comment when he jerked back as though the computer had slapped him. "Dude. You've got rats."

Now it was Ethan's turn to jump as though his computer had zapped him. "What? Where?" And then he laughed. "Not a rat." He picked up the kitten, which had managed to stretch its little body high enough that it could see over the top of the table and be caught on Zoom. "Meet my temporary shipmate. It's a cat."

Then Neil tipped his head to one side and stared at it harder. "Is it, though?"

"That's what they tell me."

"But it's missing an ear."

"It is. And before you start any rumors, I had nothing to do with that."

"What are you doing with a one-eared cat?"

That was a very good question. "I saved it from certain death."

"Temporary shipmate? Maybe you should keep it."

He shook his head. That was another hard no. "I don't have the right lifestyle for a pet."

"So, what are you going to do with it?"

"I'm going to find it a good home. I even have an idea for somebody who might need a kitten. Somebody who probably won't care that it's not perfect."

"Good luck with that. It's kind of cute though. What do you call it?"

He shook his head again. "Oh no. That's how you get stuck with things. You name them. This little critter will be no name until its new owner picks one for it."

Neil stared at him with a look that might almost have been pity. And then moved on to the rising cost of lumber.

When the call was over, he looked around to find the cat had wandered all the way to the edge of the bench and was leaning its head over as though preparing to jump down to the floor. He knew cats had nine lives but it seemed so small to be jumping that far. He scooped it up and set it on the floor himself. He watched the cat as it walked about sniffing every corner. Did it need to take care of business?

"Hold on there." He dug around in one of the bags and found kitty litter and a tray that was supposed to be the right size for a kitten. He was glad he'd never had kids if a cat was this much work.

He set out the tray and the cat nosed it a few times and then looked up at him and meowed.

"Hungry?"

He got another pitiful, little meow. He took that as a yes. He put the fancy kitten food into the new bowl and filled the second bowl with water. He was pleased to see his temporary shipmate dig right in.

While the cat ate, he figured he might as well make his own dinner.

He threw together a salad from the produce he'd bought at the little grocery store today. Then, shaking his head, he took out the walnut and raisin loaf he'd picked up at the bakery. He'd have to go early tomorrow if he was going to stock up on bread in this town. He'd eyed the selections in the grocers and seen a shelf of mass produced, pre-sliced bread that lasted a long time. Not that he minded those. But when good bread was available, well, he had a fondness for good bread.

He cut a couple of thick slices and some sharp cheddar and made a meal of it. The bread was fantastic. He cut two more slices and more cheese.

The cat looked up at him and mewed and he scooped it up and put it on the couch. Before he knew it, the little stray had climbed up onto his lap, curled up and gone to sleep. He tried not to look down and watch it sleep. He couldn't get attached. But it was one cute little kitten.

FOUR

They were up bright and early, he and the cat. He showered, dressed, and then discovered the cat had used the litter box.

"Smart cat," he said, feeling very grateful for its brains and discretion. He rewarded it profusely and then leaving fresh food and water he climbed up the ladder only to stop halfway as the pitiful meows pierced his heart. He looked down and the little, upturned face with the big, wide eyes and the single, twitching ear got to him.

"Maybe you're right. Maybe it's better if I take you so she can meet you in person." He couldn't be certain.

He piled the cat back into its carrier and made his way once more up onto deck, climbed down onto the dock and walked into town. It was seven thirty in the morning and there weren't too many people about, for which he was grateful. He probably looked pretty strange. A six-foot-three guy carrying a cat the size of a teacup.

His long legs soon took him to the bakery, where he had his first shock of the day. When would he learn? This wasn't a big city. This was Clamshell Bay. And the sign on the door informed him the bakery would not be open until eight in the morning. He set the carrier down and peered in the window feeling like an idiot. The lights were on in back, which he assumed was the kitchen, and while he watched, Cleo came out pushing a cart loaded with breads which she began stacking into the racks.

She flipped on the lights and must have caught him staring. She glanced at the clock and back at him. He shrugged in the classic "I didn't know" expression. Arms outspread, face drooping in sadness.

Even if he'd stuck with acting, he would never have won an Oscar. But he could manage the basics.

She shook her head at him even as she came towards the door and unlocked it.

"I'm sorry," he said before she could tell him they didn't open until eight. "I never thought to check your opening times."

"Well. Since you're a newcomer, I suppose I can make an exception. You'll have to wait for coffee, but the bread's fresh and hot."

"Actually, this is perfect." He said, "Could you step outside for a minute? There's something I want to show you."

She looked quite confused but stepped out. She was wearing a big white apron that wrapped twice around her middle and had a splotch of batter below her left shoulder. Once more he noticed that her body was long and lean, which made him wonder if she ate any of her own products.

"What is it? I have to get the rest of the bread out."

"I bought you a present," he said, enthusing his voice with as much positive energy as he could drum up.

She was surprised, as well she might be, they'd only met yesterday. "A present. For me?"

"I hope you like it." He lifted up the cat carrier that had been sitting on the sidewalk hidden behind his legs and brought it up to her eye level.

He saw the moment she made out what was in the cage and what it was missing. "Oh, poor thing. He's missing an ear."

"It's a she. She's very smart. She would be an excellent mouse catcher for the bakery."

Cleo put her hands on her hips and gave him an "Are you kidding me?" look. "I'd back any mouse against this poor scrap of a runt. Besides, I don't have vermin in my bakery."

"But this kitten needs a good home." He defaulted to a plaintive tone. "If I don't find it one, its little life will be over before it's had a chance to live."

"I'm truly sorry, but this isn't a child with leukemia. It's a stray cat."

"I know."

She shifted her gaze from the cat to his face. "This was the runt of that litter Janet Beamish was giving away at the pet shop, isn't it?"

He nodded. Busted.

"I heard she got rid of them all yesterday."

"All but this one. It's only a baby and was headed for certain death at the shelter. I couldn't stop myself. I said I'd take it. But I can't have a cat. I live on a sailboat."

If he'd hoped to appeal to Cleo's maternal instincts, he'd wasted his time. She looked kind but firm. "I've known loads of people with boats who have cats. It's the perfect companion."

"Yes, but I travel a lot. What would I do with it?"

"You should have thought of that before you adopted this cat."

"I did not adopt the cat. I bought it as a present for you."

She laughed. A bit derisive, but gentle too. "You might have to take it to the animal shelter. They will try to find it a home. And then..." She couldn't finish that sentence, and they both knew where it was going anyway.

She glanced into the bakery window. "I've got to get back.

The bakery opens in fifteen minutes. If you want to come in, you'll have to leave the cat out here."

"But it might get stolen."

"You should be so lucky."

True. "That's okay. I'll take it back to the boat and then be back here again for your real opening time. And a fresh cup of that coffee."

"I'm really sorry. I hope you find it a home."

He had a sinking feeling that nobody was going to want a one-eared, stray kitten. "Me too."

As though the cat had understood every word, it was uncharacteristically silent when they got back to the boat. He set the cat carrier back in the same spot on the padded bench and opened the door, but the cat just curled up in a corner of the cage. It reminded him so much of the way it had acted when its double-eared brothers and sisters had frolicked and curled up together and left it outside the circle.

"Don't worry," he told the little, furry stray. "We'll figure this out."

It looked at him with those big eyes and then curled in a ball and was instantly asleep.

It didn't take him long to head back to the bakery. By this time, it was ten after eight and a line had already formed at the till. He walked into the warm bakery, that smelled of yeast and coffee. He was happy to stand in line. He could stay here all day smelling the scents of fresh bread and cinnamon buns, pies and cookies, and all the other things that were currently filling the display cases.

While Cleo manned the cash register, a young assistant with some impressive tattoos and blue dye in her hair finished loading the fresh stock. They had an efficient system, he noted. Cleo had a friendly word for everybody. She obviously knew them all. And, from what he could tell, everybody ordered the same stuff every day so she probably didn't have to ask them what they wanted, just said, "Your usual loaf of rye and two cinnamon buns?"

"You know me too well," an older gentleman was saying as he pulled out a credit card.

By the time it was his turn, he said, "I hope you saved me a cinnamon bun."

"I promised, didn't I?"

"And a loaf of whole wheat." She popped the cinnamon bun into a bag and the loaf into another and very efficiently made him a coffee while the assistant took over ringing up bread purchases. When she reached for a ceramic cup, he said, "To go, please."

As she handed him his coffee, she said, "It is kind of busy right now."

"Oh, this isn't our date. I'll be back this afternoon for our date."

She looked both taken aback and a bit annoyed with him. "Keep your voice down. And it's not a date."

He felt better already. "Whatever you say."

She bit her lip. "And I'll be teaching a baking class until four."

"Okay. I'll see you at four."

And with a cheery goodbye, he left.

When there was a lull, Cleo reminded her assistant that she had a baking class that day. Pepper looked as though this was the first time she'd heard of such a thing as a baking class even though it was written on the schedule in the kitchen along with their deliveries and beside the work schedule.

Pepper Blake was twenty-two years old and probably as lost in her life as anybody at that age who doesn't know what they want to be when they grow up. She'd put some weird blue in her hair that Cleo suspected came from a Kool-Aid package. But she was clean, efficient, and honest. She showed up pretty close to when her shift was meant to start and Cleo had learned to be grateful, having been through some assistants that didn't have quite so many sterling qualities.

She knew she'd lose Pepper, probably in the next year or two, when Pepper decided what she really wanted. Cleo had once thought she might be that elusive person she'd been looking for. The woman who would be a partner more than an assistant and take over the bakery when she retired.

However, it hadn't taken many months to realize that Pepper didn't have the drive or ambition to run her own business, and was putting in her time. For what, she didn't know. Some day she'd figure it out and Cleo would lose her, but, for now, the arrangement worked for both of them.

Pepper went into the kitchen and Cleo followed her. It was their morning to bake cookies and the smell of chocolate chip filled the air.

"So, you'll be on your own out front, but I'll only be back here in the kitchen if you need anything."

Pepper nodded. "I know."

They worked together, lifting the cookies from the big sheets onto cooling racks. Pepper went back out front, and Cleo did a quick clean and tidy before her class started. By the time noon rolled around, she was ready. She changed into a clean apron and double-checked she had all the supplies set up for her new bakers. There were four of them. In the summer she sometimes ran classes for six or eight, but four was a nice number. The classes wouldn't make her rich, but she ran the courses because she loved baking and she genuinely wanted people to see how easy and satisfying it was to take simple ingredients and turn them into delicious and nourishing breads.

Pepper brought the first student into the kitchen from the café.

Libby Brown wasn't a regular but she'd been in a few times. Cleo thought she'd seen her with a couple of little kids. The woman looked around the kitchen nervously. "I'm the first one. Am I too early?"

"No, you're right on time," Cleo said, with a reassuring smile. Her early bird had a sweet face, and was pretty in an understated way. Cleo put her in her early thirties. She had hair that was neither blond nor brown, but somewhere in between. Hazel eyes, as though they couldn't decide what color to be, either.

"Here's your apron. You can wash up at the sink over there and then as the first one to arrive, you get to pick your spot." She'd laid out bowls, scrapers, and digital scales in four spots around the marble-slabbed workspace that ran down the middle of the kitchen.

Next, there was a knock at the door leading into the back alley. She opened the door and wasn't surprised to find Megan had come by the alley entrance rather than through the café. She wore clean jeans and a gray T-shirt advertising a lumber store. There was a streak of red paint in her hair. With her was Brooke looking ready for a garden party in white slacks and a turquoise silk shell. The women came in, and thanks to Megan's friendliness, soon got acquainted.

They all washed up and donned their clean aprons and then she checked her watch. Her fourth student seemed to be a no-show. It happened sometimes. They might show up late, they might show up tomorrow, they might not show up at all. She was philosophical. At least now she had more time to devote to each student.

Cleo could tell right away they were going to be a good group. She'd discovered that classes were like bread. You took simple ingredients—flour, water, salt, yeast—very different things, but under the right circumstances and the right atmosphere they could bake up into something pretty spectacular. This group of students looked like they might have that kind of magic. Over the weekend they'd all find out if that was true.

As they gathered around the scarred marble workstation, she beamed at them. So tidy and fresh.

"Today," she informed them, "we go back to the very basics. We're making plain, old, white sandwich loaf. But trust me, you've never tasted white bread like this. We'll also make a rustic boule which is basically a round artisanal loaf, and focaccia today. Then, tomorrow, we'll kick it up a notch. Croissants, a rustic European loaf, and then the recipe that probably brings in most of my students, I'll be teaching you exactly how I make my famous cinnamon buns."

"It's why I'm here," Megan said, patting her stomach.

"Bread is magic," Cleo said to her small but rapt audience of budding bakers. They looked so clean and unmussed with their perfect, white aprons. Not a dusting of flour or smudge of cinnamon decorated them. Yet. Three virgins.

She loved this part, because it was heart and soul of what she believed. So she repeated the words.

"Baking bread is magic. You take these ingredients that are nothing on their own and combine them, and have one of the staples of life. Bread might be simple, but it isn't easy. You need your ingredients to be exact. There are lots of recipes where you can throw a little of this and a little of that in and it'll turn out, but bread isn't like that. It's a science as well as an art and works on exact proportions.

"The flour is always proportionate to the water and the yeast and the salt. So, we weigh it. You can use an old-fashioned scale like this one," and she motioned to the Victorian scales that she'd bought at a flea market years ago. Sometimes she even used them for fun. "Or, you can do what most of us do these days and buy a digital scale. They're not very expensive and they'll give you exact measurements. Otherwise, your equipment is pretty simple. People made bread for centuries without electricity, never mind fancy gadgets, and you can too. We're going to do a lot of it by hand so you get the feel of the dough. Yes, a hook on your mixer will knead your bread without giving you muscle strain, but until you've experienced the feel of your hands in the dough and felt it coming to life, you haven't experienced one of the great joys of making bread. And so today we'll make this first loaf completely by hand, although I'll also give you instructions on how to do it with a mixer if that's your preference."

She glanced around and no one looked bored yet. This was a good sign. Some people lost interest the minute they discovered they couldn't make bread at the touch of a button. She went over flours next and then she got them all measuring and set them to work. She worked alongside them because she felt that was the best way to teach. When all her pupils had their ingredients nicely measured and placed in the stainless-steel bowl in front of them, she instructed them to get their hands right in there. She dove her own hands into her bowl to demonstrate. Oh, how she loved that feeling. The water was still puddling as the flour resisted getting too closely involved. The yeast was acting like a guest invited to the wrong party. Refusing to engage. The salt was like a sparkle that got everyone talking. She mixed and squeezed and turned, and encouraged them to follow her example.

Megan got right into it. She was clearly used to working with her hands and having them mucky. She had excellent muscle tone and kneaded the dough as though showing it who was the boss. Libby was a little more tentative, as though she might encourage her ingredients to mix rather than force them, but she was doing an acceptable job. It was Brooke who had Cleo smiling to herself. The woman looked like she'd never got her hands dirty in her life. Her nose was slightly wrinkled and her mouth turned down as though she were doing something absolutely distasteful, bordering on disgusting.

Bakers weren't born, she reminded herself, they were made. In this case, taught.

She didn't say anything, just let them all get on with it. When her dough was nicely mixed, she went around and checked on her students' progress. "Nice work," she said to Megan. She showed the others. "See how her ingredients are already looking like dough. This is very good."

Libby's dough was still very wet. "Remember, you're the boss." Libby glanced up as though this were a completely foreign concept to her. She seemed like she wasn't very often the boss of anything.

She went last of all to Brooke. As she had suspected, her ingredients still hadn't mixed properly. She tried to be encouraging.

"You've got to get in there and squish it around between your fingers. Roll it, turn it, do whatever you need to do to incorporate all the ingredients together. You should end up with a fairly sticky but consistent mess like what's in Megan's bowl."

Brooke looked as though she was being asked to wade naked through Jell-O. But, she wasn't a quitter. At least not yet.

"It's so messy." She pushed her hands back in, and once more that giveaway wrinkled nose. She probably didn't even notice she was doing it. But, with everyone watching her, she tried a little harder and managed to get her dough into a ball.

"All right," Cleo said, going back to her own bowl. "Now comes the fun part. Now we knead." She gestured behind her at the big Hobart mixer. "You can get a machine to do it and save a lot of time and effort, but first you should get the feel of doing it by hand. You may find you love the hands-on effort so much you never bother with a commercial mixer. I find hand kneading is excellent for stress relief. Either method is fine.

"We're working on a beautiful marble slab. A lot of baking instructions will tell you to throw flour on the board to make the kneading easier. We're not going to do that. The whole point of measuring your ingredients exactly is not to end up with a loaf that is too heavy. Or too anything. It will feel wet at the beginning, and that's fine. It's normal. Don't panic. As the yeast begins to work and the flour stands up to its job it will turn into bread dough. Just give it a chance, and help it along a little."

With that she eased her wet lump of dough out of the bowl with a scraper and plopped it onto the counter where it made a sound like a frog jumping off a lily pad into a pond. She began to pull the edges towards her and push them back again, still mixing at this point.

She nodded and the other three followed what she'd done. Libby had made bread before, she could tell right away. This wasn't a foreign process for her. Megan was too heavy-handed, Brooke too light.

They kept working and then she showed them how to knead properly, folding the dough towards her using her palm to push in and away, around and around. Occasionally she'd pick the ball of dough up and throw it back down onto the marble. Megan seemed to have an instinct and was soon kneading the dough as though she'd been doing this for years.

Brooke was the most interesting baker to watch. She began to take on a new personality as her dough gained elasticity and lost its stickiness. She was banging and thumping on that dough as though she were punishing it. That was a woman who harbored a lot of anger. And yet, on the outside, everything about her, from her appearance, to her home, to her marriage, to her position in the community was dazzlingly perfect. What did a woman like that have to be angry about?

Libby was still too tentative. As though she didn't want to hurt the dough or its feelings. Cleo walked over to stand beside her and said, "You can't be a pleaser with the dough. You have to be the one in charge."

She realized she'd said those very words before and received an identical, almost scared gaze back. How would this woman's children ever learn to respect her if she couldn't master bread dough?

She stepped in and showed her, pushing and pulling the dough until it began to change, then she stepped back and gave Libby back her dough.

"Thank you," she said in a soft voice. "I've never been very good at being assertive."

"This is the perfect place to learn."

When she was satisfied that all the dough was sufficiently kneaded, they put them back in their bowls and covered them, and she put them in the proofer.

"Now we tidy up our space and ready for the next task."

She showed them how to use the scraper to scrub all the bits off the marble surface, and then they all washed up and turned to her expectantly.

She wasn't a slave driver. "Now it's coffee break."

They looked surprised, and she said, "There's a lot of standing on your feet when you're baking. Don't be surprised if your legs and your back hurt tonight. I recommend a hot bath with Epsom salts."

And many a night she had spent soaking in a bath after a long day in the bakery.

There was a table in the corner where she sometimes sat to do her paperwork, or to take a break. The table had been rejected as not good enough for customers since it had a broken-off corner. She could have taken them out front for coffee but she'd learned from other baking classes how much they enjoyed the insider's view of the bakery. It was special to sit back here and sip coffee and gossip, knowing their dough was in the proofing oven and the scents of baking were all around them. It didn't matter that their aprons were spattered. Today, they weren't customers, they were bakers.

"What'll you have?"

"Just black coffee for me," said Brooke, the former model. So predictable.

"Tall Americano okay?"

"Yes, fine."

She raised her eyebrows at the other two. "I also have tea if you prefer."

"Could I have a cappuccino?" Megan asked.

"Oh, that sounds lovely. I'll have one too," said Libby. She hoped that was what the woman really wanted.

She went out front to find Pepper and give their order. Since it wasn't busy, she returned to the kitchen and sat down trying not to sigh as she was finally off her feet for the first time since she'd started work at five thirty this morning.

They settled at the table talking to each other, stiffly the way new acquaintances do. "This is great," Megan said. "I've always wanted to bake my own bread. Of course, I'll eat too much of it, but then a day at work for me is like going to the gym."

"What work do you do?" Libby asked.

Megan grinned at her. "So glad you asked. Here's my card." Shamelessly, she dug into her jeans pocket and pulled out a business card and handed it to Libby. She didn't bother giving one to Cleo or Brooke. Cleo had Megan's cards on the community bulletin board inside the bakery, and Megan was currently working for Brooke. "My specialty is bringing historical interiors back to life, so taking a run-down old Victorian and saving the original features but also making the home feel modern and comfortable. I also refinish furniture and paint."

"And she's excellent," Brooke put in. "If you need any work done."

"Thank you," Libby said, rising to put the business card in her wallet. "Our house is quite new, but you never know."

"How about you?" Megan asked Libby. "What kind of work do you do?"

"I was a nurse but after my children came along, I was able to give up work and stay home." She sighed in bliss. "I love being a stay-at-home mom. I'm so lucky my husband does well enough that we can afford it."

"Aww. How old are your kids?" Megan asked.

Libby needed no further encouragement to pull out her phone and show a photo. Megan made appropriate cooing noises at how cute they were while Libby said, "My son, Tyler, is eight. Mia is three."

Megan passed the phone to her and she said how cute they were. They were, too. Tyler was skinny with a big grin and Mia had a sweet expression and her mother's looks.

She passed the phone to Brooke who barely glanced at the screen and mumbled a phrase that had the word "sweet" in it, before returning the phone to Libby.

Pepper brought their coffees on a tray and put the pot of sugar and the milk and cream on the table with them. Cleo had chosen a tall Americano as well and reached for the cream.

Then, like a magician pulling a rabbit out of a hat, she reached over for the plate of cinnamon buns she'd saved specially for this class.

Megan threw a fist in the air. "Score. Your world-famous cinnamon buns. I took this class especially so I could learn to make them."

She laughed. "And you will. Help yourself."

Megan plopped one big cinnamon bun on her plate. The pure white icing caught the light and looked like a ski slope at the beginning of the day.

Libby, predictably, took the smallest bun on the plate. Not that there was much difference between them. It was infinitesimally smaller than the others, but visibly so. What happened that made her think she didn't deserve more?

There was a silence. Brooke was staring down at the plate,

unmoving. Cleo picked up the plate and offered it to her. Still, she didn't say or do anything.

"Don't you like cinnamon buns?"

She looked up and her beautiful face, famous for selling everything from swimsuits to face cream, looked bereft. "I don't know."

There was an emotion in the air, as fragile as a blown bubble that would burst any minute. Megan was already chewing her first bite and she swallowed noisily. The plate still hovered in the air as Cleo didn't know what to do with it. Put it back on the table? Keep offering it? Brooke hadn't said no, and she hadn't said yes, she'd only said she'd never eaten a cinnamon bun before, but in a really peculiar manner that seemed imbued with drama.

Megan turned to her. "What are you waiting for? Trust me, one bite of these and you'll be hooked."

Brooke glanced up and those beautiful eyes looked misty. "I look at that plate and I see three hundred and fifty calories."

She was good. They were closer to four hundred but Cleo wasn't going to add to her emotional burden.

"So? The way we're working today, you'll burn twice that," Megan promised cheerfully.

Brooke shook her head and the light caught the silvery gold of her hair and made the large diamond studs in her earlobes sparkle. "Ever since I got discovered when I was fourteen years old, I've lived with a calorie counter in my head. I look at that bun, any bread, and I see an enemy."

Cleo put the plate gently down onto the table so it hardly made a sound.

She didn't know what to say. No one did. Brooke rubbed her forehead with her eyes closed. "That's why I'm taking this course. I can't keep seeing bread as my enemy."

"No," Cleo agreed, speaking gently.

"I don't even model anymore. Who cares if I get fat?"

More like who would care if she got to a normal weight?

Libby might not be the strongest woman at the table, but she was clearly a nurturer. She said, in the tone she'd probably use to one of her children who'd fallen and scraped their knee, "Anorexia is a disease. But it's curable."

A tear slipped out from under Brooke's closed eyelids and trickled slowly down her cheek. She managed to cry and still look beautiful.

"I'm not anorexic. Not bulimic either. Just programmed. And I need deprogramming."

"Does it really matter? You seem to be at a healthy weight. Maybe you don't need to push yourself to eat things you're not ready for," Libby suggested.

"No. I need to gain weight. My doctor thinks it might be one of the reasons I can't conceive." Another tear followed the first one. "I can't believe I'm telling you all this. I don't even know you people and I'm baring my soul."

In Cleo's experience, bread-making classes tended to do that. Libby, who seemed to have taken charge of this whole situation, was doing a splendid job. She tore off a small piece of the cinnamon bun and put it on Brooke's plate. "Try one bite."

She opened her eyes and laughed shakily. "I must sound crazy. Some days I think I am crazy." She lifted the piece of cinnamon bun and before she even put it in her mouth, she studied it and then she held it under her nose and smelled it as though it was the finest perfume, and only then did she put it slowly into her mouth.

It was like a religious experience. None of them dared say a word. She watched Brooke's expression light up as she chewed. Cleo had eaten hundreds of cinnamon buns, probably thousands in her life, and never had she experienced such ecstasy taking a single bite. There was a lesson to her in this. Stop and taste the bread.

Brooke's eyes flew open again, and she said, "Oh my."

Megan burst out laughing. "You look like you just had the greatest sex of your life."

Brooke reached for the rest of her cinnamon bun. "Don't tell me you've ever had sex that was as good as this."

Then they all started laughing and the upbeat mood was restored.

By quarter to four, each student had a brown paper bag containing their sandwich loaf, a rustic boule, and a rosemary and olive focaccia. The three women left by her kitchen door that led into the alley. Not that she'd asked them too, but she was strangely nervous to think of them bumping into Ethan on their way out. If he even showed up.

"Remember," she said as they were leaving, "Rest well. Tomorrow's a big day."

And with a chorus of thank yous, they were gone, trailing the scents of fresh baked bread and rosemary behind them.

Instead of heading home as she usually would, she went into the bathroom to freshen up.

She had a date with Nick Badminton.

Assuming he showed up.

FIVE

Ethan arrived at four, exactly as he'd said he would. After being on her feet all day, Cleo was ready for the break. Still, it felt weird to sit in the front of her own bakery. But she wasn't going to invite Ethan into the kitchen, so here she was, putting out more cookies.

She tried not to be a vain woman, but on the off-chance that he did come this afternoon, she'd taken a couple of minutes after her students left to freshen her makeup and put on a clean apron.

When he walked into her bakery, he shot her that grin that had transfixed a lot of women twenty-five years ago. Like him, it was older and not as dazzling, but it wasn't half bad either. He'd also spruced himself up a bit. He'd had his beard trimmed and his hair cut, she noted when he took off his ball cap.

He had one hand behind his back.

If he brings that damn cat out again, I will swat him.

However, when he came closer, he offered a single red rose. "For you."

She shouldn't be charmed; it was as corny as hell, but her

insides went as gooey as the topping on her famous cinnamon buns. "That's so sweet. Thank you."

"I haven't forgotten how to treat a lady right."

She took the rose and put it in a water glass and poured water from the big jugs she kept out for the customers to drink. "What'll you have?"

He shook his head. "Could you call your assistant out front?"

She was so stunned at the way he was taking over that she actually did as he asked. "Pepper? Could you come out here, please?"

Pepper came out, wiping her hands on a tea towel and looked a bit surprised, as well she might. She glanced around at the empty tables and the empty café. "What?"

Ethan stepped up. "Your boss is on a date. Could you run the espresso machine?"

She might be young, but she wasn't stupid. "You're taking Cleo on a date in her own bakery?"

"Yes, ma'am. I'm paying too."

The two women stared at each other and Cleo shrugged. He was clearly crazy, but she didn't have anything better to do this afternoon than accept red roses and cups of her own coffee from strangers. Because she was a good sport, she even took off her apron. And made sure her purple blouse, one of her favorites, was tucked properly into her jeans. She walked around the edge of the bakery case and then snorted with laughter as he rushed ahead of her and pulled out one of the wooden chairs at a table, not in front by the window, but closer to the back wall. Where they wouldn't be seen. That suited her just fine.

"Thank you."

"My pleasure. And what will you have to drink?"

"A cappuccino. Pepper could use the practice."

"Sounds good. Make that two."

A very dazed Pepper began preparing the coffee. "And I will have one of those cherry Danishes. And for you, Cleo?"

This was so ridiculous. "I'll have a chocolate chip cookie."

"And a chocolate chip cookie for the lady," Ethan said, as though Pepper hadn't heard her perfectly clearly.

The fizz and splutter of the espresso machine started up and then Pepper looked over at Cleo. "Do I charge him?"

Before she could say anything, he answered, "Of course you do." He pulled out a twenty and put it on the counter. "Here. Keep the change."

That shut Pepper up. She was very fond of tips, and this would be a generous one.

"I'll bring the coffees over as soon as they're ready," Pepper said.

Then he sat down and leveled his still remarkable gray-green eyes on Cleo's face. "You think I'm crazy, don't you?"

"Well, not crazy as in certifiable, but unusual? Definitely."

He put out his two hands. Nice hands, she noticed, but nicked here and there. Looked like he'd been working with them in some fashion. Interesting. "What I really want is to invite you for dinner on my boat. But I'm a realistic man. What kind of woman would go to dinner on a sailboat with a man she doesn't even know? This is your get to know me date. If you like what you see, I hope you'll join me for dinner."

"On your boat?"

"Yes."

She narrowed her gaze, searching for a hidden agenda. "Would you spend the whole evening trying to shove that cat on me?"

"No." His face went inscrutable for a moment, and then he said, "But if you did happen to fall in love with that cat and want to take it home, that would not be on me."

"At least you're honest."

"I always try to be." And something about the way he said it made her think that was true. Their gazes connected for the first time in a serious way. Did he even know how weird that was? A man who told the truth? Or a man who didn't lie? But, she reminded herself, he was an actor. She couldn't take what he said at face value.

However, as wacky as this first date in her coffee shop was, she gave him points for delicacy. He was right. She wouldn't go for dinner with a man she didn't even know, on his sailboat. With no one around? Not a chance.

Their cappuccinos arrived then and Pepper put down plates, the chocolate chip cookie for her, and the cherry Danish for him.

He sipped his coffee and she could see the expression of bliss that crossed his face. "I have drunk coffee all over the world. And this is some of the best I've ever had."

"Thank you."

Then he bit into the Danish and it was crazy but she had a moment of anxiety, wondering what his verdict would be. Would he like it? Would he think the cherry filling was too sweet? Once more he rewarded her with praise.

"I have to say it's not the world-famous caliber of your cinnamon buns, but this is a very fine Danish."

"Well, everything can't be world-famous, now can it?"

"No. You have to leave a few things for other businesses in the world."

They were silent for a moment and she took refuge in sipping her own coffee. For a second, she actually wished a customer would come in so she could have an excuse to jump up and end this strange tête-à-tête with a man she didn't know but felt like she did.

He said, "I know it's weird. You'll get used to it."

"What?" She said it more sharply than she'd intended to.

He looked bashful. "That guy you saw on TV a generation ago was fiction. I'm not that man. I never was."

She was tempted to throw one of the lines that that show had made famous, toss off "it's a sticky situation," but it felt like a cheap shot and she resisted.

She didn't even sing the theme song, which would have been even cheaper but kind of fun. It was running inside her head now, lots of brass and drums and a kicky melody. "Okay, then. Tell me something about yourself, that I don't already know." She'd act like this really was a first date.

He leaned back and seemed to take her question seriously. "I'm kind of a drifter," he said at last. Then cracked a grin. "Well, an actual drifter, since I currently live on a boat."

"Is that your full-time residence?" she asked. Not that she really cared, it just seemed like the obvious question.

"No. But sometimes I like to get away. I love the ocean, always have. I can think there."

She understood so exactly what he meant. She leaned forward. "I feel the same. I've never lived anywhere but on the ocean." Well, that was easy. She'd never lived anywhere but here.

"You're lucky. I grew up in Iowa. Never saw the sea until I was twelve. But it was love at first sight."

"I think I've seen the ocean every day of my life."

"You never get tired of it, do you?"

"No. Because it's different every day."

"Like the face of someone you love. All those different moods and slight changes from day to day that you barely notice and that creep up on you."

"Yes. Exactly."

"How about you? Tell me something about yourself."

What could she possibly tell this once-famous, well-traveled man about herself? "There isn't a lot to tell. I run this bakery. It was my mother's before me. I've lived in Clamshell Bay all my life."

"Really?" He sounded genuinely interested. "You don't see

that very much anymore. Everybody's moving around all the time. Looking for new opportunities. Bouncing around the globe. It's crazy."

"I don't stay here because it's the green thing to do," she said, not wanting him to think she was a better person than she was. "I stay here because it's my home. I like it." Then, lest he think she'd never been out of Clamshell Bay she said, "I went away to college." Oh, who was she kidding? She might at least be honest. "All the way to Montana."

He smiled at her and she felt he was actually listening. "Baking college?"

"No. I went for a business degree. Mom wanted me to have options even though I think we both knew I'd end up working here." She glanced around, thinking how big a part of her life this bakery had always been. "I specialized in small business management so it was useful." And she'd experienced a wider world, enjoyed a college romance that ended when they graduated. No hearts were broken but she had fond memories of Jeb.

"Don't you ever travel?" Again, not judgmental, just curious.

"Sure. I've traveled. But, honestly, after three weeks I'm ready to come back home. I miss the bakery, and my house and garden."

"Huh. I'm the opposite. After a few weeks my feet start getting itchy and my palms want to wrap around a steering wheel."

She was about to ask him about his boat when there was an almighty crash from the kitchen. And Pepper let loose with a string of curses that made Cleo very glad there were no customers in the café.

Ethan jumped to his feet. "Is she hurt? We better go check."

Cleo shook her head. "She won't be hurt. The shelf where we keep extra bread pans fell down. I thought I'd fixed it."

His eyes began to twinkle. "I'm guessing you didn't."

She waved him down. "Sit back down. It's all right. I'll get somebody in."

But he was already heading behind the display counter towards the door that led into the kitchen.

"What are you doing?"

"Relax. If you'd asked me about my hobbies, I would have told you I like to build things. I'm pretty handy."

Completely at a loss now, she stood up and followed him. What else could she do? In the kitchen, the scene was pretty much what she'd expected. The long wooden shelf on the ground, baking pans scattered all over the floor. Pepper looked guilty.

"I'm sorry, Cleo. I forgot that I'm not supposed to grip the shelf when I reach for a pan."

"Not your fault. I'm going to have to figure out a new system."

Meanwhile, Ethan was inspecting the damage. Her wooden shelf had fallen one too many times and split into two. She and Pepper picked up the baking pans while Ethan lifted the broken shelf. "You'll need a new piece of wood."

He set the broken pieces back down and knocked with his knuckles against the wall in a few places. Finally, he said, "I can fix this for you." He stood back and surveyed the wall. Pulled out his phone and as he was typing into the note function, he was muttering, "Shelf brackets, self-tapping screws. Level. Stud finder."

She and Pepper exchanged a glance. Yep, check on that last one.

SIX

Cleo pulled into the long drive leading to her cottage. As she bumped along the pea gravel, she startled a deer who was happily chomping the heads off a clump or irises that lined the drive. It took one look at the approaching car and bounded off into the bushes, still munching. Irises were supposed to be deer resistant but, in her experience, not much was off limits when they were hungry. She couldn't help but love them even though they were a complete pest in her garden.

She got out of her car and stretched her arms up over her head, looking out over her garden to the ocean. She had the pleasantly content feeling she got when a baking class had gone well. These new women were bonding and she experienced the joy of sharing something she loved to do and imparting her skills to people who appreciated them. Whether these women would go on to be dedicated home bakers, she couldn't say, but at least they would know how. And they'd be able to spot the difference between a great loaf of bread and all the rest.

She walked towards her cottage. The late afternoon sun lit up the windows so they seemed more than usually welcoming. She loved her cottage. It had been her home all her life. She'd never have been able to afford a waterfront cottage on five acres if it hadn't been left to her.

After her mother passed away, and she'd taken over the cottage, she'd made a few improvements. She'd painted over the faded red that had no doubt been wildly popular in the 1950s, and now the cottage was a cheerful butter yellow, and the faded and chipped forest green trim had been replaced by a happy color somewhere between lavender and blue. The two-bedroom cottage wasn't large, but then it didn't need to be. There'd only ever been her mom and her, and then briefly her husband and her.

Now it was just her.

The camellia was blooming against the side of the house in happy bursts of red. The clematis that climbed over her front porch was beginning to flower, the purple a nice contrast with the lavender paint.

While her waterfront property didn't feature a walk-on beach, she actually preferred it this way. Her home sat on a bluff overlooking the ocean, with a long ladder of stairs heading down to her dock. The coastline here was rocky. There wasn't a sandy swimming beach, so very few people ever came this way.

More than one person in her life had asked her if she wasn't lonely living out here all by herself. The truth was she loved it. She was so busy all day talking to people and baking that it was a relief to return home. She didn't arrive in the dark. It was nearly always daylight when she got back because she started work so very, very early.

However, beneath her contentment was a twitchy feeling she barely recognized because she hadn't felt it in so long. It was like tiny fingers tapping all over her body, and especially on the back of her neck.

It took her a minute to spot the cause.

Ethan.

He'd walked into her life. Well, technically sailed into her life, and for the first time in a long time she'd seen herself reflected back by an outsider. A stranger. Someone who didn't live the way she and her neighbors did.

The moment she'd said she didn't like to be away for more than three weeks, he'd looked at her with the oddest expression on his face, as though she'd admitted to collecting old transistor radios or had a hobby rescuing rats.

Oh, he'd been perfectly polite, but for a man who'd made his living as an actor, he sure hadn't been able to disguise his true emotion. Not disdain, more confused surprise. Was she incredibly dull for living in the same town and the same house she'd been in forever? Did she seem like a small-town nobody because she hadn't trekked the Himalayas or sailed the Greek Islands?

Well, she wouldn't want to live on a sailboat either with no land under her feet. No sense of tradition or history or place. No roots.

They could not have been more different. She'd pretty much written him off as a rich former celebrity who could afford to be a drifter. And then he'd offered to build her a new shelf. Even the way he'd handled the broken wood and knocked on the wall looking for the studs made her believe he knew how to do it. Okay, it wasn't rocket science, but still, she'd never imagined a man she'd watched catching criminals on television would end up doing odd jobs in her kitchen.

She hadn't been wowed by a man in a long time. Sitting across and having coffee with the guy she vaguely remembered from a hit show had been fun. Like one of those fantasies a person has when they bump into a celebrity they've always admired. It had been pleasant, and definitely fleeting. But when he'd talked about shelving, fetching brackets, a drill and a hammer, the vision had become real. He was no longer a guy she'd once had a TV crush on. He was flesh and blood and promising to fix a shelf in her kitchen.

Making her believe he was a man she could rely on.

That was a very dangerous thing for a woman like her.

She perfectly understood that he was bored and possibly lonely on his boat and wanted some female companionship. He had a few days to kill before his water pump was ready and she was available. No doubt he had a woman in every port. No doubt.

She supposed she should be flattered that he'd chosen a woman in her fifties rather than a twenty or thirty-something. However, if he was already getting under her skin just from buying her coffee in her own café and promising to build her a shelf, then she needed to be very careful about the next step. As in, there'd better not be a next step. Because it was far too easy to fall under the spell of a charmer only to find yourself tripping down the rest of the stairs and landing in a very painful heap at the bottom. She'd done it once. She wouldn't do it again.

She walked in and flipped on the lights. Oddly she imagined seeing this place through Ethan's gaze. Not that she had any plans to invite him here. It was part of the strange mood she was in. The home that felt comfortable to her and so cozy, would probably seem shabby and poor to him. The old wood stove had been in the same corner since before she was born. It still worked, so she didn't see a reason to replace it.

She could probably do with a new couch, but the old, green, velvet one was comfortable and a friend had knit her a beautiful throw that hid the tiny tear.

The coffee table was a roadside find that she'd painted herself with milk paint. Her TV wasn't particularly large and it wasn't plasma, but she did have one. The dining area had a small, square table suitable for entertaining four people. Also painted by her in milk paint. Rustic or pathetic?

Now she was doubting herself. Also, it was pretty clear that table hadn't seen any entertaining in some time. It was piled with mail and bills and magazines. She was usually more tidy than this. She went through to the kitchen. Again, to her it was home. To a discerning jetsetter it probably looked like she pumped her water from a well down at the bottom of the garden. The farmhouse sink had been there long before farmhouse sinks had become popular. She had replaced the ancient, cracked pale green Formica countertop with granite, but she hadn't changed out the cupboards. She'd only painted them. They were solid wood. Sure they didn't have roll-out drawers and there was no appliance garage or slide-out pantry cupboard. But, again with the milk paint, she'd painted them robin egg blue. The best part, the heart of the kitchen, was an island with a kick-ass gas stove.

She decided to get over herself, and quick. She showered in the old-fashioned bathroom. Was it retro or sad that she climbed into a clawfoot tub and pulled a shower curtain all around her? Still, she felt better for a shower, and emerged, not stepping into the worst of her sweats like she usually did, but slipping into a pair of well-worn jeans and a white cotton shirt.

She put on a light sweater and headed outside. The May evening was cool, but her garden was hard at work. Thanks to the deer, rabbits, and who knew what else liked to eat her home-grown produce before she got there, she'd had to fence the whole thing in chicken wire. She opened the gate and shut it carefully behind her. A few more slugs had drowned in little dishes of beer that she put out. She didn't want to poison, so she did what her mother had done and drowned them in beer. At least they died happy.

This was one of her favorite parts of the day, walking along, seeing what was growing, what needed a little help, and harvesting whatever was fresh for dinner. You couldn't do that on a boat.

She picked some very early baby kale, a few leaves of chard that had overwintered, and some of the fresh basil she'd just planted. The smell of her fresh herbs soothed her, as did the timeless sense of things growing as they did year after year.

Having closed the gate into her garden carefully behind her, and taken her harvest into the kitchen, she walked out to the gazebo that faced the sea. This was the best view on her property. When she'd done the renovation, she'd run electricity out here so she could put up an outdoor heater that meant she could sit out here all winter if she wanted to. She didn't need to switch the heater on this afternoon. There was warmth in the late afternoon sun.

She opened the small fridge and took out a lime-flavored sparkling water and sat in the big wicker chair and looked out at the ocean, her feet propped up on the low wicker table. A seal popped up, searched around, seemed to give her a nod and then dove back under. A fishing trawler went by, and then a sailboat. The sailboat made her wonder about Ethan. He'd said he might invite her for dinner on his boat. Maybe she should invite him here for dinner. He must be dying for a home-cooked meal served on dry land.

Even as the thought appeared, she squashed it. Bad idea. Bad, bad, bad idea.

Ethan had his world and she had hers. And there couldn't be two people whose worlds were more different.

Back inside she prepared her salad, sliced a loaf of the seven seed bread that had been left over at the end of the day, and pulled out the cold salmon still left from the fillet she'd cooked up yesterday.

Nutritious, simple, and there was nothing lonely about putting up her feet in front of the TV and watching the news.

SEVEN

They were halfway through the class on Sunday when there was a knock on the bakery door that led to the back lane.

She wasn't expecting a delivery. She glanced around her group of students. "Is anybody expecting a visitor?"

They all shook their heads. She ignored it, thinking whoever knocked was probably at the wrong door when the rap came again, more insistent this time. They were kneading the sweet dough for cinnamon buns and her audience was rapt as she described all the different ways they could use sweet dough.

"Keep kneading," she said. She wiped her sticky hands on her apron and went to the heavy back door. She kept it locked because it seemed a sensible thing to do, even in a safe, small town. The lock made a thunk and then she opened the door. And took a step back when she saw Ethan Crisp standing there.

The power of his presence hit her when there was nothing distracting her but a very uninteresting back lane she'd seen far too many times already. She knew he was gorgeous, but every time she'd seen him before now, she'd been superimposing the older Ethan over the young TV star Ethan. This was the first time she'd noticed him as an extremely attractive, older man. Sure he could do a lot more with himself, but even a little on the scruffy side, he pulled at her. And that made her surly.

"Ethan! What are you doing here?"

He looked a little taken aback at her tone, and maybe a tad embarrassed. "Sorry to bother you. It didn't occur to me that the bakery wouldn't be open on a Sunday."

He was so charming, so endearing, that even though she didn't want to, she found herself warming to him. "The grocery store's open, you could try them. I don't sell bread out of the back door. Especially when I don't have any freshly made."

He held up a hand. "No. No. I'm not here for bread. Though, if the front of your bakery had been open, I admit I would have got some fresh. I'm here to invite you for dinner."

It was the strangest experience. Her heart seemed to leap forward towards him even as some instinct for self-preservation pulled her back, all but shouting the word "No. No!" inside her head.

"Dinner?" She parroted the word back at him, trying to buy herself a few seconds to think how she could answer him.

Even as she stood there feeling like a fool, Brooke came up beside her. "Ethan. I heard you were in town. How are you?"

If Cleo had been shocked to see Ethan at the back door, Ethan was about ten times as shocked to see Brooke Mattson inside the bakery kitchen. "Brooke? This is the last place I'd have expected to find you."

She laughed, but it was an uneasy sound. "I haven't been on a catwalk in a long time."

"I know the feeling. Not that you couldn't still kill it," he said as though worrying he might have dissed her attractiveness.

She laughed again, more naturally this time. "Don't tell me you signed up for bread baking lessons? The class is almost over. I can recommend it, though."

Now it was his turn to look alarmed. "No. I buy my bread. I don't bake it. Not that it isn't a great pastime, but I prefer carpentry."

"That's right. Kyle and I are really excited to get involved in the latest project."

He cast a glance Cleo's way as though he wished she hadn't heard that. What? Why shouldn't all the rich people in the area get together for projects? It was nothing to do with her.

Brooke leaned forward and kissed him on both cheeks. "You didn't answer my question. Why are you here?"

He seemed like a man who wished he was in any location but this one. He was always so sure of himself that the uncertainty made her warm to him. Once more he cast a glance at her face and then back at Brooke's.

"I came to ask Cleo for dinner."

Her surprise was evident but she quickly covered it up. "Dinner? That's fantastic." She put a hand on his arm. "And I can tell you all the best places to eat in town. There are two—"

He interrupted her before she got any farther. "No. Dinner on my boat."

Brooke's beautiful eyes opened wide in her beautiful face. Standing by, watching these two winners in the gene pool lottery, reminded Cleo of how very ordinary she was. "Oh. You're cooking?"

He looked amused now. "I do, you know. My repertoire may not be wide, but the few things I cook, I pride myself on doing well."

"Okay. I'll leave you two to it. But when you get a minute, come by the house."

She stepped back to the table where the other two were not even pretending to work on their dough. Cleo could feel their ears straining her way just as easily as though she could see them.

He leaned in. "Is this as embarrassing as I think it is?"

Oh yeah. "A little."

He motioned his head and she couldn't believe she hadn't thought to step outside into the alley instead of putting on a floor show for three very nosy, amateur bakers. She stepped over the threshold and instinctively glanced up and down the alley to see if anyone else was there. There wasn't a soul, unless you counted a tabby cat nosing around the industrial garbage bins.

"Look. Don't feel pressured. But I'd really like to cook you dinner. No strings or anything."

She'd fully intended to turn him down. But she knew damn well the minute she went back into that kitchen three women were going to be all over her. Besides, she really did want to go. She hadn't had a date in so long she didn't even know where her razor was if she actually wanted to shave her legs. If her dating life was a door, the hinges would be so creaky they would shriek every time the door was opened.

She had to ask him. "Do you have a woman in every port?"

His laugh started deep down in his belly and his whole mouth opened as his head fell back. It was such an infectious sound she found herself joining in even though she didn't think it was remotely funny. When he had himself back under control he looked down at her. And she could see he was still genuinely amused, but it was kind of an amusement directed at himself, not her.

"Oh no. Oh, most definitely no."

Well, that made her feel better. "Okay. Just so you know, I don't do this."

There was a clatter and the sound of something scraping and he turned to look behind him to see the cat had jumped up on top of the trash bin and was trying to claw its way inside. He turned back to her. "You might not believe this, but I don't either."

Oh, how she wanted to believe him. But it was only dinner. "Fine."

"Is there anything you don't eat? Are you vegetarian or anything?"

"I eat pretty much everything. And, I'll bring the bread," she said.

His grin was back. And he looked genuinely excited that she'd accepted his invitation. "I was hoping you'd say that."

"Okay then."

"Right. My boat's on A dock, slip space 7. It's called *Vagabond*."

Of course it was.

"I'll see you tonight."

He turned away and then looked back. "Come to my place around six?"

"I'll look forward to it."

And then she wondered what she'd done. She almost called him back to change her mind, but there was a bounce in his step that made her think that he was actually looking forward to this. The cat jumped down from the trash can and brushed against his legs. She watched as he leaned over to scratch it behind the ears. She realized that she was really looking forward to their dinner date too.

She went back into the kitchen of her bakery and caught the tail end of animated conversation cut short like a cleaver had come down, bang.

Three pairs of eyes turned to her. "Well?"

She put her hands on her hips. "Well, if you don't give bread dough the attention it deserves, it will let you down."

Libby and Megan immediately turned their attention back to kneading their dough, but Brooke wasn't so easily cowed.

"And? Are you going out with him? I would love to have dinner on his yacht. Do you know how private he is?"

She didn't want to be flattered. It was foolish. A woman could get herself in trouble imagining more to a date than was intended. Still, she was flattered. But not interested in being the subject of local gossip. So, she tried to sound as casual as possible, as though former celebrities asked her out routinely.

"It's a friendly dinner. I kind of helped him out with something and I think he wants to thank me."

Brooke gave her a very knowing look and then snorted. A surprisingly unladylike sound coming from someone who'd graced the catwalks of Milan and Paris wearing the most divine gowns ever created in recent history. "You thank a person for a favor by sending them flowers. You don't invite them to a private dinner on your boat."

The other two dared to look up. She shook her head and dropped the act. "I shouldn't even be going. What am I doing? I'm a very ordinary woman, a baker who lives in a little, no-account town. And he's..."

"He's Nick Badminton," Megan finished for her.

"Exactly."

Brooke looked around at them in her apron that wrapped nearly twice around her slim body. "You know, obviously I was never a movie star or anything, but I did mix in that world for a while. Celebrities are people too. I know that sounds like some corny thing you'd see on a T-shirt, but it's true. And the really successful ones develop a hard shell. They have to. Ethan built a lot of walls around himself. For him to let you in? It's something. I don't know what. But if he invited me for a private dinner on his boat—" and then she realized what she was about to say and hastily added, "and I wasn't married," she blew out a breath. "You couldn't keep me away."

"Me either," Megan put in. "And I never even saw the show when I was a kid. I watched the whole series online. You know it's like a cult classic, right? He was smokin' hot then, but even now, that's a seriously hot, old dude."

Libby looked up with something almost like distress in her eyes. "Cleo is a seriously hot dude too." When they all laughed, she blushed and said, "I didn't mean to suggest that you're old. Or a dude. I mean, obviously you're not old. I meant that he'd be lucky..."

Cleo put her out of her misery. "I knew what you meant. And thanks."

Libby tried again. "I was trying to say, he'd be lucky to get a date with you as well."

She felt so much better. Like her mom had given her one of the pretty Band-Aids for a boo-boo. "That might be the nicest thing anyone's said to me in a long time."

They didn't talk about anything but baking until the dough was ready to rise. They were all pros now at scraping the dough off the marble surface and tidying up their area. Now it was coffee time.

They all settled with coffee and today she put out slices of lemon loaf. To her absolute delight Brooke didn't hesitate today. She didn't take as big a piece as everybody else, but she did take one.

They all very carefully didn't comment on the fact.

Megan looked at her and said, "What are you going to wear?"

She looked down at her apron, her well-worn jeans and the comfortable, rubber-soled shoes she wore for work. "What do you mean what am I going to wear?"

"For your date," Megan said, as though she might have forgotten.

"I hadn't really thought about it. A clean pair of jeans, I guess. Some sort of top."

Megan glanced at the other two students, as though seeking support. "Shouldn't you dress up or something? You're having dinner with a movie star."

"No. I'm really not. I'm having dinner with a guy who's in

town for a few days. A drifter who lives on a sailboat." She had to keep that straight in her mind. Ethan wasn't the man she'd longed for all her life and finally stopped believing would one day show up. He was a wanderer. Footloose and fancy-free.

"I can't believe you're being such a snob," Megan said, her eyes going wide. "Who cares where he lives?"

Snob? "No. This isn't about him not being able to afford a house. I think it's the life he prefers. He told me he doesn't like to stay in one place for very long. I may not actually be one of his women in every port, but there's no long-term future here. That's all I meant. If we started anything, I'd know it was only temporary."

Megan looked at her like she was crazy. "Who cares? Long-term is totally overrated. Live in the now. Enjoy him. Sure, he'll move on, but so will you."

Oh, to be that young. And that carefree. She'd never wanted to be the kind of woman who enjoyed a man and moved on. She'd always wanted to enjoy a man and deepen the relationship until it evolved into something permanent. Maybe that's why she'd made such a terrible, disastrous marriage. She'd imposed a pattern where none belonged. If there was ever a guy she should have enjoyed and moved on from, it was Travis.

Well, she wasn't someone who couldn't take advice from a much younger woman. She wouldn't take Megan's casual sex advice, but she was open to wardrobe tips from someone who'd dated in the last decade.

"What should I wear?"

Before Megan could say anything, Brooke interrupted. "It's a casual dinner on a boat. You don't want to wear anything fancy. Besides, he likes you. *You.* Not some phony version of you."

She felt so relieved. "So I can wear my nice jeans and a top I feel comfortable in?"

"Absolutely. You just need me to give your makeup a bit of a touch-up."

"Touch up my makeup? I'm not wearing any."

Brooke chuckled in a slightly evil fashion. "Exactly."

"Oh no. I want to look like myself."

"Isn't that what I just said? You want to look like yourself, but the prettiest version of yourself."

The prettiest version of herself.

"I'll screw it up. I'll put on too much makeup. Besides, most of my stuff's so old, I'll probably get a skin rash and end up scratching all night."

Brooke looked like she'd just sucked on a raw lemon. "No and no and no. I will come over and I'll do your makeup myself."

"You'd do that for me?"

"Sure, I would. What are friends for?"

Cleo loved the casual way Brooke referred to them as friends. Yeah, she and her supermodel pal who was going to pop over and do her makeup. "Okay. If you're willing to paint me, I'm willing to be your blank canvas."

"Do you want to borrow anything from me?" Megan asked.

"Like what?" Megan mostly wore overalls and boots.

"I don't know. A bag? A necklace?" Seeing Cleo's expression, Megan laughed. "I dress up when I go out."

Libby jumped in. "Oh, I have a beautiful Birkin bag. My husband brought it back from one of his trips. I've barely ever used it. I'll bring it over and you can borrow it."

With her luck she'd drop the overpriced handbag overboard. "That's really kind of you, but I don't think so."

"But it's not fair," Libby whined, probably imitating her three-year-old. "Brooke gets to come over and do your makeup. We want to do something too."

"Are you telling me you're angling for an invitation to my makeover?"

"Yeah," Megan said, as though it were obvious. Libby nodded.

She put a hand to her stomach. "I'm nervous enough."

"Exactly why you need some girl time," Megan said, looking around. "Am I right?"

Brooke looked at her and shrugged with an "up to you" expression. Cleo surveyed the eager group and felt like she was back in high school getting fancied up for prom.

Well, if they were all converging on her cottage for a makeover party, she needed to get one thing clear. She pointed to each of them in turn. "All right. But on one condition. Nobody says anything. This whole dating thing is in the vault. I mean it. You know what this town is like for gossip."

The three of them looked at each other and there was a very knowing smirk passing between them.

"What?"

Megan said, "People are already talking. You were seen having coffee together in your own coffee shop when there was no one else around. He bought you a flower."

Libby nodded. "A rose." She all but whispered the word, giving it the same reverence as if he'd shown up with an engagement ring.

She was shocked. "Are you telling me Pepper's been blabbing my business?"

"Not Pepper," Megan said. "Skylar was going to come in and buy some muffins and saw you two looking so cozy in the back of the café that she turned away and warned everybody else not to come in."

She'd wondered why the café had been so quiet yesterday afternoon.

She put her hands to suddenly hot cheeks. "This is so embarrassing. And then when he sails away everybody'll think I got rejected." *Again.*

"No. Every woman in this town is jealous. Better to have loved and lost and all that," Brooke said.

Megan jumped in. "Anyway, it's not a loss. I'm telling you. Enjoy him while he's here. And when he ups anchor, he leaves no strings, no commitments, no broken heart, no demands. You'll be free, with some great memories."

That seemed like such a cynical attitude for somebody so young. However, Megan had a point. If all of Clamshell Bay already assumed she was having a romance, she might as well have one. Maybe she could relax enough to even enjoy it.

After reluctantly agreeing that they could all come to her cottage and help her get ready, Cleo tried to get her wayward students back to learning mode. "We'll make our dough for classic French croissants while we wait for the cinnamon buns to rise." She was a little worried that Brooke might faint when she saw the amount of butter than went into a croissant, but if the former model was counting calories in her head, she didn't say anything.

While the croissant dough rose, they moved on to rolling out the now risen cinnamon buns. Cleo showed them how to roll out the dough into a rectangle. That done, they mixed melted butter with brown sugar and cinnamon until the kitchen smelled like comfort and sweetness.

She said, "It's up to you if you want to add raisins. Personally, I love the raisins and think they really add something. But, up to you."

She found that inevitably people tweaked her recipes and somehow ended up with something individual. It was again one of the joys of baking for her. While she hoped she taught them how very important it was to be specific with the measurements and the proportions, there was always room to play in things like flavorings and toppings, even shapes. For instance, when they made their round rustic loaf, each of them scored the bread in an individual way.

They rolled the dough, stuffed with the cinnamon, butter, sugar, and raisin mixture, sliced it and placed the rounds on a sheet to rise once more. She was pleased at how much more comfortable Brooke had become with having a hands-on relationship with dough. She worked with precision so her buns had a uniform shape. Megan's were more carefree, so there were spaces where the snail was unwinding slightly. Libby snuggled hers too close together, as though she didn't want them to get cold.

Same ingredients, same method and yet the results would turn out as individual as her bakers.

By the time the end of the class rolled around, Cleo was feeling a little freaked out about her date tonight. What had she done? Usually she spent Sunday evenings with her feet up watching a movie on TV. Now, she had a bunch of women coming over to her house, and then she was headed to a man's boat to have dinner. This wasn't her life.

But, today it seemed like it was.

When class ended, she helped each of them pack their treats into one of her cardboard bakery boxes. Croissants flakey and glistening with butter, cinnamon buns plump and decadent. She bagged the savory European loaf each of them had made. Not a single disaster and everyone's bakes had turned out respectably.

After doing a final clean, which they insisted on helping her with, they all left together. They had their bags and boxes of goodies and she had a European loaf to take to Ethan's boat as well as four fruit tarts left over from the day before.

After telling them all how to find her place, though they probably already knew, she said she'd meet them there.

Megan said, "I'll bring the margaritas."

Cleo stopped dead in her tracks. "Margaritas?"

"Yeah. Girls' night."

She shook her head. "I can't drink margaritas. I'm going out for dinner, I don't want to show up drunk."

"You're such a lightweight. Virgin margarita for you then. Which leaves more tequila for the rest of us."

She had no idea whether Megan was joking, but Brooke's words to her were to jump in the shower the minute she got home, to wash her hair and leave it loose. She felt panicky already.

"But I always keep it tied back so it stays out of my face."

"You're not going to be baking bread this evening. Let your hair hang loose."

"Let it all hang loose," Megan offered before cracking a grin and taking off at a run down the alley.

"Watch your cinnamon buns," Cleo yelled after her, as the box of goodies bounced along.

Libby checked her phone and wore a slightly worried expression. "And I'd better run home and check on my children. Make sure the babysitter can stay."

"Hey, you don't have to come."

Libby shook her head. "No. I want to. I'll check on them and then I'll be right over to your house." Then she looked a little bashful. "Most of my friends are mothers with children the same age. It's so nice to talk about something but tantrums and play dates."

Megan drove by in her beat up, old, red truck and waved. Libby walked more sedately to a Mercedes station wagon, and Brooke minced her way in her high heels towards something so expensive Cleo wasn't even sure what the brand was. Was that a Porsche? A Maserati? A Ferrari? Whatever it was, it was silver and looked like it could beat all the other cars on the Autobahn.

Cleo locked up and headed to her own slightly beaten up SUV. It was good enough. Certainly good enough for her limited number of bread deliveries.

As she drove home, an unfamiliar feeling gripped her chest.

She tried to diagnose it as she took the curves of the road with the practice of someone who's been doing it most of her life. Was it heartburn? No. Anxiety? Partly. Finally, it hit her. She had girlfriends coming over to her house to help her get ready for her big date with a man she'd had a TV crush on for years.

The feeling, God help her, was excitement.

EIGHT

When she reached the cottage, she left the door wide open so the women would know to come on in. As she followed orders and undid her braid, she wondered if she was making a massive fool of herself primping for a man who moved in the same circles as Brooke, the supermodel. Her mirror reflected a middle-aged woman with wrinkles, a softening jawline and plenty of silver threads in her fading red hair. She peeled off her clothes and stepped back to see more of her body. She tried to be generous but time and gravity were doing their work, softening bits, moving others south. The thought of a man seeing her naked had her jumping into the shower and wrapping the curtain around herself so the curtain rings jingled as though they were laughing at her. As the water pounded over her she wondered, for about the fiftieth time, what she was doing.

She might have tried to cancel but the women were on their way to help her get ready. She was committed now. She bypassed the bar of Ivory soap for one that Pepper had given her for Christmas. It smelled like lily of the valley and was decadently rich. As she smoothed it over her skin the steamy water began to smell like an aromatherapy session. She breathed deeply, trying to relax. To enjoy the end of a hard day and to thank her tired muscles for holding her up for all those hours. Maybe she didn't have a polished hardbody, but, aging and imperfect as it was, her body did its job well.

She shampooed her hair, applied conditioner, and almost defiantly shaved her legs. By the time she'd toweled off, she could hear voices in her front room. They didn't sound like a bunch of grown women, they sounded girlish and excited and once again she was reminded of prom night.

However, when she came out of the bathroom she saw that Brooke at least was taking this very seriously. The woman had brought an entire suitcase of cosmetics, hair products, and goodness knew what else. She directed Cleo to sit in her big easy chair where the light was best. Megan, true to her word, had a bottle of store-bought margarita mix and another of tequila. In something like panic, Cleo reminded her that she didn't want tequila in her margarita. She was going to keep a steady head on her shoulders tonight if nothing else.

Megan just nodded and shamelessly opened all her cupboards looking for the blender. She found it, and ice, and soon an atrocious racket burst out of the kitchen area.

Meanwhile, Brooke was plugging in a very professional looking blow dryer. She pulled out a round brush and set them aside on the table beside Cleo.

"I'm going to cleanse and moisturize your face first."

"Is that really necessary? I just showered."

"Yes. Beauty begins with the skin," Brooke explained as though repeating a lesson. No doubt because she was. When the banging and crashing of ice cubes being pulverized stopped for a minute, she called into the kitchen, "Megan, bring Cleo a tall glass of water." And she said, "We moisturize from the inside first."

Cleo leaned back and put her feet up on the footstool and gave herself over to this experience. Her life seemed to get crazier and crazier. Now she was being made up by a woman whose face had graced all the glossiest magazines. In a strange reversal it was as though Cinderella was giving the fairy godmother a makeover. And, no doubt the poor fairy godmother deserved it. Her feet probably hurt too.

After something wet and soothing that smelled like cucumber had been rubbed all over her face, Brooke massaged cream into her skin, complimenting her on her fine pores.

"Thanks."

"And while that's sinking in, I'll do your hair," she said. She sounded like she was giving lessons now. And Cleo was perfectly happy to let someone else do the instructing. She'd just lean back and be pampered. It was heaven. Next thing she knew, she had a cold glass of water in her hand, the ice cubes clinking against the side of the glass. She was thirsty and drained half of it. She barely put that glass down and Megan was putting another in her hand.

"Virgin margarita, as ordered. However, if you change your mind, there's plenty of tequila to go around."

"I'm good for now." She sipped it and enjoyed the lemon-lime flavor just fine. Megan had even salted the rim of her glass. "Fancy."

Brooke turned on the blow dryer and for some time there was too much noise in her ears to talk. She was vaguely aware of the other women chatting away to each other until the blow dryer went off and Brooke was putting hot rollers in her hair.

The other two sat at their ease in her small living room, sipping their drinks.

"It's so beautiful here," Libby said, gazing out the window at the view.

"I do love it," she said. Then hastened to explain to them that it had come to her from her mother. She didn't want them thinking she was some property mogul in Clamshell Bay.

"How nice that it's been in your family for generations," Libby said.

"It probably sounds really old-fashioned, but Mom and I were best friends as well as business partners." She wondered what her mom would think of her getting fancied up for a date with Ethan Crisp and was pretty sure she'd approve. Her mom and she had often watched *Badminton Run* together and the Ethan crush was mutual. Her free-spirited mother would be siding with Megan right now, telling her to enjoy the man with no thought to the future. Exactly how she'd ended up pregnant with Cleo. And, as her mother would be the first to say, that had turned out to be the best thing that ever happened to her.

Libby continued. "We haven't lived in Clamshell Bay all that long. We moved around a lot and then we found this place when we were on holiday and fell in love with it." She picked up a round glass fishing float from the table beside her, put it down again. "I don't know how I got so lucky sometimes. Victor is so good to me." She sounded almost as though she were trying to convince herself as well as her listeners.

"That's nice," Brooke said, as she smoothed yet another product on Cleo's face.

Libby pulled out her phone. "This is my house," she said, as though she couldn't help herself. She flipped through the photos on her phone and once more passed it around. They were treated to a view of her children once more, standing in front of a grand-looking new build in a hillside subdivision on the outskirts of Clamshell Bay. A lot of the old townies considered the buyers of those homes the nouveau riche, coming into their pretty seaside town and ruining it with their monster houses. Cleo tried to be more charitable. Everybody had to live somewhere and she was just grateful she'd been lucky enough to be born and raised here.

Libby suddenly looked embarrassed. "I'm sure it's nothing compared to your home," she said to Brooke.

Brooke was using a damp sponge to wipe foundation onto Cleo's cheeks. She glanced over her shoulder. "Money's great, but it's not everything." Her smile was sad. "I'd give up all our money to have two beautiful children like yours."

"I'm sorry," Libby said. "I don't mean to keep pushing my children in your face."

Brooke's movements grew brisk now and Cleo could almost feel the emotion coming through those capable fingers right into her bloodstream. Libby and Megan couldn't see Brooke's face, but she could. The longing was so raw she averted her gaze, feeling as though she were intruding on something very private.

Into the suddenly heavy silence, Brooke said, "I'm thirty-seven years old. I'll be thirty-eight soon. We thought we had lots of time. We started trying for a child when I was thirty-five. Two years ago. I'm healthy, Kyle's healthy, and nothing. Two years." She blinked her beautiful eyes hard. "Now it's fertility doctors and thermometers and sex scheduled like it's a doctor's appointment."

"That must be hard on your relationship," Cleo said.

"You have no idea. Sometimes I'm not sure if it's all worth it. And then I see a baby in a carriage or hear a child in the grocery store calling out mama and my heart breaks." Her voice went husky at the end.

"I'm sorry," Libby said again. She seemed to say that a lot. From her guilty look, Cleo had a feeling she was one of those people who got pregnant the minute she thought about it.

Megan had nothing to contribute to this conversation. She was busy on her phone swiping and texting. Cleo suspected she was online looking for a good time relationship, not a long one. And why was that any of her business? Megan seemed perfectly happy with her choices.

Then she noticed that Libby was also gazing at her phone and beginning to look anxious.

"Is everything all right at home? Do you need to go?"

Libby jumped as though she'd been caught doing something she shouldn't. "No. Everything's fine. The babysitter has no plans tonight, so I can stay as long as I like. It's just that I haven't heard from my husband. Victor flies to Europe and Southeast Asia a lot on business. He can't always check in as frequently as he'd like, but it's been over a week since we heard from him. I know I shouldn't worry, but I can't help it."

Cleo had no idea what to say to that. Megan glanced up. "What does he do that takes him away traveling like that?"

"He's in the import-export business," Libby said. And then as though she needed to provide more information, she added, "He finds opportunities all over the world. And, he runs his own business, so all the responsibility lies on his shoulders. I wish he was home more, but, as he keeps reminding me, it's how we afford for me to stay home and the children to go to any activity they want to." She said again, "I'm very lucky," as though repeating it made it more true.

When Brooke finished Cleo's hair and makeup, Megan said, "Wow, Cleo, you are a babe."

She laughed. "No one's called me that for a very long time."

"It's true, though, you are."

Cleo was flattered, but felt Brooke deserved most of the credit. She did look better than she had in a long time, though. She was so accustomed to keeping her hair braided and out of her face that she forgot how it felt curling free down her back with some effort put into it. Same with her face. Brooke had managed to make her look natural, but...polished, she supposed was the best word to describe her appearance. It was so subtle that Cleo could almost have believed she wasn't wearing any makeup—except that she never looked this good. Her eyes seemed larger, her skin fresher, and her lips softer. The word *kissable* floated through her mind but she ignored it.

Not content with doing her face and hair, Brooke insisted on a preview of Cleo's clothing choices. Now all the women followed her into her bedroom and sat on the bed noisily as she opened her closet door. She imagined Brooke had a walk-in closet that lit up, like something she'd seen in one of those fantasy home shows on TV. But Brooke didn't seem to pity her wardrobe. Instead, she reached in and started pulling things out. "Oh, this is nice with your eyes," she said, holding up a soft green linen top, then turning Cleo to show the others. "What do we think?"

"Color's nice," Megan said.

"Linen creases," Libby added.

They went through a few more shirts but in the end the green linen won.

"Okay, scoot," she finally said, "Or I'll miss this dinner."

They laughed and all wished her well.

"Hey," she called after Brooke. "Don't forget your makeup."

Brooke turned, half laughing. "It's not hygienic to share makeup. That's for you."

Cleo felt terrible. "No. I can't accept—"

"I get so many samples sent to me, still. I have more cosmetics and beauty products than I'll use in my whole life. Enjoy it."

"You look beautiful," Libby said.

"Hot mama," Megan agreed, and the three of them left, walking so close together anyone would think they'd been friends their whole lives.

She heard the three of them crack up giggling about something and smiled even though she had no idea what was so funny. Her, probably.

NINE

Ethan couldn't remember the last time he'd entertained a woman onboard *Vagabond*. Come to think of it, he never had. He'd only owned the sailboat a couple of years. That explained it.

But why Cleo? Of all the people to invite on his boat, why had he chosen her? Brooke and Kyle would have been happy to drop by for a visit. But he wanted Cleo. There was something about her that drew him.

Further than that he didn't feel like going. He put a lot of effort into the salad he made from the freshest greens he'd been able to find at the market.

"Are candles too much?" he asked the cat.

His feline companion seemed to ponder the matter, sitting on the bench seat and watching him in the galley, then she sneezed. He laughed. "Okay. Not dinner candles. I'll put lanterns out. That's a compromise. Says, 'I like to see what I'm eating,' not, 'Come below and check out my cabin.'"

Maybe he should have taken Cleo for dinner at the pub or the fish and chip place. Was cooking her dinner too intimate for a first real date? But he had reasons for preferring to eat aboard *Vagabond*. And good ones. Mostly, he didn't want a lot of nosy locals spying on him and the local baker. What they both did in their private time was their business. Not that this was as private as he might have hoped. He cringed inside recalling that moment when Brooke Mattson had appeared at Cleo's side when he was trying to ask her out. Maybe calling Brooke a nosy local was going too far, but she had seemed pretty interested in her baking instructor's business—and his.

He wondered if she was finding life a little boring without a runway under her feet. However, he doubted she'd gossip about him and Cleo to anyone but her husband. Brooke knew first-hand how hard it was to keep a private life private when your face was plastered on magazine covers or a TV screen. Still, he'd have preferred she not know anything about him and Cleo. There'd been a look in her eye he hadn't entirely trusted. Like she was a matchmaker or something. He really hoped the former model developed a passion for baking, or any hobby but playing Cupid.

He checked his phone a couple of times to see if Cleo had canceled and then remembered he hadn't given her his number. No way she could cancel, then. But she might be a no-show. He found himself anticipating an evening with an interesting woman and really hoped she turned up.

"Think I've been at sea too long," he said to the cat.

He must have been. He was talking to a cat.

Cleo found *Vagabond* with no problem at all. The yacht sported a sleek navy-blue hull, gleaming teak in the cockpit. Ethan was sitting on the deck in the built-in couch with cushions uphol-stered in blue and white striped fabric, obviously waiting for her. Like her, he'd changed into better jeans. He wore a cream-colored denim shirt and wraparound sunglasses that hid his expression from her. His smile didn't, though.

"Cleo. Welcome."

He stepped out of the cockpit and reached out a hand to help her climb onboard. She didn't need the help, she'd been around boats all her life, but it was nice. His hand was work-roughened, though she shouldn't be surprised since he'd told her that carpentry was a hobby. And his hand was warm. If she really let herself think about it, there was a zing of attraction as their palms touched. So, she wouldn't let herself think about it.

She let go of his hand the minute she was up on deck.

He said, "You look great."

And thank you, Brooke. She almost parroted back, "You look great too," but he must know that by now. God had not stinted in the looks department with this one.

Soft music was playing and a vase held a small bouquet of flowers on the table between the built in benches. He said, "I thought we'd have a pre-dinner drink up here, before it gets too cold. Then we'll head down for dinner. That all right with you?"

"Absolutely. Perfect." She handed him the bag. "There's bread in there, and I also put in a little something for dessert."

"Thank you. What can I get you? I have beer, wine, gin and tonic, one of those weird pre-mixed cooler things just in case, and sparkling water and fruit juice. I wasn't sure if you drank alcohol."

That was so thoughtful of him. "I'd love a glass of wine. White if you have it."

"Coming right up." He went down below.

She settled in the comfortable couch and looked around. The view was different from her place, but just as nice. A small fishing boat was coming in and she raised a hand in greeting.

Ethan came out with two glasses and a chilled bottle of wine. The label looked French and expensive. "You did not get that here," she said.

"Even though I don't always remember when bakeries are open, I do know that the wine selection in small towns isn't always the best. At least, not off-season."

"Is this something fancy?" She wouldn't know fancy from... well, she wasn't a woman accustomed to the finest vintages.

He shook his head. "Not fancy. But nice. At least I think so."

He poured them both a glass and handed her one. Tapped his glass to hers so it made that wonderful clink of glass on glass. She knew a lot of sailors who only allowed plastic on their boats and she was glad to find Ethan wasn't one of those. She'd be really careful not to drop her glass and break it.

He went back down below again and came up with a plate of antipasto. She could see that most of it had come from the local market, but a couple of things he must have had with him. There were olives and hummus, thin-sliced charcuterie, cheese and crackers.

"This is nice," she said. She sipped her wine, which was crisp and perfect, popped an olive in her mouth and leaned back. Then glanced around. "Where's the cat? Don't tell me you actually found it a home." No doubt he'd be relieved to be rid of the kitten, but there was something so endearing about him with that little stray that she was almost sorry to miss seeing them together.

Before he could answer, there came a piteous meowing from down below and Ethan shook his head and rolled his eyes heavenward. "As you can hear. She's still here. I'm going to have to teach that cat how to climb a ladder."

To her delight, he got up and climbed below deck to retrieve the small kitten and hiked it back up. The kitten looked over at her with pure green-eyed jealousy and then settled in Ethan's lap, just a tiny bundle of fur with its butt facing her way.

Cleo laughed. "She doesn't like to share you."

He looked at the tiny thing. "I need to find her a home before she gets too attached."

Cleo didn't say what she was thinking, which was it was too late, she suspected for both of them. Instead she stretched her legs out a little farther and sipped her wine. "It's so nice to get off my feet."

Above them the rigging creaked in a puff of wind. She moved her toes toward her and away again trying to work a kink out of her calf. He watched the movement.

"Must be hard work standing on your feet all day."

"Pretty physical, too. I definitely don't need to join a gym."

"Sorry I barged in on your class today. I didn't know."

"That's okay. It gave the bakers a thrill."

"I didn't mean to make things awkward for you," he said.

She thought of Skylar spreading the news that she and Ethan had been seen having a coffee date. No doubt at this very moment, some sharp-eyed local was reporting that she and Ethan were sitting on his boat. Together. Alone.

Well, if she was going to live in a small town, she was going to be talked about. The middle-aged baker having a date with the washed-up actor.

"Did you always want to be an actor?" she asked him. Maybe it was a personal question, but he'd lived so much of his life in the tabloids and celebrity magazines he must be used to it.

He gave a short spurt of laughter that sounded genuine. "It was the last thing I would have chosen for myself. Acting found me."

When she thought about how competitive an industry it was, she found that a little hard to believe. "Acting found you?"

"It's true." He stroked the tiny cat with one finger and she wondered if he even realized he was doing it. The cat did, however, and it looked blissed out, its little body rumbling as it purred. For just a moment she imagined being the one under that caressing hand, and then had to yank her thoughts back.

"I was a carpenter building sets on a sound stage in LA when I was discovered." He put air quotes around "discovered" and made a face.

She shook her head at him. "I'm guessing most of the carpenters who work in LA are hoping to be discovered."

"Maybe. But I wasn't." He told the story like he'd told it a hundred times before. With ease and self-deprecating humor. "This woman had been eyeing me up like she was measuring me for a suit. I don't want you thinking I was a cocky, young stud, though I probably was, but I definitely noticed her watching me a lot when I was working. Anyway, finally she came up and introduced herself. I assumed she was going to ask me for a drink or something, instead she asked if I'd like to do a screen test."

"Wow. That really happened? That isn't some story out of your press kit?"

"It really happened. The guys were laughing and jeering and I thought, what the hell? So, I did it."

"Were you like a natural?" She pulled her feet up under her now, getting more comfortable as she listened to the voice that had mesmerized her from her TV set. She reached for a slice of smoked salmon and a cracker.

He looked at her in horror. "Hell no. I was terrible. Reading lines somebody else wrote while a camera was recording me and strangers watching? Judging? Making notes? It was awful. The director was a man and I knew he wanted to get rid of me right away, but she persisted. They brought in a woman to run lines with me and that was better. The woman turned out to be a local casting director and she got her way."

"Because you were so pretty," Cleo said, teasing. Though he

had been. It wasn't only that, though. She could understand a casting director following Ethan around, making him into an actor. It wasn't only his looks, he had something else. A kind of emotional honesty, maybe. Gorgeous men came and went, but he had something indefinable that she suspected couldn't be taught.

"Anyway, they tried me out with a bit part on another show. I played the younger brother of a killer. I didn't have many lines, I had to go around acting like a handyman. That was easy, because I am a handyman. Though I don't usually do my work half-dressed."

Her lips were twitching and she could feel his young man's embarrassment at being treated like a piece of meat.

"But the pay was great. Ten times what I made in a day as a carpenter. And less chance of banging my thumb with a hammer."

"So, you became an actor."

"Yes, I did. There were a couple of other small parts, and they did audience testing, which I still really don't understand. And next thing I knew, I was Nick Badminton."

"An instant star."

He looked deeply uncomfortable. "Maybe a star, but I was never an actor. Everybody warned me not to read my reviews, and mostly I didn't, but you can't help noticing sometimes what people are saying about you. Especially when they say it to your face. I was stiff, unnatural, and never did understand what getting into character meant. They ended up cutting a lot of dialogue so I had more action and less talking."

"I remember that show so well. I feel like they wrote some of those lines deliberately to play into that sort of awkwardness you had around the language."

He'd been gazing past her and now his gaze locked on hers. "That's very astute of you. I think you're right. They couldn't turn me into Marlon Brando, so they fed me lines that were easy to say and so corny that even Brando would have sounded like he couldn't act if he had to say them."

She'd only ever seen *Badminton Run* from the living room side of the screen, never thought about it from the other side.

Now he'd started talking he seemed happy to continue, and she was happy to let him. "My co-star was, luckily for all of us, a real actress. Tessa Draycott helped me so much. She'd coach me through my lines and made it feel more natural. After the first year the studio was only too happy to hire me acting coaches and all the other malarkey, but by that time the audience had grown used to my style. They call it style when you do something so badly it stands out and people start to love it."

This she understood. "It's like when I overbake bread and call it dark golden."

"My acting was definitely in the overbaked bread category."

"And then the show ended and you never acted again, did you?"

He shook his head. "I didn't."

Then he scooped the cat off his lap and stood, all in one graceful motion. The kitten made a *brrp* of annoyance. He said, "Do you mind looking after the cat while I fire up the barbecue?"

"Not at all."

The cat was less than pleased with this change in arrangements but did reluctantly settle in her lap. Its fur was silky soft and while she didn't get the robust rumble Ethan did, after a minute or two, the cat began to purr softly.

Ethan turned on a small barbecue attached to the rail.

"Do you need some help?"

"I think I can manage."

She watched anxiously at first, but he was clearly more than used to his barbecue. He said, "You probably eat seafood all the time, but I thought I'd do a sort of surf and turf. I found some nice fat scallops at the seafood store, and even I can't screw up steak and potatoes."

"Sounds amazing."

So, frankly, was watching him work. He had an unconscious grace about him and he was still a fine-looking man. It was no hardship to sit here and watch Nick Badminton cook.

He served up dinner and they sat, still up on deck, companionably chatting. She told him about her baking class and how she was hoping to turn out a few more home bakers.

After dinner he made coffee and as it was getting chilly, they drank it down below with the fruit tarts she'd brought from the bakery.

She'd been on plenty of sailboats in her time, but this was more luxurious than most. The galley was like a high-end kitchen, the woodwork gleamed, and the built-in furniture was way more comfortable than most boat upholstery. "This is nice," she said, looking around.

"I like it. My home away from home. There are roomy cabins fore and aft and two heads." Though he didn't open any of the closed doors leading to the cabins.

Even so, as he complimented her extravagantly on the pastries, she began to grow the tiniest bit anxious. Would he expect her to stay? She hoped not. She barely knew the man, and she'd never been a woman who had sex on a first date. Even less so now she was older. He'd been a celebrity and no doubt accustomed to women throwing themselves at him. Did he have unrealistic expectations?

But he didn't put any moves on her. He sat at a respectable distance away and he told her about some of the places he'd been on his boat. It sounded like a lonely existence, but he didn't appear lonely. As though he'd heard her unspoken thought, he said, "It's the one place I relax completely. Now that *Badminton Run* is on streaming services, even younger people are starting to recognize me." He made a wry face.

"The price of fame?"

"More like a mortgage that never gets paid off."

"Would you do it again?"

He put his mug down on the teak table. "I don't think anyone's ever asked me that before." He paused to think. "How do you answer a question like that? If I hadn't taken this road, which would I have taken? Would I still be building sets? Maybe I'd have crewed on big yachts as a way of seeing the world. Impossible to know. But, yes, I believe I'd do it again."

He turned those world-weary but still remarkable eyes on her. "How about you? Would you take a different path? If you'd known then what you know now?"

She opened her mouth to say one thing she wouldn't have done was marry Travis, but, like he had, she wondered how her life would have gone differently. Her marriage was part of the tapestry of her life. A dark thread that maybe helped her appreciate the lighter parts more. Still, she couldn't be quite so certain. "I don't know. I married the wrong man. Do I wish I hadn't?" She gave a soft chuckle. "When he left, I definitely wished I'd never set eyes on him."

"I was thinking about the bakery. It's not like you chose your career any more than I did, if it was your mom's business."

She sipped the last of her coffee, partly to cover her embarrassment that she'd talked about her failed marriage when he'd been asking about her career. She set down the white china mug. "Huh. Like you, no one's ever asked me that before." She tried to imagine doing anything else and couldn't. "I think it was in my blood. I used to love helping out at the bakery, even when I was little. Sometimes I'd sit in the back coloring or doing a puzzle while Mom and her assistant baker worked. I never knew my father. Mom was very independent, a hippy, though she hated labels. She said my father was a commercial fisherman who spent some time in Clamshell Bay and then left before she knew she was pregnant, though I'm not sure she tried very hard to tell him he was a dad. She wouldn't have wanted the interference."

"She wanted you all to herself, I guess."

"I think so. Anyway, I spent a lot of time in the bakery. They'd let me help with simple tasks and always slip me treats." She smiled, transported back to that time. Her mom must have struggled financially, but she never seemed stressed. "No doubt I'm conditioned, but the smell of the bakery always makes me feel like I'm where I'm meant to be." She tried to explain this nebulous concept. "It's part of my roots."

"They're good roots."

A huge yawn had her slapping her hand over her mouth. "I've got to get up early, I should get going."

"Before you go, I've got something for you."

While she'd been worried he was going to try to seduce her, had he had a less flattering agenda? "If you shove that cat at me one more time—"

He put his hands up in surrender. "No. Promise. Hold on."

He got up and went to a closet so cleverly built in she'd have missed that it was even there. He brought out a gleaming shelf. It was made of oak and much nicer than the one that had fallen down in her bakery.

If he'd offered her a string of emeralds she wouldn't have been as excited as she was at a new shelf for the bakery. "That is beautiful," she cried out.

"I'll bring it by tomorrow and install it. When's a good time?"

If the man wanted to be her handyman, she wasn't going to turn him away. "Any time after three it slows right down."

"I'll see you tomorrow."

He walked up behind her onto the deck and she had that awkward moment of wondering whether he'd kiss her good-night, and whether she wanted him to. And what was she, sixteen years old?

He merely said, "Drive safely."

"Thanks for a really nice evening."

And then she left. Unkissed. Did that mean he was trying to take things slow? Or that he didn't find her kissable? She hoped it was the former, worried it was the latter. Resisting the urge to text her new friends because she really wasn't sixteen years old. She just felt like a boy-crazed teenager again.

TEN

The next morning Cleo found her step was lighter and the morning rush was more of a pleasure than usual. Everyone seemed to be in such a good mood. Or maybe that was just her?

She'd had a date. With a former television star. He'd been nice. Regular. If Ethan had been a single man who'd chosen to retire to Clamshell Bay she might be seriously interested. But, just as well, he wouldn't be staying. Still, until his water pump was ready and he left town, she could enjoy spending time with him. He hadn't known her forever like most people in Clamshell Bay, and he treated her like an interesting woman. Made a nice change.

The morning rush ebbed and she sent Pepper out to tidy the tables while she restocked the bread and front bakery cases. A customer came up to the counter and she glanced up ready to take an order only to find Brooke standing there with a very expectant grin on her face.

"Well?"

"Well what?" she said, glancing around to make sure no one could overhear them.

"How was your date last night?"

"Shush." Then, since Brooke didn't move, she was about to describe her date in as few words as possible when the door opened and in came Libby. She looked a little embarrassed as she came up and said, "I ran out of bread."

Brooke turned and laughed. "No, you didn't. You're as nosy as I am."

She had the grace to blush at least, but nodded. "Well? How was your date?"

"You two are terrible."

"Absolutely," said Brooke. "Nothing exciting ever happens around here. You're it."

She threw up her hands in exasperation. "At least come in the back. I don't want everybody in town hearing my personal business."

She hustled them through and then a voice said, "Wait, I'm coming too."

She turned around and, naturally, Megan was coming through the door. She had yellow paint in her hair and on her overalls. She must have rushed out in the middle of a job. Coincidence that all three should show up at the same time? She doubted it very much. Surreptitious texting had been at work, she was certain.

The four of them gathered around the break table in the kitchen. It was sort of nice to have three friends anxious to hear how her date had gone. They weren't here for gossip, she realized, they wanted to know because they'd become part of this odd adventure. She found she was only too pleased to talk it through.

"What did he cook you? Can he cook?" Megan wanted to know.

She described the meal and they were suitably impressed with his culinary skills.

"What did you talk about?" Brooke wanted to know.

"He told me about his career, how he got his start. We

talked about our lives. You know, first date stuff." She paused. "The strange thing is, though, I already knew so much about him." She stopped and frowned. "I made the mistake of asking him why he stopped acting. He never answered the question. He jumped up and started cooking."

"Neatly ending the conversation," Brooke said.

"Exactly. Do you know what happened?"

Brooke hesitated. "Only from gossip."

"I remember when the show ended there was speculation that he and Tessa Draycott had a big romance that went south. Is that what happened?" Cleo asked. She hoped not as Ethan had been married at the time. He'd said his marriage ended because he stopped acting, but what if he'd also had an affair with his co-star?

"No. She had some problems. Maybe drugs? Or it could have been alcohol." As sorry as Cleo was that Tessa Draycott had a drug or alcohol problem she was secretly relieved that Ethan hadn't had an affair with his co-star while he was married.

"Oh, what a shame. She was in the middle of a brilliant career," Libby said.

"She was. But she wouldn't be the first celebrity who ever imploded thanks to that lifestyle. And she probably won't be the last."

"Whatever happened to her?" Megan asked.

"I honestly don't know. I've seen her in the odd TV series, where she has a pretty small role. But definitely, after *Badminton Run*, her star burned out."

"And Ethan walked away from the show," Cleo said. She was sorry Tessa'd had problems, but much more interested in the male star and Brooke obviously knew him personally.

"I wouldn't feel too sorry for either of them. Even twenty-five years ago, being a star in a popular series like that was a fast-track to wealth."

"He doesn't live like a rich guy," Cleo said, thinking of the worn T-shirts and jeans he favored. Though his boat was definitely high-end. Probably a hundred and fifty or two hundred thousand new.

Brooke opened her mouth and then shut it again. "Who can say?"

Megan pointed to a misshapen muffin not good enough to sell abandoned on the counter. "Can I eat that? Didn't have time for breakfast."

Cleo nodded.

Megan polished off the rhubarb and blueberry muffin so fast Cleo popped two more muffins from the cooling rack into a bag and put it on the counter beside Megan, who said, "Score!" She leaned closer. "Speaking of scoring, did you, you know?" She made a leering face and pushed her index finger through a circle created by the thumb and index finger of her other hand, in case Cleo found "you know" too subtle.

"What? Have sex? Of course not. Not on a first date."

Megan looked at her with pity. "Cleo. He's only going to be here a few days. If you don't tap that now, you won't get another chance."

"I'm not really the tap that sort."

"I always say, make hay while the sun's shining."

Libby said, "Are you going to see him again?" A much better question.

"As a matter of fact, he's coming in this afternoon. He built me a new shelf for the bakery."

Everyone but Megan looked swoony.

Megan shook her head looking sad. "Anybody with a hammer and some nails can build you a shelf. But it's not every day you get taken to bed by Nick Badminton."

Ethan strolled up Main Street headed for the marine store, which also seemed to double as the town's hardware store. He needed to get the brackets for the shelf he'd built. On the way he passed the pet store and on impulse went in. The woman recognized him, of course.

"How's the kitten working out?"

He grimaced. "I haven't been able to find it a home yet."

"You should put a notice up at the bakery. Cleo keeps a community bulletin board in there. It's the go-to place if you want to rent a room, sell fishing gear or, give away an animal."

"Why didn't I think of that?" He'd seen the big board, even glanced at the ads briefly. "Brilliant."

"There's one in the grocery store as well, but Cleo's is pretty much the heart of town."

"Could you put up a note here, too?"

"I could. Although, I have to be honest, anybody who wanted a kitten pretty much took one already. And I feel I'd have to mention that it only has one ear."

"It's part of its charm," he said, bristling to the poor little thing's defense. "Also, you can say that it's a very smart cat and it's already litter trained."

"It is?" she said, looking impressed. Which made him feel pretty good because a woman who ran a pet store ought to know. "I'll definitely mention that to anyone who's interested." She said, "How would a prospective cat owner get in touch with you?"

He thought about giving her his cell phone number, but old habits died hard. And, the odd person did still like getting in touch with him for all the wrong reasons.

Instead, he went with, "Could you take any interested person's name and number and I'll get back to them?"

She seemed to understand and nodded. "Sure thing."

While he was in the pet store, he might as well get the cat something to play with. It made such a piteous ruckus every time he left it alone, which was hardly ever. She showed him three that she thought would be suitable for the kitten and he bought all three.

That done, and feeling he'd made a step towards finding the cat a home, he continued on to the marine store. Filbert Marine was about as busy as last time he'd been in. Not very. The same guy was behind the counter. He didn't need help though in finding what he wanted. He picked up the brackets and took them to the counter to be rung up.

Before the guy did so, he asked, "Any news on my water pump? It's Ethan."

"Right. Right." The man seemed to hesitate and then punched something into the computer. Scanned the screen and shook his head. "It's on back order. Looks like it's going to be a few more days."

"Okay." He wasn't in a big hurry. This was as nice a place as any to spend a few days. Still, he'd like to get that job done. He preferred to keep his boat in tiptop condition and always ready to set sail. However, he'd spent enough time in small towns to know they didn't operate the same way as big cities.

The man rang up his purchases. "I'll give you a call when that part's in."

"Appreciate it."

ELEVEN

Cleo could have hung up a shelf herself. She knew how. But what time did she have between running a bakery and keeping a cottage on five acres going? Between getting up at four thirty, working at the bakery all day and then afterwards checking on her herbs and vegetables, keeping the books. It was a lot of work. So, she hadn't got around to fixing that shelf. Didn't mean she couldn't have done it.

However, even as these thoughts went through her head, she was honest enough to know she wouldn't have done as good a job as Ethan. Nor, frankly, looked as good doing it. Even Pepper, at half her age, was shooting quick glances at the long streak of man using a power drill like it was an extension of his arm. He was wearing his oldest jeans and a shirt that wasn't even good enough for the charity bag. That moth-eaten, stained shirt's next stop was either as an oil rag or trash. Didn't stop her appreciating what was underneath, though. And, since Ethan was facing away, she could enjoy the odd glance without being caught.

When he reached up, she could see the muscles in his back shifting. Once the shirt hiked up far enough that she caught a glimpse of an intriguing couple of inches of tanned skin.

Then she went resolutely back to mixing dough to stop herself acting like a sex-starved spinster.

When he was finished, had checked the level and found the bubble to be in the perfect center, he nodded with satisfaction and stepped back to admire his handiwork.

"I think that'll be solid," he said, gripping the shelf and pulling down on it.

From what she'd seen, a major earthquake wouldn't budge that thing. The bakery would fall in around it and all that would be left after the big one would be a shelf still attached to the remains of that wall.

She and Pepper both complimented him extravagantly on his handiwork and collected the tins that normally belonged there. She realized to her delight that, now, she could even put heavy things up there if she wanted to.

Pepper looked at Ethan with dreamy eyes. "It's so nice finally getting that shelf fixed."

"I was going to fix it," Cleo said, stung.

"You always fix it and it falls down again. We needed a proper handyman."

How could this woman be so young and so sexist? "I was going to hire someone."

"Who?" She turned to Ethan. "The only handyman we have in town is Rudy Lindquist. And Rudy only calls himself a handyman to stop his wife nagging at him. He's the laziest guy ever. He likes to surf, he likes to play, and he likes to drink. To hire Rudy, you have to pay in advance to get him to show up for a job, then he pretends to work for half an hour, says he needs a different tool or a kind of glue that he doesn't have and goes away again."

In spite of herself Cleo was laughing. "He's not that bad."

"Name one thing in town he's ever actually fixed."

"Old Marge's clothesline that fell down."

"And he only fixed it because the mayor got so mad that he was taking advantage of an old lady that he hauled him out of bed himself and stood over him until he finished the job."

Cleo turned to Ethan. "You see? That's all I would have had to do to get my shelf put up properly."

He packed up his tools and by that time they were nearly finished with the kitchen cleaning. Everything was prepped for the morning.

He said, "All that effort made me hungry. Could I interest you two ladies in dinner in town? I've checked out the menus thoroughly. If you're not inclined for the world-famous fish and chips, I hear the burgers are good at the pub. They have a vegan burger if that's an issue," he said, looking at Pepper.

Pepper looked at Cleo, her eyes wide. "I'd love to, but I have to get home to my boyfriend. But Cleo's free."

She glared at her assistant. What was she doing throwing her boss under the bus like that?

She looked at Ethan to find his face serious, but his eyes were twinkling as though he was laughing at her. She flapped her hands helplessly. "I can't go out for dinner with you in town. People will gossip."

"From what I've seen of this town, people are already gossiping."

"It's true," Pepper stuck in. "I overheard Arlene Overfeld and Scott Bixby in the grocery store at lunch." She turned to Cleo and put her hands on her hips like a mother who'd caught her kid staying out past curfew. "You were seen going onto Ethan's boat last night."

She was furious with herself for blushing, but blush she did. "Well, I hope they also saw me getting off Ethan's boat."

Her young assistant shrugged her shoulders. "Plenty of time for something to have happened." Then she cracked up laughing as Cleo went after her flicking a tea towel so it snapped back. "See you tomorrow."

"Not if I fire you."

"Nobody else would work for you."

It might have gone on for much longer except that Pepper, having had the last word, was now out of earshot.

She folded the tea towel and felt like she didn't know what to do with her hands. If she hadn't already cleaned the bakery, she'd start an extra batch of dough just to do something with all this nervous energy. When she risked a glance up at Ethan's face, he was looking at her with a somber expression. "Am I causing you problems?"

She shook her head, immediately feeling foolish. Who cared what a bunch of small-town busybodies said behind her back? "No. This is a small, gossipy town. There'll be some funny looks and sly innuendos and then Burt Tupperman will get so drunk he falls off his boat again and the town will have something else to talk about."

"Look, I'm sorry. I don't mean to embarrass you. I didn't feel like eating alone."

He'd made her dinner last night. And made her this beautiful shelf and put it up. She didn't want to be ungrateful. "Tell you what. I need to change anyway." She glanced at that disreputable old T-shirt, "And so do you. Why don't you come to my place for dinner?"

"No. That's okay. Besides, my boatmate would be really unimpressed if I left her any longer."

She thought maybe he was a little embarrassed too. How were two fifty-something adults acting like bashful young teenagers? She said, "You can bring the cat. Just so long as you swear an oath that you will take it back again at the end of the evening."

He still looked uncomfortable. "I pretty much invited myself. You don't have to do this."

And now that he was pushing her away, she realized she did want to have him over for dinner. He was good company, she liked him. And, Megan was right. He wasn't going to be here long. He couldn't cause her very much trouble. Why shouldn't she indulge herself? Oh, she wouldn't sleep with him. She wasn't crazy. But a few dinners? Somebody interesting to talk to? To cook for? "Please come."

"I'll go pick up some food at the grocery store. You weren't expecting me."

She walked to the big, industrial fridge, opened the door, went inside and pulled out a plastic bag. Walked it over to him and opened it.

He looked inside. "A slab of raw fish. Not what I was expecting."

"Mitch O'Grady brings me fish in exchange for bread. He likes to fish and I like to bake. It works out. He caught a twenty-pound halibut and brought me some of it. He also brought me a dozen lemons. I'll make a lemon sauce. With capers," she added, as though that might clinch the deal.

"Nice. And that is definitely too much fish for one person."

"Definitely."

"Okay. What time do you want me?"

"Give me an hour."

"Where do you live?"

She gave him the address. "It's a small cottage at the east end of the bay. About a ten-minute drive from here. Just stick to the coast road. You can't miss it."

"What color is your house?"

She looked at him like he was crazy. "What color? Do you think Google Maps cares?"

He shook his head. "I'll be coming by boat."

She couldn't believe she'd forgotten he didn't even have land transportation. "I could pick you up."

"No. I'll take the skiff over."

"Great. My dock is the one with the blue fishing floats on it. The cottage sits on a bluff. It's blue and yellow."

"I've seen it. Pretty place. Be over in about an hour."

She helped herself to enough of tomorrow's prepared dough to make focaccia, and with the ease of long practice, plopped it into a round baking tin and covered it with plastic wrap. He watched her as though fascinated.

When she'd picked up the bag of fish and the one with lemons, she let him out into the back alley, turned out the lights, came out behind him and shut and locked the door.

"Do you want a ride down to your boat?"

He shook his head. "It's a ten-minute walk. Besides, we have your reputation to think about. What would Arlene and Scott think if they saw you with me again?"

She didn't bother to tell him that him driving his skiff over to her place was going to be all over town anyway ten minutes after he tied up to her dock.

TWELVE

Cleo pulled into her driveway wondering what she'd done. She didn't have men over for dinner. In fact, she rarely invited people to her cottage. She was social in town, where she had to be, and enjoyed it. She liked her customers, she liked talking about their lives, a little banter over the espresso machine, hearing their problems and chatting about new grandbabies and planned vacations during the slow times.

But, when her work day was over, she retreated to the peace and tranquility of her cottage. Now, in the last few days, it felt like it was being overrun. First those pushy students had all ganged up on her and ended up in her space. Okay, it had been fun having her makeup done by an expert and the company of women as she got ready for a date. But still, her world was getting all messed up ever since Ethan sailed into Clamshell Bay. Now he'd wrangled himself a dinner invitation.

He had done her a solid favor. The least she could do was cook him dinner as a thank you. Before he overstayed his welcome, she'd make sure to remind him that she had to get up long before dawn.

She put the fish in her kitchen fridge, the bag of lemons on her counter, then started a mental schedule.

Trying not to think about how shabby her little cottage would look through his eyes, she concentrated on a quick tidy up. It wasn't that her cottage was ever dirty, but she still had books and papers and unread magazines dumped all over her dining table. With less than an hour until Ethan arrived, she pulled everything off the dining room table and shoved it all in her spare bedroom, which had somehow become more of a storage room than the guest-bedroom-cum-office she'd planned.

Now her table looked bare. A vase of flowers, that's what was missing. Lilac, bluebells, and irises would make a quick bouquet. When she went to fetch her garden clippers from the potting shed with its door that wouldn't quite close, she jumped when something moved in there. She didn't have time to investigate and tried to convince herself it was a squirrel. That's what came of not having doors that shut properly. If it wasn't deer treating her garden like a smorgasbord, it was squirrels using her potting shed as a storehouse. There were raccoons nesting in the trees, eagles and seagulls who dropped shells on her roof to crack them open, and otters had been known to treat her dock like the love shack. And people worried that she lived alone?

She cut lilac, bluebells, and a couple of pink and white peonies that had just come into bloom, stuck them into an old jug made of green Depression glass and placed them in the middle of her table. The irises and a couple of white calla lilies she left long-stemmed and put into a tall crystal vase that had been a wedding present. That she placed in her small living room.

Already, the place looked so much better. She should really treat herself to flowers all the time.

Then she got busy in the kitchen. She made focaccia, fetching fresh rosemary from her herb garden, which went on the top of the bread, along with olive oil. She pressed her fingers into the dough making dimples all over it then finished with flaky sea salt and a sprinkle of fresh parmesan before sliding the bread into the oven. She made a simple salad from more of the early greens, and she set brown rice on. Dinner wouldn't be fancy, but he wasn't going home hungry.

She'd make the sauce for the fish as she was cooking.

Dessert. She hadn't done anything about dessert. She glanced at her watch. Twenty minutes until he was expected to arrive. She had a brownie recipe she'd been making so long she'd memorized it decades ago. She could have made it in her sleep. Soon the kitchen smelled like heaven, if heaven were made of chocolate, and she really hoped it was.

And then with only ten minutes to go until her hour was up, she dashed into the bathroom. She showered in five minutes, keeping her hair out of the spray of water as she had no time to dry her long hair. It was back in its usual braid and there was no time and no Brooke to recreate last night's look. Once out of the shower, she dried in record time, dressed in a pair of casual navy cotton trousers and a white T-shirt. Brooke might argue, but she had no intention of wearing one of her nicest tops when cooking.

There was no way she could manage the makeup job Brooke had done, but she used the gifted cosmetics sparingly and so quickly, Brooke would probably faint if she saw her in action.

Too bad. The last thing she wanted was for Ethan to think she was primping for him.

She heard the rumble of an outboard before she saw him, and walked out and down the path to greet him. She watched as he maneuvered the little skiff in and tied up at her dock. Out came a cat carrier and what looked like an overnight bag. Instantly her spine went as solid as a steel rod. Oh, he'd better not be getting any ideas. Had she been putting out some lonely, desperate vibe?

She walked to the end of her garden to meet him as he came up the steep stairs that led up from the dock to the bluff where her property sat.

"Nice place," he said, looking around.

"Thanks. What's in the bag?"

It didn't come out sharp or anything, but he must have thought it was an odd question.

"I brought some wine, and I didn't have time to feed the cat so I brought some cat food. Hope that's okay."

Immediately, she could have kicked herself for even thinking he'd be so desperate to sleep with her that he'd brought an overnight bag packed with his toothbrush and clean socks, or whatever he carried for booty calls.

Because she felt bad about her suspicions, she said, "Let me take the cat. How did she make out on the journey?"

"The sound of the motor drowned out the meowing, but I'm guessing there was meowing."

"She'll get used to it."

"Won't have to. Unless a mariner adopts her."

She put the carrier down on the grass and opened the door. The cat poked its nose out cautiously and daintily stepped out, sniffing the grass as though it had never seen dry land before.

"Do you think it'll run away?" he asked, looking anxious.

"I don't think that cat's going five feet away from you. She probably thinks you're her mother."

He sent her a baleful look. "I'm the cat sitter until we find her a permanent home. By the way, I meant to ask you if I could put up a notice in the café letting people know that this cat is free to a good home, including the carrier, food, and toys."

"You bought her toys?"

"Not because I was planning to keep her," he said. "Because she gets lonely when I leave her on the boat."

"Sure. Bring it by tomorrow and I'll stick it up."

"'Preciate it."

"Come on, I'll give you the tour of the cottage, it won't take long. Then I thought we'd sit outside while it's still nice." She gestured to her gazebo area.

"This is a beautiful place."

"I've always loved it here."

She led him in and stopped herself from apologizing for the shabbiness of the furniture or the old-fashioned aspects of the cottage. It was her home. He could like it or not like it. She checked to see how he was reacting and caught him with his eyes closed and a look of bliss on his face. When he opened his eyes, he said, "I smell chocolate."

She grinned at him. "I'm making brownies for dessert."

He moaned softly and put a hand to his stomach. "You are ruining me for other women."

She had no idea how to react to such a flirtatious statement, so she pretended she hadn't even heard it. "This is the living room. And the dining room." The bedrooms were off a short hallway behind the living room but she left them off her tour. "Bathroom's through there," she said, pointing to the closed door. And then she walked forward into the kitchen, where she checked on the brownies by peeking in the oven window. They still had twenty minutes to go, which she knew perfectly well, but checking on them gave her something to do as he entered her most cherished space. The focaccia would be ready in about ten minutes. Perfect.

"Why am I not surprised that the kitchen is the nicest room in your house?"

She almost said, "You haven't seen my bedroom yet," and then stopped herself in case he thought she was coming on to him.

But it was true. She loved the kitchen, but her bedroom was her sanctuary. For a woman who was on her feet so much she cherished her time in bed. Especially as she had to get out of it so very early most mornings.

He looked at the pale blue cupboards, the open upper shelves where she kept her baking supplies. "You bake all day for a living, and then you come home to bake?"

"What can I say, it's a sickness."

"Then I hope you never get better."

He'd brought the bag in with him and now set it down on the floor and pulled out a bottle of wine. "Luckily I knew what we were having for dinner. Can I put this in your fridge?"

"Sure. Yes."

Then he looked puzzled. "Is it too much? Too much wine? Because we don't have to drink it."

"No. It's fine. I don't drink every day, but then I rarely entertain. It's a really nice treat."

He also took out brand new cat food bowls and the premium kitten food that the pet store sold.

She decided to end the tour there. Showing him her bedroom would just be too weird. And he seemed perfectly happy to settle in the kitchen.

He wandered over to the kitchen cupboard that hung askew. "I could fix this for you."

"That's all right. I can fix it myself. I just haven't got around to it."

He shrugged as though he didn't mind either way. "Okay. Offer stays open if you change your mind."

It would be too seductive to say, *Yes, please.* He might have bedroom eyes, a killer bod, and ooze charm, but seriously, what made Cleo weak at the knees was to watch that man with power tools.

She said, "Why don't you pour us both a glass of that wine and we can take it down to the gazebo. The bread will be ready to come out in about five minutes."

She showed him where to find glasses and he very kindly didn't comment that yet another cupboard door didn't fit properly.

She led him back out into the back garden and they headed towards the gazebo. He settled so easily in one of the wicker chairs and they sat companionably looking out at the water. She'd barely taken her first sip of wine when a sound split the air, like a baby screaming. She and Ethan both jumped up and headed towards the sound. A tiny ball of fur practically flew out of her potting shed. Its black hair sticking out as though it had been electrified. Ethan ran and scooped up the cat.

"What happened?"

For answer, the kitten clung to him as though he really were her mother.

Holding the cat, he opened the door wide and peered inside then jumped back almost as startled as the kitten had been.

"What is it?"

"You've got a skunk in there."

Not squirrels then. "Just one?"

He looked at her, startled. "How many skunks were you expecting?"

"So long as it's not a mother with babies."

"I'd say it's single. But it won't be for long if you leave the door open like that."

Did he think she didn't know that? "It wasn't like I invited a skunk to take up residence. The door doesn't shut on the potting shed."

He peered at it from a safe distance. "You need a new door."

"I know. It's on the list." Though when she'd get around to it, she had no idea.

"I'll go feed the cat. She's looking a little freaked out." The kitten was clinging tightly to Ethan, its eyes still huge.

"I'd say she used up one of those nine lives just getting frightened to death."

"Your place suits you," he said, after the cat had been fed and was happily snoozing in his lap. The brownies were on the cooling rack and they were back under the gazebo. She could hear the distant bark of sea lions.

"You mean old and run-down? And falling apart?" Some days that's exactly how she felt.

"No. Beautiful, and very grounded. That's what I meant. You know, everyone says your bakery is the heart of the town. And they're right. I see the same people going there every day. They're not just there for bread and coffee. They go to meet their friends and chat to the nice ladies behind the counter. Find out what's going on in town." He held up his hands. "Find homes for stray cats."

"That's a very nice thing to say. Thank you."

"It's true. Though, I have to say, you could use somebody around the place to fix it up."

She immediately felt her goodwill clamp down. "The last time I had a man around the place it didn't end so well."

"I'm sorry about that. But, I'm going to make you a proposal."

She looked at him warily. "And the last time I said yes to a proposal, that didn't end up so well, either."

He chuckled. "Not a marriage proposal. Here's the thing. My water pump won't be in for a few more days, which pretty much leaves me stranded here. I don't mind, it's a pretty little town, but I have a lot of energy. Apart from the water pump there's not much to do on my boat that I haven't already fixed. You'd be doing me a favor if you let me fix that door and a couple of things in your kitchen. I'll come by when you're at work. You won't even know I'm here."

"You'd do that?" The thought of Ethan working on her cottage was both thrilling and terrifying. She knew he'd do a great job, but they barely knew each other and some instinct was warning her this might be a bad idea. Oh, but to have kitchen cupboards that hung properly...

"Absolutely. I believe I said I like to work with my hands. I am a trained carpenter. I have references if you'd like."

"I pay the people I hire. I don't take favors."

He raised his eyebrows in a skeptical fashion. "Sure, you do. Everybody takes favors. It's how the world works. Take tonight's dinner, for example. Fisherman brings you a fish. That's a favor. You give him bread. Returning the favor."

He had a point. "It's more the barter system. If I accept your work around the house, how will I pay you? How will I return that favor?"

"Nothing easier. I eat. You're a baker. I see a pretty good barter arrangement in our future."

"You're going to fix my door for bread?"

"Well, you could sweeten the deal with cinnamon buns. And I'm partial to pie."

When he turned on the charm he was hard to resist, and yet the little voice warning her to beware was faint but persistent. "I have to think about it."

The thought of him working around her house felt oddly intimate. She was almost certain the voice was right and she ought to say no. But then she thought of getting those things fixed that drove her so crazy she'd considered hiring Rudy Lindquist. Anything was better than that, even if it meant a washed-up actor would be hanging around the place wearing a tool belt.

Oh, no. The picture was too appealing. Way too appealing.

His eyes crinkled in an almost-smile. "You're thinking about it. I can tell. Tell you what. Your friend Brooke who's taking your class. Call her husband. Kyle Donovan. He'll vouch for me."

Did he think she had the local billionaire on speed dial? "I barely know him. He almost never comes into the bakery. In fact, I barely know her."

"You two looked pretty friendly when I came by the bakery the other day."

In spite of her confusion over his offer to be her unpaid handyman, she was pleased he'd noticed how well she and her bakery students were getting on. Happy students spread the word to other potential bakers. More than that, she felt as though she'd made some new friends over the weekend. "We have kind of bonded. Sometimes my baking classes are like that. Everybody gets along really well and friendships are born."

"Well? Give Kyle and Brooke a call. I'm pretty sure they'll tell you I'm a regular guy. No hidden agenda."

"And you'll take that cat with you when you leave?"

"Unless I've found it another home, yes, I will."

"I'll think about it," she said again. She suspected she'd be able to think more clearly when he wasn't standing in front of her looking like the middle-aged hero of her middle-aged dreams.

He pulled out a cell phone and began to scroll and suspicion bloomed in her belly. "What are you doing?"

"No time like the present." Before she could stop him, he held up a hand. "Kyle? Ethan here. Yes, the contractor told me that. Yeah, we can talk about that tomorrow. Listen, I'm with Cleo Duvall. The lady who runs the bakery in town? I've offered to do a few jobs around her place and understandably, she doesn't find me trustworthy."

"That's not true," she yelled from the background, wondering what Brooke's husband must think of her. He was the richest man on the island, possibly in all of the Pacific Northwest, apart from Bill Gates, and Ethan was asking the guy for a character reference?

He chuckled softly. "Well, just tell the truth." Then he handed her the phone.

"Are you insane?" she asked him in a low voice.

His all-too-innocent expression was belied by the twinkle lurking in his eyes. "I want the job, that's all."

She shook her head at him. And took the phone. "Hello, this is Cleo Duvall speaking."

Kyle Donovan had a nice, rich voice with an edge of humor to it. "Cleo, it's nice to speak to you. I'm sorry I haven't been into the bakery as often as I should. I've been watching carbs. But my wife may change all that, thanks to your baking school."

She smiled even though he couldn't see her. "I'm glad she enjoyed it."

"So, Ethan. I can definitely tell you that he's a good man. He won't steal from you. He's a pretty good carpenter. I've seen his work. And if he gives you any trouble at all, you tell me and I'll take care of him."

"I appreciate it. I'm really sorry we bothered you. I had no idea he was going to phone you."

He chuckled in a slightly villainous fashion. "It's okay. Now he owes me one."

She passed the phone back to Ethan, who said, "Thanks, bro," and ended the call. He looked half amused and half eager. "So? Am I hired?"

Oh, what the hell. It was him, Rudy, or spending the foreseeable future with doors that didn't fit and animals using her potting shed as a nursery. "You can start tomorrow."

He put his fist in the air. "Yes," which startled the cat on his lap so it jumped. Once on its spindly legs, the kitten used Ethan's chest like a climbing wall until she was snuggled right over his heart.

Dinner was more fun than Cleo could have imagined. Somehow discovering a skunk living in her potting shed tore the last shreds of awkwardness from between her and Ethan. He'd already borrowed a tape measure and measured for a new door while she seared the halibut and made a sauce of butter, lemon, wine, and capers.

They ate inside and she put the fire on so that it blazed merrily in the corner, adding to the atmosphere. She had lots of candles and lanterns because it wasn't unusual for the power to go out here. All the flickering lights added romance to the atmosphere and hid the imperfections in her house.

She wasn't even sure what they talked about. It seemed like anything and everything. Bands they'd liked, books they'd read, places he'd been. Places she wanted to go. The one thing, oddly, they didn't talk about was television shows. She pretty soon got the idea that he didn't go in for them. She wondered if he'd seen too much of what went on behind the curtain and the magic was spoiled.

By the time they got to her decadent brownies served with homemade ice cream it seemed perfectly natural for him to jump up and make the coffee while she pulled the dessert together.

He acted like it was the best brownie he'd ever tasted. And quite possibly it was. She was not modest about her baking talents. He suddenly looked up at her. His eyes were mysterious in the flickering candlelight.

"Does your ex-husband still live in Clamshell Bay?"

She was a little startled by the change of subject. "Why? Are you worried he'll beat you up?"

"Nope. Wondering how anyone was fool enough to let you go."

And there it was, right there. The reason she couldn't trust him. Flattery was a dangerous thing. It weakened a woman's defenses.

"I don't know where he is," she said honestly.

"Not an amicable breakup then?"

"Let's just say, he found the grass was greener on the other side of my fence."

At the time her husband had left town and her, in the company of the wife of one of their neighbors, she'd thought she might bolt herself inside her house and never come out. It wasn't that she'd loved Travis so deeply; by that time she'd seen through the charm and good looks to the seedy character that lurked beneath.

It was the humiliation that was the most painful part. Knowing she'd be the subject of gossip and that all of Clamshell Bay was laughing behind her back. Assuming she hadn't known her husband was cheating on her. She'd guessed, but she hadn't thrown him out. She hadn't stood up for herself, not even to confront him. What was the point? He'd only have lied. But at least she should have had the moral victory of chucking him out on his ass, not waited until he disappeared along with a woman who was both younger and curvier. What a cliché.

What she said was, "It stung for a while. But I'm better off without him."

He ate another bite of brownie and ice cream, and to prevent him asking her any more personal questions, she asked, "How about you? Your marriage didn't last either, did it?" She'd read about his break-up in People but didn't want him to think she'd been too interested in him outside of Thursday nights in *Badminton Run*.

He nodded. He took a few moments and then said, "It's hard to explain, but from the minute my face was plastered on TV every week, I was suddenly God's gift to women. It's not good for a man. Especially a young hothead. Goes to your head. But I was shrewd enough to know that most of the women wouldn't have cared if I was a secret Nazi so long as I was famous." He screwed up his face as though he was in pain. "I can't believe what an arrogant ass I sound."

She didn't have that much trouble believing him. Even she

was a little star-struck, and he hadn't been a star for a quarter century.

"Frankie Kaplan played a con artist on three episodes of the show. She was funny, swore like a Marine and seemed more grounded than most people in show business. We hit it off and it was easy. We went to parties together, she came along to awards shows where I never won. We'd been together about six months when we took a few days off, went to Vegas and got married. I didn't want a media feeding frenzy so we got married first, then told people."

Right. She did remember now. Headlines like *Secret Love Match* and *Con Artist Steals Nick Badminton's Heart* had been plastered on magazine covers and in newspapers.

"What happened?"

He shifted in his chair as though the wooden seat was uncomfortable but she suspected it was the topic. Well, he'd chosen it. She waited.

"What happens to most Hollywood couples? After swearing we'd be different, and our marriage would last, we got divorced. Truth was, the marriage worked when I was a star, but after I left acting, Frankie didn't know what to do with me. She still loved acting and wanted me to stick with my career but I was done. And, pretty soon, so were we. She never wanted kids so nobody got hurt."

He didn't sound too broken up, but then it had happened a long time ago. Still, she said she was sorry because she always felt sad when couples broke up.

"It wasn't so bad. I wouldn't say we're still friends, but we're cordial. She married a stunt man and became a stepmom to his three kids." He didn't sound bitter so maybe he hadn't wanted kids either.

"After that, I hit the road. Went traveling, always looking for places where *Badminton Run* wasn't on TV, and somehow I got into the habit of drifting. Guess I never stopped." Warning bells went off in her head one more time. A man who was in his fifties and still drifting wasn't going to come to harbor any time soon. She felt a flash of sadness, because a man like Ethan who wanted to settle might be exactly the man she'd been looking for all her life.

There was a moment when they looked at each other and she felt the pull and knew he was feeling it too. He reached over for her hand and lifted it up. Her hands were not her best feature. They'd been burned and sliced open too many times to count. But he wasn't looking at her hands, he was looking into her eyes, and she thought of what Megan had said. Why not? Why not let this beautiful man who'd drifted into her bay take her to bed? Why not tap that, knowing it would be short-term and soon he would be gone?

Then he did a most extraordinary thing. He brought her hand to his mouth and kissed her wrist. It was the most erotic thing that had happened to her in about twenty years. She felt the quiver of attraction through her body. Every womanly part of her was crying out *yes, yes, yes*. She was already thinking how she could get undressed in as close to total darkness as possible so this man who likely had his choice of any woman wouldn't see the imperfections on her fifty-two-year-old body.

But, instead of drawing her to her feet and leading her to the bedroom as though they were acting out a scene from television, he let her hand go, scooped the sleeping cat out of his lap, and said, "I know you've got an early morning. We'll be on our way."

And she, who had worried that he might try to take advantage, was struggling not to let her disappointment show.

She didn't want him to go.

She clamped down on that thought. She had her pride. She wasn't going to beg him to stay.

He eased the sleeping cat back into the cat carrier and then said, "I'm going to need to either borrow your car or get a lift to the hardware store. That potting shed door is mostly rotten. I need some two-by-fours and some one-by-sixes. And some other things to fix your kitchen doors."

One by sixes? Frustrated lust was pulsing through her veins and he was thinking about his lumber order? Her ego fell another notch. "Sure. We can go right after I finish work tomorrow."

"Good. I'll come by tomorrow and take down the old door, see what I can do about getting rid of the skunk if it's still there." He didn't sound too sure of himself.

"Don't get sprayed. And please don't kill it." She had no idea what his ideas entailed but killing slugs was about as brutal as she got.

"I was hoping to lure the skunk out somehow. Maybe there's a way to rehouse it. Need to do some research on that."

"Good then." She was glad they were on the same page on avoiding skunk destruction. "I'll pick you up here after I finish work. We're closer to the lumber store going this direction."

"Suits me perfectly. See you tomorrow."

She walked out with him and before he headed down the stairs to the dock he turned. He was silhouetted against the ocean and the night sky where the first stars were appearing like a darker shadow.

"Thanks for dinner. I had a great time."

"Me too."

And the scary thing was how great a time she'd had.

And how soon he'd be gone.

THIRTEEN

Cleo went back inside and finished tidying up the kitchen. She looked at the eight lemons sitting in a bowl on the counter and decided to make some lemonade. She could imagine Ethan enjoying some fresh lemonade after a hard day's work, and besides, it gave her something to do with her sexual longing.

She flipped on the TV for company as she simmered sugar and water together, squeezed the lemons. Soon her kitchen was filled with the sharp, clean scent of fresh-squeezed lemon juice. She let the sugar mixture cool, then added the lemon juice and fresh, filtered water. She put the juice into a sealed glass jug and into the fridge.

That done, she put the squeezed-out lemon rinds into her kitchen compost, then wiped down her counters.

And, yawning, she headed for bed.

She had a little moment of self-knowledge as she crawled in between fresh, clean sheets. Why had she changed the bed today?

"You're a fool," she told herself as she snapped off the light and tried to settle down to sleep.

When Cleo returned home the next day, Ethan didn't even hear her coming. She got out of the car and slammed the door and then realized why he couldn't hear her. He had the music playing full blast and his back to her. He was hammering something and she just stood there for a minute enjoying the view. He was long and lean and in his short-sleeved T-shirt, she could see his biceps bulge as he worked, the shift and sway of his back as he rhythmically banged nails. She wondered what he was working on. He'd told her that they needed to go to the lumber yard.

The kitten was curled up asleep on the lawn a couple of feet away on his discarded jacket. It was heart-meltingly cute.

She walked forward and, not wanting to scare him, crossed into his line of vision. He broke into his wide grin when he saw her. And then paused, wiped sweat off his forehead with the back of his wrist. He turned down the music to human levels.

"Hey, honey, how was your day?" he asked.

"Not bad. How was yours?"

"I've got some ideas for our skunk problem," he told her. He pointed at his phone. "They don't like loud music or bright lights at night. Thought we might try putting a radio in the potting shed, and some motion detector lights around it. Right now, I'm working on patching the holes in the shed floor. Her den is probably underneath the shed, so first thing is to stop her getting up into your potting shed, then getting her to move out of the den."

"You're sure it's a she?"

He shrugged. "My in-depth research online suggests it's probably a female and she either has babies or is planning a family."

"Oh."

"Don't look so sad. They move dens all the time. The trick is to make this one inhospitable so they abandon it."

"You really did your research."

He seemed quite content working in her yard in the sunshine, so she decided not to feel guilty that she was accepting free labor.

"I'm going to change my clothes and have a quick shower. Do you want some lemonade? Iced tea? Water?"

"Do you make the lemonade from real lemons?"

Was he really that fussy? "Yes. I made it last night from the leftover lemons Mitch gave me."

"Did you keep the lemon peels?"

"They're in the compost. Why?"

"I'll dig them out. We'll put them in the shed. Citrus repels skunks."

She headed toward the house. "I'm on it." And she loved that he'd done so much research to help her out.

She hadn't told him about her hidden key and now she felt terrible. What was he going to do if she gave him access to her house? Steal? Snoop through her things? He wasn't like that. And anyway, even if he did snoop, what was he going to find?

The hammering resumed and she dug through her kitchen compost, retrieving the lemon rinds, which she put into one of her biodegradable compost bags. Then she washed her hands and poured him a large glass of lemonade. She took both out to her backyard handyman who looked as pleased with her old lemon rinds as he was with her homemade lemonade.

And she went in and showered. It felt good to shower the sweat and flour and dust that clung to her after a day in the bakery. Since Ethan seemed busy out back, she took the time to wash her hair. She dried off, then she threw her work clothes in the hamper and slipped on fresh underwear, her favorite well-worn jeans, and a long-sleeved T-shirt. She thought about makeup and then realized she'd only be doing it for him. So she didn't. She combed out her wet hair and left it to air dry.

They drove to the lumber store together and he chose what he needed. It had been a long time since she'd gone shopping with a man. As they walked through the lumber yard, choosing the wood and screws and new hinges, it reminded her what it felt like to be a couple, and for a few moments she wove a fantasy that they were. Especially when the older woman ringing up the order cast her a glance that without words said, "Nice going."

By the time they got back to her place it was nearly six.

"It's too late to start a project now," she said.

He nodded. "I'll just unload all this and get ready for tomorrow."

She helped him. When they got to the bag with the motion-detector lights in it, he said, "Why don't I put that up now? Won't take long and the sooner we let our skunk friend know she's not welcome, the sooner she'll leave."

"Okay. Thanks. I have payment in pie and bread." Which didn't seem like much compared to everything he'd done for her.

The pie was rhubarb and apple, made with local rhubarb that was tender and just ready to eat. She'd saved one of the nicest pies for him. The crust a perfect golden-brown.

He said, "A whole pie is a lot for one person." He didn't push, but left the words floating for her to ignore if she chose.

She grinned up at him. "I also have chicken for dinner, if you'd like to stay." And he didn't have to know that she'd run out to the store specially in case he wanted to have dinner at her place.

"I believe I would."

Over dinner she asked him if he'd heard anything about his water pump. She needed to remember that he was here on a temporary basis.

He shook his head. "Turned out Seattle didn't have one. It's back-ordered from somewhere." He shrugged. "It's not like I have a tight schedule to keep."

Right. As he kept reminding her, he was a drifter. And what drifted in on the tide, tended to drift out again.

Ethan woke up in the dark, startled, wondering for a second where he was. And then reality restored itself. He was exactly where he ought to be. In his cabin aboard *Vagabond*. She swayed ever so gently in the calm waters of the harbor. But something had woken him. And then he became aware of a strange sound. Kind of a sniffing and grinding. And as he came more fully awake, he realized that a small, warm, furry bundle was settled on his shoulder and the cat was chewing his hair. He turned to look at his tiny companion, faintly visible in the dawn light. He chuckled so his chest rumbled, lifting the cat up and down.

"You giving me a haircut? You're some Delilah."

He could move the kitten, but they were both comfortable and drowsy so he drifted back to sleep wondering if he'd be shorn by the morning. Delilah was a woman who'd taken away a man's power. He wasn't too worried that the kitten was going to do that to him. He'd make sure of it.

When he wakened fully it was to rain drumming. He got up, made coffee and decided that given the weather fixing the loose boards on Cleo's dock, which had been his project for today, would have to be put on hold.

A rain day was definitely an inside day. He'd been itching to get at those cupboard doors in the kitchen that were barely holding together. Today was the perfect day. Cleo had finally decided she trusted him enough to let him know where she kept her spare key. Progress from a woman who clearly had some issues with trust. He didn't blame her; he had plenty of those himself. Maybe it just came of enough years under your belt and enough life experience to know that leaving your heart wide open was akin to leaving the door of your bank vault swinging.

It was a wet ride over on the skiff. He packed a few dry clothes and cat food into the bag. He thought about how hard Cleo worked all day, on her feet, baking bread and serving customers. He'd been feeling bad that she kept making him dinner. Even if it was their deal. He'd only made the bargain, anyway, so she wouldn't feel bad accepting help from a friend. Because that's what he wanted them to be.

Friends.

As much as she had a confident, "I'm fine on my own" shell around her, he suspected both that money was a little tight and she had a hard time accepting favors from anyone.

He'd actually come across the town's only handyman, a certain Rudy Lindquist, in the marine store. Lindquist had a vacant look and a slow way about him that didn't inspire confidence. He hadn't been in the marine store for a customer, he'd been there to buy a new fishing rod.

If that was the best Clamshell Bay had to offer, he could imagine that if Cleo wanted anything done in the handyman department, she either had to figure out how to do it herself or trade favors. He knew she'd worried at the beginning that the favors he'd had in mind from her were of a more intimate nature. He hoped he'd eased her mind now he'd been working with her a few days. It wasn't that he didn't find her attractive, because he did. As much as he liked the long, lithe body and the frankness in her eyes, he could get sex anywhere. Friendship with a woman was a lot harder to find.

He turned to the cat. "And we don't want to mess that up, do we, Delilah?"

He banged his eyelids shut. "No," he groaned aloud. "No naming the kitten."

But even as he looked at the kitten, its one ear twitching as though picking up on the frustrated tone in his voice, he knew it was hopeless. He stroked her back with one finger. "I'm a goner, aren't I? How did I not figure it out? You're the latest in a string of wounded females." He must be getting better, though, Delilah was a lot less wounded than most of the females he'd loved.

Rain in the Pacific Northwest took itself seriously. This was not a light drizzle like you might find on a Paris afternoon, say. This was rainforest territory. So, when he and Delilah emerged, not even his Sou'wester and heavy sailing jacket could prevent them from getting soaked.

He got them in the skiff and headed out. Visibility was terrible, but, luckily, he didn't have far to go. Even so he nearly missed Cleo's dock. The bright blue fishing floats were barely visible through the rain in his eyes and the fog that hung low.

He managed to get up to the house in one piece, already thinking about what he could do to make Cleo's stairs safer in wet weather.

First thing he did was to check the potting shed and found the door still sound. The motion sensor lights had come on as they were supposed to and when he opened the door, he heard the chatter of a talk show. That inane garbage would have him moving out if he had to listen to it day and night. He hoped mama skunk was as intolerant of noise as he was. At least the floor was fixed now so she couldn't get into the shed any longer.

He fully supported local wildlife, but not in Cleo's potting shed.

He was rehanging one of the kitchen cabinet doors when his cell phone went. He turned down the music and grabbed his phone. It was the marine store telling him his part was in for the water pump.

"Hold on to it for me for a couple of days, will you? I'll be in to pick it up."

The guy at the marine store was perfectly happy to hold the part since Ethan had already paid for it. As he turned the music back up, he wondered about his curious behavior. He could have rushed right over to pick up the pump, installed it, and then he could be on his way. But where would he go? What destination was so important he needed to leave right now?

The reason he didn't want to hurry was if Cleo asked if he had it yet he could honestly answer that he didn't. She asked almost every day. He suspected she was worried that him coming here every day was like handing out charity. He couldn't explain his motives. It wasn't charity. He wanted to say it was friendship. He respected how hard she worked, and how independent she was. But no man is an island, as some famous poet had said. And her island was troubled with doors that didn't close properly, sections of fence that were sagging, and in the rain, he noticed one of the windows needed resealing.

In his life, he was free to do whatever he liked with his time. He'd discovered long ago that lounging didn't appeal to him, neither did living like some rich playboy. He still felt guilty that he'd fallen into a hit show that made him wealthy enough he could do anything he wanted. Ironically, what he wanted to do was work at something useful. He didn't do it for money anymore, but for the satisfaction. He had a feeling Cleo was the same. If she had millions tucked away, he bet she'd still live here and run her bakery. Maybe she'd hire a little more help, but her job gave her satisfaction the way building and fixing things gave him a reason to get up every morning.

As he was quick to tell her, too, she was also doing him a favor. He loved this kind of stuff. He loved working with his hands, building things, fixing them. Keeping perfectly good items out of the landfill. But he had surprisingly little opportunity to use his skills. His building project manager had taken him aside one day and asked him not to work alongside the team anymore.

"Dude, you're making them nervous. Besides, without you working here, we can afford one more guy."

Ethan had accepted his dismissal from his own worksite as graciously as he could. He understood what the PM was getting at, anyway. Part of the reason behind these projects was to give jobs to people who couldn't always get them otherwise. So, he'd given up that outlet for his energy and talents. Then Cleo had come along with exactly the kind of thing he liked to work on.

Maybe he should think about buying a little fixer-upper around here somewhere.

He thought about it. Then almost immediately shook his head. He didn't need more property.

Still, it wouldn't hurt to take a look at real estate online. Maybe when he got home.

He nearly jumped out of his skin when he felt a touch on his shoulder. He turned to face the intruder, his adrenalin surging, ready to attack, when he found a familiar face laughing.

Kyle Donovan held up his hands in defensive mode. "Whoa. I yelled, but you didn't hear me."

He turned the music down. "Sorry. Wasn't expecting company."

Kyle held up a plastic bag. "I went prawning this morning. Nothing like fresh spot prawns. There was too much for Brooke and me. Thought you and Cleo might like some."

His eyebrows pulled together. "How did you know I was here?"

The laughter was back. "Everybody knows you're here." Kyle looked around the kitchen and nodded approvingly. "Nice space. I love these old cottages."

But Ethan didn't want to be so easily sidetracked. He felt concern congealing in his belly. "Everybody knows I'm here? Seriously?"

"Ethan, if you want to be anonymous, go to a big city. You come to a place like Clamshell Bay, out of season, and everybody's interested in your business. They don't mean anything by it, there's just not much to do here. A new guy comes to town, maybe he used to be famous, starts paying attention to the local baker? Oh yeah. You're under the microscope, my friend."

He scratched his head, thinking. "I don't want this to look bad for Cleo. There's nothing going on here."

"Not my business. Or anybody else's. It's only harmless gossip. Everybody loves Cleo."

The cat was roused by the sound of voices and got up to investigate. Her legs were still a little spindly and after a nap she sometimes walked a bit crooked until she got everything straightened out again. Kyle crouched down and held out a hand, which she came and sniffed.

"Who's this?"

"Delilah."

Kyle stroked a finger under her chin. "Cute cat." He appreciated that Kyle didn't mention the missing ear.

"I was planning to give her away. She's a stray. Then she chewed on my hair this morning and I gave her a name."

Kyle looked at him with pity. "Dude. Once you name them, it's all over."

He cast his old friend a glance. "Unless you'd like a cat. I can guarantee you she's very smart, already litter-box trained, and excellent on boats."

Kyle was already rising to his feet. "No can do. We're trying for a baby. It's causing a little stress around the house. I don't think this is the right time to bring in another helpless infant."

Ethan was ready to push the benefits of learning about helpless infants on a cat so they'd be better prepared for a baby, but something in Kyle's tone warned him off. A weird frown had flitted across his old friend's face and then swiftly moved away. He had no idea what trouble at home meant, and he could tell from Kyle's expression he didn't want to talk about it.

Kyle clapped him on the shoulder. "I'll let you get back to work. But come by the house soon. It would be great to catch up."

He nodded. "Will do." Then he looked at the bag sitting on the counter. "Thanks."

Their deal had always been that he'd do handyman stuff and Cleo would cook. But maybe it would be nice for him to cook dinner for her for once.

Not wanting to presume, he phoned her to tell her about the prawns. Instead of being pissed as he'd half worried she'd be that Kyle Donovan knew he was spending so much time at her place, she sounded pleased. "I'll grab a baguette to bring home. I think there's a lemon in the bowl."

He checked. "There is." He saw it there, peeking out from beneath two bananas and a couple of apples in her fruit bowl.

"Anything else I should pick up on my way home?"

"I think we're good." And, as he got off the phone, he realized they'd spoken like a couple. The thought should have left him feeling claustrophobic and ready to run, but instead it felt good. Normal.

The next day dawned bright and sunny. That meant Ethan could work outside again. He wanted to get the rest of the dock pieces finished and it was the perfect weather for that. Delilah chewing on his hair had woken him again. He wasn't sure about this new morning ritual of hers. She was like his alarm clock. He checked his watch and it wasn't even six yet. But he was up now. He hauled his hair-obsessed sleeping companion off his chest and rolled out of bed. He stretched and put coffee on. Breakfast was toasted slices of the rye bread Cleo had given him yesterday with eggs, and then one of her blueberry and rhubarb muffins as well for good measure.

He took his coffee up on deck and watched the activity at the marina. Most were pleasure boats put away for the winter, but a few people like him were staying onboard. There were fishing boats getting ready to head out to sea. He waved a cheerful good morning to the crew. He loved this time of the day. Yesterday's rain had cleared the air and he could hear the bark of sea lions. Seagulls wheeled overhead crying and a bald eagle circled above them.

He'd had the pieces of lumber for the dock delivered yesterday. They were stacked in the shed. He'd start with that job and see how far he got. He stretched in the morning air, thinking he didn't need much gym time when he worked with his hands all day.

"Ready, Delilah?" he asked his shipmate. She'd eaten her breakfast, used the litter box and appeared ready for adventure. "You're getting bigger every day, you know that?"

She tipped her head to one side, staring at him. He might be biased but he thought that single ear gave her an avant-garde appearance, like people who styled their hair dramatically shorter on one side than the other.

He opened the cat carrier and she got right in, suggesting that she'd become comfortable with their daily skiff ride. Or, at least, she preferred a couple of short sea journeys to a day spent alone on the boat.

He skirted around colorful buoys that warned of crab traps below. He'd noticed a couple of traps and an outboard in a shed at the edge of Cleo's property. He wondered about setting the traps. He wouldn't mind a crab feed, though the way he'd been eating since he got here, every day was a feast.

He tied up at Cleo's dock, in what was becoming a daily routine, hauled the cat carrier up the stairs.

It wasn't until he was already in the garden that he saw

Cleo. She was just stepping out of the French doors that presumably led to her bedroom, the one room in the cottage he'd never seen. She had a cup of coffee in her hand and was wearing a cotton nightdress. Her long red hair, streaked with gray, hung loose and her face was soft with sleep. For a moment he took in her long, muscular legs and womanly curves. When she caught him looking, he felt awful. Like a pervert sneaking around trying to catch a glimpse of her in her underwear.

"I didn't know you started work so early," she called out, as though this was her fault.

"Sorry." Though why he was apologizing, he wasn't sure. For staring at her, probably. "I thought you'd be at the bakery." She should be. She was always at work when he arrived. As she'd told him many times, she began work before dawn.

"It's my day off."

He didn't know what to do, so he stood there. He might have remained as still as a garden gnome if Delilah hadn't meowed, letting him know she would like to be released. Right. He did and when he glanced up again, Cleo had retreated back into the house. She'd left the door open, though.

He wasn't sure whether to stay or go. She could kick him out if she wanted to, or he could carry on. By the time he'd checked that the shed was skunk free and heard the weather forecast from the radio in there, Cleo had emerged, now in T-shirt and jeans. Still holding her coffee. They glanced at each other and there was sort of an amused and embarrassed moment that passed between them.

He said, "Sorry again. I didn't realize you'd be here."

She chuckled. "I'm just glad you didn't catch me naked in the shower."

Then she looked as though she wished she'd bitten her tongue rather than say those words. But she had and a flash of heat arced between them. Definitely what you'd call an awkward moment. But sexy, too.

To break it, he said, "I can come back tomorrow and let you enjoy your day off."

She put up her free hand, waving off his offer. "No. It's fine. I mean, if you don't mind me being here."

"I'd love the company. Unless you'd rather be on your own."

It looked like they could do this polite dance all day and never get anywhere, and then she asked, "How does bacon and eggs sound?"

He grinned at her. "Now you're talking. I'll get started on prepping the boards to fix your dock. Call me when it's ready?"

She nodded. "I'll put more coffee on."

Over breakfast he suggested putting the crab traps out one day soon. She looked almost surprised. As though she'd forgotten she owned any, but she soon came around. "That's a great idea." They talked about some improvements she wanted to make and some of the tasks she had in the garden, getting ready for the growing season. He offered to help her with the dishes but she waved him away.

"Earn your keep. You get back to work out there doing the heavy, manly stuff. Kitchen's my domain."

"That is very sexist," he commented as though he were offended. And then he flexed his biceps in a he-man fashion. "But, since you've noticed my manly strength I might as well go and use it."

She laughed and he found himself grinning as he went back to work. It didn't take more than an hour to replace the rotted boards on the dock. He had a couple of treads he wanted to fix on the stairway going upstairs next, but he'd need to borrow her car and get some more lumber. He walked up and found her wrestling with a trellis. Like she'd been trying to secure the tendrils of Clematis growing up the lacy wood when it had tipped over on her.

It wasn't heavy, just awkward, and he strolled over to lend a hand. He pulled the fallen wooden structure away from her and said, "I'll fix this today, too."

She laughed up at him. "I could keep you busy your whole life working around this place."

The sun was shining down on them, a butterfly was just a flash of yellow as it wafted by. He could smell the sweet scent of lilac on the breeze.

When they righted the trellis his hand ended up over hers and she glanced up so their gazes caught. The thought never entered his mind. It was pure instinct that had him reaching for her. He let his gaze linger on her mouth so she'd know what he intended. He gave her a second to pull away and instead of retreating her lips opened. He took his time. He leaned in and put his mouth on hers and felt the spark that had flashed between them for days now explode. She made a soft sound in the back of her throat like a sigh and he pulled her even closer.

Her arms came around him, strong from kneading dough and lifting sacks of flour. He liked how solid she felt, how real.

She tasted good. Like coffee and the best bread and hot, willing woman.

The trellis sagged, forgotten. Maybe the stair project could wait.

As the kiss lengthened and deepened, he thought he might finally get to see the inside of Cleo's bedroom.

When they came up for air, he said, "How about we take this inside."

Her lips were wet, swollen from his kisses, her eyes already going dreamy. She nodded and reached up to kiss him again.

The moment was broken by a man's voice calling out. "Hey there," all friendly like. Ethan felt nothing but irritation for anyone who'd come calling at such an inappropriate moment. Couldn't the guy see what was going on and come back later?

He sighed. They both turned and he kept an arm around

Cleo so he felt her stiffen from a warm, wanting woman into something akin to a frozen iron statue.

The man walking forward was a little younger than him, wearing dark sunglasses and a flashy grin.

Cleo pulled away and took a step back. Instinctively, he shifted his body so he was in front of her, as though she needed protecting.

The guy with the lantern jaw and the set of pearly whites said, "I'm Travis Smith. Looks like you're boning my wife."

FOURTEEN

Ethan wasn't rendered speechless very often. But if the guy standing there claiming Cleo as his wife had belted him in the solar plexus, he couldn't be more stunned.

He turned to Cleo to see what she had to say about this. Her face told him it was the truth. She looked pale and mortified.

"You're married?" he asked her.

That seemed to rouse her out of her stupor. She passed him a quick glance, seemed all confusion and guilt, and then said to the guy calling himself Travis, "What the hell are you doing here?"

The grin was back, but there was no amusement behind it. "Can't a man say hello to his wife?"

She pushed herself around Ethan and planted her hands on her hips, her legs a couple of feet apart, kind of an anchoring stance, the way he'd do when the boat was pitching so he didn't get knocked over. "You haven't been my husband since you walked out on me two years ago. Now get the hell off my property."

The guy shook his head. "Now that's a funny thing. I don't recall a divorce."

She made a sound of fury. "Because I couldn't track you down after you two took off. And how is Linda Preston anyway?"

"Now, honey, you're jumping to conclusions. If Linda Preston left town around the same time I did, that was a coincidence."

"Bullshit."

Ethan had never heard her swear before. He glanced at her. Her face was flushed and there was stress in every line of her body.

"That two years when you forgot where you lived. What did you have, amnesia?"

"Come on, Cleo. Things weren't great between us. I needed some space. I'm sorry I took so long to come back. But I want to try again." His voice went soft and intimate. "We were good together once."

"I want you to get off my property right now."

He stood his ground. "I believe I have a legal right to be here."

She made a sound like Delilah did when she bolted her food and it came back up. "Why don't I call the sheriff? And let him decide?"

Travis held up his hands and took a step back. "I don't want any trouble. Take some time to get used to the idea that I'm back. We'll talk later." And then he turned to Ethan. "And you might want to find another bedpost to hang your hat on."

His hands formed themselves into fists. Twenty years ago, he'd have launched himself into battle. But age and experience had taught him physical violence was rarely the answer. All he said was, "I'll be here as long as Cleo wants me."

It wasn't what he'd meant to say, but after the words were out, he knew he meant them. The two-bit charmer turned around and sauntered up the gravel drive. Like he was in no hurry. He got about a hundred yards up and then turned and yelled out, "I like the new colors you painted the place."

They both watched him until he was out of sight. Interesting that he hadn't driven a vehicle to the house so they could have heard him coming. There was something sneaky about his arrival. He couldn't have walked here. There wasn't a bus. He must have driven and parked on the road, exactly so he could surprise Cleo.

He turned back to find Cleo curled in on herself with a hand held to her chest as though her heart was hurting. He said, as neutrally as he could, "Hey, are you okay?"

She nodded but he could see she wasn't. She was still pale and her hand was trembling.

"Is that your ex?" It was the stupidest question of the century, but he didn't know what else to say. In case she wanted to talk about it, he wanted to be here for her.

"Yeah. And technically he's right. He is still my husband. But only because I couldn't find him. I figured he was gone for good. I never thought he'd come back."

"No offense, but I'm guessing he's not back here because he loves you and he couldn't live without you. Not after two years."

"No. And I wouldn't take him back if he was." She let out a huge sigh. "If you want to leave, I understand."

"I don't." He was still reeling from finding out she had a husband kicking around, but he was surprised by his own reaction. After the first blast of disgust that she'd lied to him, he quickly caught on to the real story, and gone from outraged to sympathetic. If they weren't going to be lovers, and as of right now that was clearly off the table, he hoped he was her friend and enough of a friend not to take off when she was in trouble.

"I think I need to make some coffee. And is it too early for brandy?"

"Under the circumstances, I think brandy would be an excellent idea."

They went into the kitchen and she tried to scoop coffee into the French press, but her hand was shaking so much she was spilling coffee grounds all over the counter. He took her gently and sat her down on the old green velvet couch that he could tell was her favorite. Delilah was snoozing on the windowsill in the sun. He scooped her up and carried her over and put her on Cleo's lap. There was something about a purring kitten that could soothe a body.

Then he went back into the kitchen and made coffee. It probably wouldn't be as good as hers, but he didn't suppose either of them minded. Besides, it gave them both a few minutes to process what just happened.

He dug around in her scanty liquor cabinet. There was no brandy. He found some Bailey's Irish Cream. Figured that was as good as anything. He measured a healthy slug into both their mugs and brought the coffee out to the living room.

"Thank you," she said, closing her hands around the mug as though it was a cold day and she'd been sledding and needed the warmth. She took a sip of her drink as he sat quietly watching her. "I never lied to you. I never said I was divorced."

"But you did call him your ex," he reminded her gently.

She nodded. "He is my ex."

"In every way but legally, I'm guessing."

"Now that he's back, I can at least serve him with divorce papers."

"Why do you think he's back?"

Delilah was having trouble settling, no doubt picking up the jittery energy. Cleo stroked her back until she sat. She wasn't ready to curl up yet, but she sat, her one ear twitching, her eyes wide and alert. "I don't know, but I can guarantee it's not good news."

"Do you want him back?" He had to ask.

Her response, "Hell no," had the cat jumping to its feet again in alarm.

"Sorry, Delilah," she said, softening her tone.

"Is there any chance he's sincere and wants to try again?" He didn't think that for a second but he was curious how she viewed the sudden reappearance of Travis Smith in her life.

She laughed, but not a humorous sound. It was cold and bitter. "No. I do not think he is sincere. I expect he's run out of better options." She sighed. "I acted like a wimp toward the end of our marriage. No doubt he thinks I'm a pushover. But I don't intend to be. Not anymore. At least now, I can divorce him."

Ethan had a bad feeling about this. "Oceanfront property in this area has increased a lot in the last few years."

Her eyes squeezed shut. "I know. And Washington is a community property state."

"How good is your lawyer?"

She shrugged. "He's local. He handles wills and estates, property transfer, the odd divorce. He's part of the community. Not a friend, exactly, but he's been our family lawyer for years."

"Look, I don't want to butt in where I don't belong, but I could make some calls."

She still looked stunned. She glanced up at him and back at her coffee, and then just nodded. "Thanks."

He couldn't stand seeing this strong, feisty woman looking like a rag doll with all the stuffing pulled out of it.

He went over and sat beside her and gripped her hand. "Hey. You'll get through this. It's not the end of the world."

Her smile wobbled around the edges. "It just brings it all back, you know? What a fool I was. I can see through his phony charm in a second now. But eight years ago, I was forty-four. I'd lost my mother and business partner to cancer and I was mourning her."

"That must have been awful."

"One of the worst times of my life. And there was Travis

making everything seem better. He was sexy and charming and flattered me. He could be so much fun and outrageous, exciting. Everything was a game to him. He took me to an escape room, parasailing, hiking to places I'd never known about. After the dark times I'd been through, it was like a time out. I didn't think about the future, how I was going to pay the medical bills, manage the business on my own. I played."

She shook her head, looking back. "He was gorgeous, a few years younger than me and he reeled me in like a fat trout. His proposal was probably the most romantic thing that had ever happened to me." She stopped to take a breath. "He chartered a small plane and had us flown to a remote island. For a picnic! There was no one around but us on this sandy beach. He had a real picnic basket and in it was a blanket to sit on, a tablecloth, champagne, glasses, all this beautiful food." She tipped her head back to stare at the ceiling. "He got down on one knee. Pulled out this ring box. I hadn't seen it coming. We'd only been together a couple of months. And I fell for it. I was old enough to know better and as foolish as a sixteen-year-old with a high school crush."

"What does Travis do? Does he have a job?"

"He came here to open a fishing charter business for tourists. He had all these grand sounding plans. He made it sound like he'd been running a similar business in the Bahamas and had wanted to come back home. It sounded plausible. I had no reason not to believe him."

"I'm guessing, from your tone, that he lied?"

"Well, he had been in the Bahamas, but he didn't own or manage the company. He was one of their fishing guides. He got fired for not showing up one too many times. Which I found out later, when I was trying to track him down."

He heard the self-blame in her tone and reached out to put a hand on her knee. "Hey, you couldn't know. And you were grieving. That makes people vulnerable."

"And, in my case, gullible."

"So, you married him."

"Yes, I did," she said, sounding tired. "The lawyer I talked to said that theoretically, because I'd inherited this house and property from my mother, it could be considered my sole asset, but because he lived here with me he could claim he made improvements which he really didn't, that muddies the waters. And, you're right, in the last few years this property's tripled in value. I could lose my home."

He didn't say anything, but he was worried that any debts her runaway husband had accumulated might also be considered joint property.

"Look. I'm no lawyer. But I certainly know some good ones. He left you, and you couldn't find him. Hopefully that'll be enough."

"I never thought I'd see his weaselly, cheating face again."

He was glad to see that her color was coming back and so was her fight.

She turned fiery eyes on him. "My mother worked her butt off to buy this place and build the bakery, I have worked my butt off to keep it. I am not giving up my home without a fight."

FIFTEEN

Cleo felt physically battered, the way she'd felt when she'd been stopped at a red light and a car that she hadn't seen coming hit her from behind. As though an explosion had happened right in front of her. She had to concentrate simply to breathe.

There was Ethan, offering her a shoulder to cry on. An hour ago, they'd been halfway to the bedroom. She couldn't believe how her emotional landscape could go from bright, promising spring to dead of winter in a couple of minutes.

Underneath all of that, anxiety was beginning to gnaw at her. What was Travis doing back in Clamshell Bay, and what could he possibly want with her?

Ethan spoke and she had to concentrate on his words. She still didn't get it. "I'm sorry, what did you say?"

She felt like a fool, but his eyes were full of understanding as he gazed at her. "I asked if Travis has friends in Clamshell Bay? Other reasons to visit besides you."

"I don't think so. He never did start that business and if any of my friends spotted him walking toward them, they'd cross the street. But, obviously, he had a whole other life I knew nothing about."

"What if I sleep over for a couple of nights?"

"What?" And then she shook her head. "I know what happened in the garden earlier might lead you to believe—"

"No," he interrupted her. "I'm going to sleep on your couch. Cleo, I don't trust that guy. I saw your face when he showed up. He's trouble and I don't want you here alone where he can get at you."

She suspected he was right. Travis had always been trouble. He just fooled her at the beginning with charm and good looks. Now another man with genuine charm and better looks was proposing to shack up in her living room? Her voice went clipped. "You want to sleep on my couch."

"I do."

"Why?"

"Because we're friends." His eyes lit with a sort of remorseful humor. He leaned forward and ran his thumb along her lower lip. "Maybe more than friends. Heading in that direction, anyway. But not today."

Travis had some bad timing. He'd arrived so fast after she and Ethan started kissing that she hadn't even had a second to process what had happened. Now she did. She might be out of practice, but she was pretty sure that kiss had been amazing. And she had a pretty good idea where it was going to lead them. It wasn't as though she hadn't thought about it. In fact, she'd thought a lot about breaking her dry spell with Ethan. He was still a fine-looking man. And he was right, there was something building between them. Maybe it wouldn't last. It was time she stopped worrying about the future. Would she have grabbed his hand and led him into the bedroom? Had Travis not appeared when he did, she was pretty sure she would have.

Megan would be so pleased that she'd taken her advice to "tap that."

Now the only thing she wanted to tap was her sense of contentment and serenity that she had built up over the years.

That Travis had managed to pull to pieces in the first second she saw him standing there, staring at her kissing another man.

Was Ethan right? Would her ex-husband— No. She had to stop herself even thinking of him that way. Technically, and legally, he was still her husband. She shut her eyes against the certain knowledge that she'd been very foolish. She had consulted a lawyer after Travis took off. But not knowing where he was made things more difficult. She'd meant to be free of Travis legally and forever but it was negative and unpleasant and even thinking about him filled her with such humiliation that day after day passed.

There came a time when she stopped thinking about him every day with that sick feeling in the pit of her stomach. She'd removed all traces of him from her home, from her life, and as much as she could from her memory. And now he'd turned up again, like a bad penny, her mother would have said. Her mother would have had a lot to say about a daughter who would be stupid enough not to make sure that when Travis walked out the door she'd shut and locked it behind him.

But did she really need Ethan sleeping on her couch like a very attractive, nice smelling watchdog?

"What do you think he's going to do to me? Even if he does decide to show up again?"

"I don't know." He took her hand. "Maybe nothing. But I need to do this, Cleo."

She could see he meant every word.

Still holding her hand, he brought it up and down a couple of times so her fingers tapped against his thigh. "I want to tell you a story."

Could this day get any weirder? "Okay."

"As you know...No, I can't start the story there. You'll have to forgive me. I never tell anyone this. But I need you to understand." He seemed like he was shuffling through memories as though they were a pack of cards and he was trying to pull the right one. Finally, he chose one. "Back when I was doing *Badminton Run*, I got to be friends with my co-star, Tessa Draycott."

She nodded. She remembered that they'd been talked about as a romantic item in the media, though they'd both denied it.

"Unlike me, she was the genuine article. An actress who'd trained at Juilliard and knew how to speak a line to give it resonance, and just with a tiny movement of the muscles in her face she could convey so much emotion. I was never going to be an actor and everybody on set knew it. She could have made my life hell, but she didn't." He fell back in time, seeing Tessa walk into his trailer after he'd blown another scene. She'd say, "What if you didn't know the next line?"

"What do you mean?" Everybody knew he couldn't act, so he did everything else to make sure he didn't screw up. No one memorized their lines more faithfully. She sat across from him with her script and said, "You're all but telegraphing the next line, waiting to deliver it. Imagine if you didn't know what I was about to say, so you had to listen. Like in this scene. I don't think it's a good idea to confront Bradford at his warehouse and you do."

"Right." He knew all this.

She settled back and crossed her very attractive legs and sent him a cool look. "I think the scene could be so much better with a little more rehearsal."

In his opinion they'd rehearsed plenty, but he respected her opinion. He nodded slowly.

"Good. I'm going to suggest to the director that we work over the weekend to make sure we get this scene right."

He'd been furious. "But I have plans. I told you. I'm going home for my parents' wedding anniversary. It's a big deal."

"A bigger deal than your career?"

He'd been outraged. Argued with her. Stood up and paced the small trailer, poking a finger at her to emphasize his excellent arguments. At the end of ten or fifteen minutes, she'd given him her dazzling smile and stood. "Now, when we run that scene again this afternoon, remember exactly how you felt in the last ten minutes you were arguing with me. Use it. The irritation in your voice, the testy body language. The emotional outrage."

His jaw had dropped as he saw her self-satisfied smile and knew he'd been manipulated. "You conned me."

She laughed. Not the well-modulated laugh she learned at Julliard, but a shriek of amusement that was about as attractive as the sounds of seagulls fighting. "We'll make an actor of you, yet."

Ethan related the story to Cleo. "As much as she could, Tessa helped me. I'll never forget that. And it makes what I'm about to tell you seem so much worse."

She was starting to think she didn't want to hear this story. She had enough problems of her own, she didn't need to hear him admit to wrongdoing. She already had her black hat in Travis. She really needed a white hat in Ethan, and not a gray one.

"This was long before the Me Too movement. Our show producer was one of those guys who strutted around wielding his power over the people in his shows, particularly the women. Behind the camera, in front, didn't matter. Tessa was vulnerable. She'd just got divorced before we started shooting *Badminton Run* and I believe part of what made her such a good actress was being more open emotionally. Anyway, he got to her."

Her stomach clenched in sympathy for this actress she'd never met.

"At first, I didn't clue in to what was going on. Tessa seemed different, more jumpy. He'd take her to lunch and seemed to spend a lot of time with her. I assumed it was mutual."

Oh, she was getting a bad feeling about this. "And it wasn't?"

He shook his head. "I was walking by her trailer and I heard them. The things he said to her were awful, and I waited until he left her trailer and then I went in. She was a mess. He'd thrown her against the side of the trailer. Called her names and sexually assaulted her."

Cleo had heard of stories like this, of course. Who hadn't? But they'd always been distant to her. Women who'd worked on screen, but she'd never known anyone personally who'd been a victim. Her sympathy was roused along with deep-seated fury against men who treated women badly. And Travis got lumped in that category as well, so her fury was both old and rekindled and fresh as a newly lit fire all at the same time.

"What did you do?"

She could imagine how he must have felt.

He squeezed her hand tighter. She wasn't even sure he realized he was doing it. "I did nothing." The words seemed to come from somewhere deep inside him and he spat them out like bullets. Then he repeated himself. "I did nothing."

She wanted to ask him why not, but she kept her mouth shut. He'd tell her when and if he was ready. She could tell he was looking back into the past and he didn't like the view.

"I was ready to go punch his daylights out. Call the cops. She begged me not to. Other women had lost their careers by not doing what he wanted. Well, you've seen the media. I don't have to tell you. It was an awful secret for decades as these women put up with this abuse in order to continue with their careers. I tried to talk her into pressing charges or letting me do something. But she begged me not to say anything or it would ruin her career. And so I didn't."

"I'm so sorry." She didn't really know who she was sorry for. The poor woman who'd put up with a producer abusing her, or Ethan, who in those days would have been younger and no doubt more idealistic and hotheaded than the man she knew now.

"I feel guilty about it every single day. I should have done something to protect her."

"But she begged you not to. You were only following her wishes."

He turned to her. His eyes were bleak. "And don't you think that somewhere deep inside myself, I was pretty relieved? If I rocked that boat, Tessa and I both got tossed out." He shook his head. "But now I look back and I don't think that would have happened. If both of us had stood up and gone public about what was going on? While we had a hit show? Maybe a lot of women would have felt empowered to come forward then, rather than waiting decades."

Even in the midst of her own pain, she felt his. She reached for his other hand so that they were angled towards each other on the couch, their hands clasping each other's, Delilah shifting to get more comfortable.

"You're taking an awful lot on yourself. Sure, maybe it was convenient for you to respect her wishes. But you were still respecting her wishes. Her life, her body, her career. Those were her business."

The bleakness in his eyes didn't lighten, but he did smile at her a little. "The kicker is? She lost her career anyway. She started drinking. Heavily. The last season, she was drunk more than she was sober."

Cleo didn't really remember much about that last season of *Badminton Run*, but like a lot of shows, it seemed to lose its spark and then got canceled. She'd never realized why.

"I'm so sorry. I never knew that."

"Nobody knew that. We kept it very quiet. She was so fragile, she couldn't take any more. I did manage to get her into rehab. That was the first time."

"I'm so sorry. How is she now?"

He shook his head. "Up and down. She tries. Every once in a while she'll check herself back into rehab. I just think her demons never leave her alone."

"I'm sure I've seen her in a few things."

He nodded. "She still acts, occasionally. Bit parts. It keeps her going. She's still an amazing actor. But I think of the career she could have had. Should have had. It makes me furious. And guilty."

"I'm so sorry," she said again. Inadequate words but all she had.

"That's why I want to sleep on your couch for a couple of nights. I'm not walking away from another woman I care about who needs me."

She was touched. Hearing him admit to caring about her warmed her all over. Still, she shook her head. "If Travis finds you sleeping here, he'll use it against me somehow. You know he will. He's greedy and lazy, but he's not violent. And those motion-detector lights you put up will warn me if he gets close. I'll be on the phone to the sheriff's office before he can knock on the door."

He opened his mouth to argue some more and she stopped him by leaning forward and kissing him. When she pulled slowly away, she said, "Thank you for being there for me. For reminding me that there are good men out there."

"Cleo, I—"

Her phone rang. It was Pepper at the bakery. Oh, no, what else could go wrong today? She picked up the phone dreading to hear of some supply shortage, power failure, some disaster with the bakery. What she got was Pepper saying in a low, breathless tone, "Travis Smith was just in here. I thought you should know that bastard is back."

He must have come to the house first then. She was positive this was true when Pepper continued, "I wanted to warn you, in case he tries to come by the house."

"He already did. But thank you for trying to warn me. How's everything else?"

"Everybody's buzzing about Travis being here. He's going around as though he's some war hero back to be given a medal by the people of the town. I can't get over him having the nerve to show his face here, never mind act like anyone wants to see him. Cleo, everybody's on your side."

Even as she felt foolish for getting so emotional, she felt the burn of tears at the back of her throat. Just knowing people here cared about her that much made Travis's return more bearable.

"Thanks. What did he want?"

"He came in. No, he swaggered in, like he owned the place, got himself a cup of coffee and started talking to people as though he'd only seen them the day before. So friendly. I'm sorry. I didn't want to serve him, but I was so shocked and he was all smiles and jokes, you know what he's like."

"It's okay. You did the right thing."

She could feel her blood starting to boil again. Her hand clenched the phone so tightly she was afraid she'd break it and forced herself to relax. She could picture him too. Travis the charmer, no matter what he did, always thinking that bad boy grin meant he could get away with anything. He'd gotten away with too much already in his life. She was proud and grateful that the people of her town weren't falling for him anymore.

"Is he still there?"

"No. He left. He seemed surprised that nobody wanted to talk to him. But, Cleo, nobody did. Well, a couple of tourists who didn't know any better chatted to him about the fishing.

After he left, they had to come up and tell me how friendly everybody was in this town. I nearly puked."

Her lips twitched even though she was having one of the worst days of her life. "Let me know if he comes in again."

"Don't worry. I will."

She ended the call and turned to Ethan. "That was Pepper. She said Travis was in the bakery trying to charm everybody. And she used a term that made me very uncomfortable. She said he walked in like he owned the place." She put a hand to her forehead as though checking for fever. "He probably thinks he owns half the place. Because we're a community property state in Washington and I never divorced him." How could she have been so stupid?

Ethan looked ready to pick a fight. But she watched him take a breath and let it out. Take another breath and let it out. Then he said, "Cleo, you're not alone. You're older, you're stronger, and you're not freshly grieving. We'll figure this out."

The burn in the back of her throat was back. "But this is not your problem. You don't owe me anything."

"So? Can't a friend help a friend?"

As the burn intensified, she realized she didn't want to be just friends. It was easy to be independent and tough when nothing bad was going on. It was times like now that she recognized the power in having a team, even if it was only two people.

She probably couldn't afford to hire his fancy lawyers, but then again she probably couldn't afford not to.

He picked up his phone and was going through his contacts when her cell phone rang again. Brooke. "I'll make some calls. Okay if I use the spare room?"

She nodded and picked up. "Cleo! I just came from the bakery. Pepper's probably already called you, but I wanted you to know that your ex is back."

"How do you know that? You weren't even living here when he left."

There was a burble of laughter from the other end of the phone. "Are you kidding? It's all anybody can talk about."

"Yeah. Pepper called me, but I already knew. Travis had the nerve to drop by the house today."

"What? What did he want?"

Oh, it was so hard to speak through tightly gritted teeth. She opened her jaw wide and closed it again just to get some movement there. "He said he wanted to try again."

A spurt of disbelieving laughter. "Did you fall for it?"

Why would Brooke, who hadn't lived in Clamshell Bay when Travis wooed, married and left her, be so certain Travis was a bad man. "How do you know he wasn't sincere?"

"I'm sorry, honey. I met him."

Another wave of humiliation washed over her. Brooke could see in one meeting beyond the slick charm to the calculating man beneath. How had she been so fooled?

Before she could speak, Brooke said, "Kyle wants me to tell you that he can get some buddies together and they'll drive him out of town if that's what you want."

She was glad Brooke couldn't see her smile. Even more happy that Kyle couldn't see it, as she pictured his elegant, slim body that he kept toned with regular squash games launching himself at Travis. She doubted Kyle had ever been in a fight in his life outside of a boardroom. Then she wondered if a guy with that much money had thugs for hire. She really didn't want to know.

"Please tell him thanks. I'll keep that in mind. But he's to stand down until I give the order."

"Roger that."

She couldn't help it, she was starting to feel better. They were about to hang up when she heard a male voice speaking behind Brooke. "Oh. Kyle also says to tell you that if you need a good lawyer, he's got one on speed dial."

Did she tell them that Ethan was here? Oh, what the heck. No doubt Travis would blast it all over town anyway, if he thought it would make her look bad. "Thanks. Ethan was here when Travis dropped by the house. He's on the phone right now in the bedroom tracking down a lawyer. *Spare* bedroom."

Then she closed her eyes tight. What was she doing? She was fifty-two years old and whether she was sleeping with Ethan or not, it was her business. Except that no doubt Travis was branding her as an adulteress. Over one kiss.

At least it was a great kiss.

SIXTEEN

After that the calls came one after the other. She thought about turning her phone off, but she answered every call for two reasons. One, it was nice to hear that everyone in Clamshell Bay had her back. And two, she didn't want anyone deciding on their own to get rid of Travis. She needed to do that herself. With divorce papers signed.

Megan called about half an hour after Brooke did. "Hey, heard about Travis. How are you doing?"

"Not bad. Not great."

"Listen, I was thinking. I could bring my toolbox over and stay the night at your place for a few days. Or, you could come here if you'd rather."

She was snagged by the toolbox. "What are you going to do with your toolbox?" Was she planning to fix stuff?

"Girl, I'm pretty handy with a hammer. If Travis tries anything, he'll have to go through me first." She seemed to think about it for a minute. "I also have a pretty lethal staple gun."

"Thank you, I'll keep that in mind." If there was anyone who would be thrilled to hear that Ethan was staying over it would be Megan. She said, "Ethan offered—"

She was about to say she'd refused when Megan let out a whoop so loud Cleo had to pull the phone away from her ear. "Awesome. Okay, I know you're in the depths of despair right now, but I have to ask. How was it?"

"Megan!" she said with as much outrage as she could muster. "All we've had so far is one kiss."

"Man, you old people. You'll die waiting for him to make a move."

She wasn't that old. "I like to take things slowly."

"A kiss, huh? How was that?"

After making sure Ethan was still in the spare bedroom, she let satisfaction seep into her tone. "As good as any sex I've ever had."

The chuckle in her ear was pure evil. "Wait till he gets you naked in that bed. I predict that guy's going to rock your world."

She laughed and they ended the call. What she didn't share with Megan was that Ethan had already rocked her world.

And she wasn't sure that she could ever right it again.

Even Libby phoned her. "Cleo, I heard about your ex coming back into town. I'm so sorry. Is there anything I can do? Do you want to me to come over and stay with you for a few days? I'd have to bring the kids. Or you could come and stay with us."

Libby had gone back to her home and family when the weekend baking class ended. "How did you even hear about that?"

"Both Brooke and Megan called me. We're all worried about you."

She'd never had a baking class that turned into a solid friendship so quickly. But she could feel the goodwill of those three other women propping her up. And it helped.

Once more she explained that Ethan was staying a couple of nights. And, unlike her other two callers, Libby said in her soft, tentative manner, "If you're uncomfortable at all about him staying, we'd love to have you here. Right now it's just the kids and me. The guest room's very comfortable and you'd have your own bathroom."

"It's fine. And since I'm sure you're thinking what the other two were, you're just too polite to ask, no, we haven't done the nasty. We've shared one very nice kiss."

There was a tiny pause, and then Libby said, "I always think a kiss tells you everything you need to know."

When Ethan came back into the room he had to wait while she assured Janet Beamish at the pet shop that she was really okay and didn't need a place to stay. Janet said, "I liked Travis a lot when you two first got together. But, the way he treated you, that wasn't right. Now I wouldn't trust that man farther than I could throw him."

"Thanks. It's nice to know I wasn't the only woman in town who was fooled."

"Trust me, you weren't. He's still a good-looking guy, but back then? He was smokin' hot."

Hot on the outside and not so hot on the inside.

She got off the phone to find Ethan was making notes in a notebook he usually had in his toolbox or shoved in his back pocket. He glanced up.

"My guy knows a guy. He's tracking down the best divorce attorney in the state. I told him you want an appointment this week."

She stared at him feeling numb and disoriented. "Is there a rush?"

He came towards her and put a warm hand on her shoulder. "I know this is hard for you. But the sooner you get moving, the sooner you can get rid of Travis. I think you and the whole town will be glad when he's out of here."

"How do you know the whole town is anxious to get rid of him?"

"You think you're the only one getting calls? I've had three texts already today. And I hardly know anyone in town." He counted off with his fingers. "Text from Janet Beamish at the pet store. A text from Kyle. And, most interesting of all, I got a text from Filbert Marine. Eugene Filbert wants me to watch out for you. This is a guy whose name I didn't know until he texted. Our whole relationship has consisted of me buying things and him ordering them or ringing them up."

"Small towns," she said.

"Cleo, people here care about you."

"I have to go into town," Cleo said to Ethan. It was something she rarely did on her day off. She liked to putter around at home, lounge in sweats all day if she wanted to, tidy and garden. Cook for pleasure. Today, she'd have taken her handyman to bed.

She couldn't even think about that now.

What she wanted to do was hide out here forever. Close the bakery, never show her face again. Have all groceries, books, clothes, everything she could possibly need for the rest of her life delivered to her cottage. Her sanctuary.

But she had her pride. Travis would not crush her a second time. So, she'd get dressed, put on that makeup Brooke had given her and go into town with her head held high.

Cleo thought of herself as a sensible, mature woman. Somebody people relied on and told their secrets to. The time after Travis had left had been one of the darkest of her life. It wasn't that she had been so desperately in love with him. By that point in their marriage, the rose-colored glasses she'd worn when she first fell for the guy had fallen from her eyes.

She could see her husband clearly. He still lived to play and have adventures, but he was shallow, vain, greedy, and manipulative. Also lazy. He'd traded on that charm and undeniable good looks. There was an unspoken agreement in their marriage, all his and none hers, that she did all the hard work, provided the comfortable home and warmed his bed, and he provided his fine physique and good-looking face. More, it seemed, was not required.

For the first few months, okay, more than a year, she had felt that was a perfectly fair exchange. She'd still been awed that a man like that would want a woman like her. Not that she was plain, exactly. But she felt dull next to his dazzling presence. He was the sun in his own universe and she was some distant planet barely getting enough reflected sunlight to do whatever distant planets did.

In her case, work.

While she'd been up in the wee hours heading to the bakery, she'd leave him comfortably snoozing in bed. He was evasive about how he spent his days. He had claimed to be researching his fishing charter business, then decided it wasn't economically feasible. He told her he was day trading. So whenever she came home and found him on the computer, he had a ready excuse. He was working. And, if she asked him to do anything useful, he'd argue that he was tired from busting a hump trying to make a living.

Except that he wasn't. It was she doing all the work, she who bought the groceries, paid the taxes, did all the cooking, cleaning, and still, he seemed to expect her to put extra effort into her appearance when he was around. And always, but always, to be in the mood.

For the first year or so blind lust had carried her along. But at some point, she'd begun to grow fatigued. She was managing on too little sleep. If she tried to go to bed at ten o'clock, he would pout and beg her to keep him company. "Babe, I hardly ever see you," he'd complain, and pull her close.

And then she discovered, as the haze of lust wore off, that there was a slow-burning anger buried so deep inside her she hadn't noticed it. When had she realized he was taking advantage of her?

Perhaps it was the time she asked him to pay the electric bill because she was short on cash.

He had looked at her as though she'd asked him to give her a kidney that he would remove himself with an ice-cream scoop and a rusty saw.

As his intense blue stare bored into her and as the silence lengthened, she grew increasingly uncomfortable. Finally, he said, "I do not think you understand the nature of my business. I do not have spare cash. It's all invested, it's all for our future, babe."

She looked forward to a comfortable retirement as much as anyone. But she was never going to make retirement age if she didn't slow down. When she asked him to fix the back fence he told her he hated nagging. She was starting to remind him of his mother. But this time she'd insisted. Then he'd made the hugest production out of going to the lumber store for boards and banging them up so ineptly that the fence fell down again shortly after he'd left.

Had she known he was cheating on her?

Oh, that wash of humiliation again even as she thought the thought. She probably had known on some level. But, she was a proud woman. She wouldn't admit defeat until she had to. However, by year five of their marriage, it was pretty clear things were coming to an end.

Truth was she'd been thinking a visit to an attorney was in order, but it was admitting defeat so she kept putting it off.

And then one day she came home from work and he was gone. Gone. His truck from the driveway, clothes gone from the dresser. His toiletries from the bathroom.

She'd looked around for a note and there wasn't one.

She'd called him and discovered his phone was no longer working.

She could have hired a private investigator but by that point she was so happy to see the back of him she didn't really care where he was.

The hardest thing though had been doing the walk of shame. She went into the bakery the next morning with determined cheer. It might be brittle, but it was enough to hide the awful truth. At least she'd imagined so. Until Bud Preston had burst into the bakery looking frantic. He wanted to know if anyone had seen his wife.

And that's when she'd discovered that her ex hadn't left her quietly, so she could tell the town some feasible story she'd make up, and do it on her own timetable. Oh no. He'd plunged her into a mortifying scandal. People who probably wouldn't have said anything stepped up and admitted that they'd seen Travis and Linda Preston at various times and in various places they had no business being together.

It was Pepper's aunt who saw the couple driving out of town, "sitting so close together he must have given her a bruise when he changed gears."

Bud moved away a few months later.

And that had left Cleo to bear it all alone. Although it was easier not having to look the other spurned spouse in the eye. Not having him ask one more time if she'd heard anything of Travis. Share that he hadn't heard from Linda, and then he'd lean forward over the bakery counter where she was trapped and spew the details of some new horrid story he'd heard about his wife and her husband. Listening to the account of how her husband had made a fool of her did her no good. She had plenty of fury and humiliation already. She did not need more.

But Bud was a different character. He seemed to enjoy getting himself all worked up again, and apparently believed she felt the same way.

So, in a way, it had been a relief when he'd left town. Unlike his runaway wife and her runaway husband, Bud made sure to leave a forwarding address.

And so, she'd lived down the awful humiliation of having married a man who was despicable in every way.

She'd regained some sense of peace and had rebuilt her life. And now, when she was thinking maybe there was hope for her, Travis had to show up. He had to bring all her stupid mistakes crashing back on her like a rogue wave.

SEVENTEEN

Going into town that afternoon was one of the most difficult things Cleo had ever done. As though he could sense her discomfort while she got herself ready, Ethan said, "I'll come with you."

She shook her head in a most determined fashion. "No. I'm going into that bakery and I don't want to feel like I'm leaning on you or hiding behind you. I have to do this on my own."

His eyes sort of squinted up a bit as he gave her a skeptical look. "You sure about this?"

No, she wasn't sure at all. "I'm sure."

"I hate to ask this. But is Travis inclined to violence?"

"No." At least she'd been spared that. "No. He was a loser, a cheater, a moocher, and the laziest man I've ever known. But he never hurt me in any way but emotionally."

"I still want to pound his head in." As he said it, his hands fisted. Much as she appreciated that he was on her side, the last thing she wanted was violence. Besides, Travis had always been so proud of his physique. The only truly energetic thing he'd ever done outside the bedroom was working out. She suspected he was still in fine shape and the last thing she wanted was for Ethan to get hurt.

She pulled a full breath in, imagined a string pulling up from the middle of her head the way her yoga instructor had taught her. "The first time I walk into the bakery will be the hardest."

"I know it." His smile was a little crooked. "And I also know that in this town, the word will have already gone out." He waved his phone at her as evidence. And she could see there were several new texts that had arrived since they'd been talking. "I don't think you're going to find yourself alone with that lowlife for a second. A lot of people have your back, Cleo. This community loves you."

This community loves you. The words felt true. Sure, she knew the townspeople loved her coffee, and her cinnamon buns were good enough to keep her business going and her bakery packed with her neighbors. But this was a new view of herself. Not as a woman dumb enough to fall for a truly worthless guy and then not even be able to hold on to him, but as someone they cared about.

He could obviously see the doubt running through her mind and he nodded as though she'd asked a question and he was answering. "It's true. I've been in a lot of small towns. There's often one person or place that is the beating heart of the town. In Clamshell Bay? That's you and your bakery."

She shook her head as though that was the most ridiculous thing she'd ever heard. "It's because everybody comes to my bakery. It seems that way."

"When I was looking to find a home for Delilah, Janet Beamish told me to post a notice at the bakery. She called the bakery the heart of this town. Not me."

Warmth swirled around her chest. And it pushed out some of the bad stuff.

"I have to go. Even though it's my day off, I don't want

anyone thinking I'm cowering in this cottage." She was honest enough to add, "Even though that's all I want to do."

"I'm serious. I'd love to come with you."

Once more she shook her head. More definitively this time. "Please understand. It's not that I don't want your company, but this is something I have to do alone."

"I'm not going to be far away."

"You're not going to hang around me like some weird stalker, are you?"

"Wow. I've never been called a weird stalker before." He looked down at his hands still holding the phone. "I've had a few though."

Her mouth tilted up as though it wanted to smile. "Not a weird stalker, then. I just don't need you to hover."

"Understood. All I meant was, I'll be somewhere close by. Maybe visit at the pet store, or pick up a few things at Filbert Marine, but a text, a call, a smoke signal will find me. You need me, I'm there."

And for a woman who had prided herself for so long on being completely self-sufficient, for a beautiful second she opened herself up to the idea of having someone in her life she could truly lean on. Someone she could trust.

"Thank you."

And then, as though it was the most natural thing in the world, he kissed her. Not a kiss of passion like the earlier one, more a kiss of comfort and companionship. Probably the kind happily married people exchanged all the time. The message was, we're in this together.

Then he backed up a step. "And, when this is all over, I fully intend to pick up where we were so rudely interrupted in the flower garden."

That did surprise a laugh out of her. She'd thought that fleeting moment of mutual passion would be forever gone thanks to her horrid ex's horrid timing. To think that Ethan still wanted more from her added another glow of warmth.

Not that she'd take her relationship with Ethan any further. The universe had sent her a big, fat reminder about her bad track record with men, having Travis show up just at that particular moment.

Still, it had been so nice to feel like an attractive, desirable woman again. She had a feeling she'd be reliving that moment for some time.

————

They left the cottage together. Cleo got into her car and drove off and Ethan and Delilah headed to the dock.

Before he got into the skiff, he called Kyle. The man who ran a multi-million-dollar publishing and entertainment empire immediately picked up and said, "How's Cleo? We're all worried about her."

That was one of the reasons he always got on with Kyle. Wealth and power never got in the way of him being a regular guy.

He watched a bald eagle circle overhead looking for prey. "She's taking it on the chin, but I've got to tell you, I'm worried about her. I didn't like the look of the ex. Slicker than owl shit."

"Yeah. I never knew him personally, but people don't have a good word to say about him around here. What does he want? Why is he back?"

"He told Cleo that he wants to come back home. Make their marriage work."

There was an expletive and a rude sound of disbelief. "You've got to be kidding me. Isn't she divorced?"

The eagle swooped down low over the waves and then rose up again. Ethan pictured a fish swimming near the surface suddenly sensing the eagle-shaped shadow and diving deep to live another day. "He took off and she couldn't find him. So, no, she didn't divorce him. I like Cleo, but I don't think it was burning love that brought Travis back here."

"You think he wants money?"

"That's my guess."

"Damn. Did she have a prenup?"

"I didn't ask but I don't think so."

"Not good."

They were in full agreement there but he couldn't believe Travis could still make a claim. "Her husband abandoned her. Doesn't a guy running off with another man's wife trump some law that's meant to keep people from fighting tooth and nail over their great-aunt's dinnerware?"

"You'd think so. But there are times that somebody gets screwed over royally. And, in this case, it could be Cleo."

"Yeah. The bakery and house were her mother's though, and willed to her. Aren't they exempt from a later claim by a spouse?" He suddenly recalled where he was getting this information. It was from an episode of *Badminton Run*. Great. He was quoting legal facts from a corny PI show that was a quarter century old.

Ethan heard tapping as though Kyle was banging his fingertips against some surface. "I'm no lawyer, but my guess is that poor woman's in for a world of hurt."

"I'm a peaceable man, but I've never felt a stronger urge to knock a man's head off his shoulders."

"Sounds to me like you've fallen for more than Cleo's world-famous cinnamon buns."

Ethan wasn't big on sharing his feelings, particularly not with another guy. He managed, "She's a good person. I don't want to see her get hurt."

"You sure there's nothing more going on?"

He had a strong feeling that the extremely unwelcome Travis was going to make sure everybody in town heard how he'd found his wife making out with another guy. He might as well be the one to tell Kyle himself. "He caught us at an awkward moment."

"How awkward?"

"Not what you're thinking. We were outside working in her garden and one thing led to another and suddenly I was kissing her."

He'd never forget that moment as long as he lived. Even as he'd felt her body yielding in his arms and her lips soft and tentative beneath his, he'd felt, not just the wanting but something more profound. Something he didn't yet care to name. And then that sack of crap had made that snide remark, turning a promising moment acidic. For that alone he wanted to knock that smarmy grin off his face.

"What can I do?" Typical Kyle, he liked to cut to the chase.

"I need the best divorce attorney in Washington State. I have some leads, but my connections aren't as good as yours."

Kyle didn't bother to argue. His network was incredible. "Leave it with me. I'll have a name within the hour."

"Even better if you can put in a good word."

"Consider it done. Cleo should probably move fast. Tomorrow okay?"

"I like the way you work."

Cleo had to give herself a pep talk from inside her car. Her hands were shaking and the fact that Travis could still mess with her equilibrium like this made her furious. She pulled the rearview mirror and angled it so that she could see herself, or at least a slash of herself, the eyes and part of the nose.

"Pull yourself together," she said to the mirror, steely-eyed and tough. "He's not worth it. You're strong. You're independent. You have friends. You will find out what he wants and you will get rid of him."

That felt like an agenda. She needed an agenda. Steps to follow. "You will find out what he wants and you will get rid of him." The eyes in the mirror looked back at her and moved up and down as she nodded briskly. And that was enough to get her out of the car. It didn't stop her hands shaking or her heart from beating uncomfortably hard. Even her breath didn't seem to be flowing in and out in any sort of regular pattern. But she was on her feet and she was striding towards the bakery. That was good. She entered through the back alley, as she always did. And found Pepper running in for a last few loaves. In spite of her misery, she was shocked.

"Are we that low on bread already?"

Pepper sent her a half-panicked glance. "Ever since Travis was spotted in town, it's been crazy busy in here. Everybody's asking how you're doing and what can they do to help. Then, since they're standing there, they feel like they have to buy something." She took a breath and suddenly grinned. "It's awesome."

That was nice. But she really wanted a slow, quiet afternoon where she could accustom herself to the glances of pity that she knew she'd receive and the offers of help she didn't want.

People meant well, but nobody could fix this. She went back to her agenda. She'd find out what Travis wanted and she'd get rid of him.

Her phone rang a little while later. A local number. Egan and Associates, Attorneys at Law. They'd settled her mother's estate. It was the last time she remembered dealing with them.

"Hello?"

"Cleo?" She didn't see Oliver Egan very often. It was his wife who came into the bakery. Oliver was the only lawyer in town. His voice was dry and impersonal. As close as a human voice could be to a legal document. "Thought I ought to tell you, Travis Smith was in to see me today."

"What?" His voice might be as dry and careful as a legal document, but hers sounded like a hysterical foghorn in her own ears.

He went on as though she'd hadn't interrupted. "He wanted to engage my services. He wants to know about divorce and community property laws."

She slumped back against the counter and her eyelids closed as though not seeing a wall of shelves crammed with baking trays might make a difference. "Oh no."

The impersonal voice went on. "Naturally, I told him we couldn't help him. I informed him that your family had been clients of this firm for years."

She would not cry. She would not stand in the bakery kitchen and blubber like an overwrought child. She had cried every tear for Travis she was going to cry.

But her voice wasn't quite steady when she said, "Thank you."

"It's a business policy. If you require my advice, my assistant will make time for you."

"Would this afternoon be convenient?"

There was a pause and she pictured him checking his schedule, or perhaps asking his assistant when he was free. He came back with, "Come by at five."

"Thank you." On this day of highs and lows she found comfort that people in Clamshell Bay cared about her. Whether they were buying muffins and checking that she was okay or offering legal help. Travis could flash his pretty teeth and fake charm to get what he wanted but these were her people as everyone was quick to let her know. She was going to be okay.

In spite of her tough talk with herself, she spent more time in the kitchen than out front. She tried serving customers but it was too hard. The glances of pity and offers of help, the commiseration and outrage, were almost more than she could bear. She was too raw. She worried that the next person who offered her a shoulder to cry on would drown in her tears.

So, she worked in the kitchen. Making dough, baking cookies even though they weren't on today's schedule. She needed to bake.

At a quarter to five, she got ready to leave. To her shame, she glanced up and down the alley before shutting the door behind her in case Travis might be lurking. He wasn't. She drove the short distance to the lawyer's operating purely from cowardice. She could not stand the idea that Travis might be lying in wait for her somewhere. She wasn't tough enough to handle the encounter. Besides, she didn't want to say anything he could twist and use against her. Better to stay away.

However, there was no sign of Travis, not on the drive and not lurking in the parking lot.

Oliver Egan had occupied the same restored historical house in the middle of town for longer than Cleo could remember. He'd been her mother's attorney. Well, he was pretty much everyone's lawyer in Clamshell Bay. He drew up the wills and settled them. Did most of the legal work for mortgages and property conveyancing. He was the one you dealt with when your funds were in escrow. Oliver Egan wasn't a specialist of any sort, he was a generalist who had been taking care of the dull, routine legal affairs of the people in this town so long that he had become an expert on small-town law, she supposed.

However, she doubted he'd ever come across a case quite like this before. Well, she didn't have to hire him. At the moment she just wanted to talk to him. Rather than some cold legal shark in Seattle that she didn't even know, she could get some advice from Mr. Egan. He'd known her all her life and her mother before her. He'd written her mother's will and been the one to do the legal work that was required when she passed away.

He might not be an expert on divorce law, but he knew all about her family's legal affairs.

Besides, Travis had gone to him. With any luck Travis had shown his hand. That ex-husband of hers combined greed, laziness, and stupidity in almost equal measures.

She walked in the front door of the old house, which was now a reception area. The big fireplace hadn't seen burning logs in probably fifty years. Instead, a floral arrangement of silk flowers, meticulously dusted, filled the space. The old oak floors clicked and creaked beneath her feet until her shoes hit the area rug that might have been original to the house.

A mission style leather couch and two chairs sat in the area that she supposed was meant for conversation, although the seating was arranged in far too military a fashion to promote easy conversation. This was a room meant for waiting. A couple of fishing magazines and a virgin copy of the *Wall Street Journal* sat on the coffee table. A large desk with a modern computer sat at the end of the room, and behind it was Mrs. Egan, the lawyer's wife.

"Hi, Lettie, I'm here to see your husband."

"And I'm sorry to hear about your troubles," the older woman said. "You go right on in, honey."

She nodded, feeling oddly comforted by the brisk manner that still managed to convey plenty of sympathy. She didn't need directions. She knew exactly where his office was. She walked forward to what would have been the dining room in the old days. The couple had renovated the main floor, putting in a heavy oak door, and behind that was Oliver Egan's office. She knocked softly and then opened the door when he called, "Come in."

She took a quick breath to center herself, and then she walked in.

The last time she'd been here had been the sad occasion of

telling him that her marriage was over. Before that had been the sad business of clearing up her mother's affairs.

Presumably some people must come into this office filled with joy. The ones just starting out, buying their first houses, perhaps. She'd never had that experience. All her times in this office had been unfortunate, to say the least.

Even though Clamshell Bay was a casual place where jeans and shirts and sneakers and ball caps were the norm, Oliver Egan went to work every day in a suit and tie. People might mock him gently, but they respected him too.

He rose as she entered and came forward with his hand held out, as though they were strangers. "Cleo. I'm sorry about this business."

And it was a business, of course, to him. To her it might be a broken heart, broken promises, and a string of betrayals, but in the end when she sat in front of her lawyer it was business, and the sooner conducted the better.

She took the leather chair he indicated. He put his hands together on top of his highly polished mahogany desk and looked at her expectantly. "What can I do for you today?" he asked as though he didn't know perfectly well.

She couldn't help but notice that there was a tissue box within easy reach that looked to be freshly opened. That did not fill her with confidence about how well this meeting was going to go for her.

She knew exactly what her problem was, but she didn't quite know where to start. There was silence for a minute. He seemed in no hurry to break it, just kept looking at her with that attentive but impassive expression.

Once she started speaking, she knew she'd begin a course of action that was going to cause her anger, frustration, and probably more humiliation. So, she was in no hurry to launch that particular ship.

Then she remembered that Mr. Egan charged by the hour and pulled herself together.

"I think you know why I'm here," she said, with absolutely no imagination, but at least it had given her boat a little push out. "My husband, Travis Smith, is back in town." She stumbled over the word husband, stopping herself from adding the "ex" which was how she always referred to Travis.

He nodded. "He came to see me today, as I told you."

"He left me. He took off with another man's wife, ruining both our marriages. As you'll recall, I couldn't get hold of him and wasn't able to track him down. He never came back. I've always assumed our marriage ended at that moment."

He nodded gravely. "Do you have a record of all the ways and the various instances when you attempted to contact your husband?"

Like her, he said husband, not ex-husband. Her stomach was getting that queasy feeling, like she might be coming down with the flu.

"Absolutely. I have a whole file folder full of the times I tried."

He nodded again. He'd been the one to advise writing all that down, probably in case this day ever dawned.

"Look. It's desertion, right? I know that Washington State is a community property state, but I couldn't divorce him. I couldn't find him."

He seemed to be debating something, and then he said, "Since I refused to take Travis as my client, technically there is no attorney-client privilege. I can tell you that he came in with a very different story."

She'd known it. She'd known the second she saw that smug, self-satisfied face. When he'd given her that false smile and said he was hoping for a second chance, she'd known.

"What is his story?"

"He says he left with you being perfectly aware that he was going away for a while."

She felt like she was choking on something. "With another woman?" The words came out too loud. She had to control herself. Getting angry wasn't going to help.

"According to Mr. Smith, he merely offered Linda Preston a lift when he found her waiting at the bus stop. He claims he dropped her off in Spokane and they parted ways." The dry voice had no inflection. Oliver Egan must know that was a lie, but, unlike her, he wasn't letting emotion get in the way of doing his job.

She was almost gagging on the lies being fed to her vicariously. She wanted to burst out with angry speech again, but it was pointless. The best thing she could do was listen and wait. The lawyer gave her a single nod as though approving of her restraint.

"He said he only meant to be gone a few weeks. You'd been worried about money, he said, encouraging him to find employment."

Not all her restraint was enough to stop the bitter crack of laughter.

"He claims he always intended to come back, that he's always believed you were man and wife and his intent is to resume the married state."

Evil, rat bastard.

She felt ill. Truly ill.

She clasped her hands tightly in her lap. "Bottom-line it for me. What's the worst-case scenario here?"

"Travis will try to claim a portion of your assets. And, there will be a possible claim for spousal support."

She thought of the varicose veins she'd developed from all the years of standing. The time she tore her rotator cuff hauling a fifty-pound bucket of icing awkwardly. Her mother's life's work and her own.

"That's bad."

He moved his hands flat against the desk and she noticed how very neat his hands were. The nails cleanly cut. In a town where so many of the year-rounders sported the rough, nicked hands of hard work or fishing.

"I gave you the worst-case scenario. If you engage me in this matter, I will do everything I can to protect your assets and income. You must be prepared for a fight."

EIGHTEEN

Cleo walked out of the lawyer's office with a hollow, stunned feeling of shock. Oliver Egan had told her to prepare for a fight, and somewhere inside her was a cowardly impulse to run away instead. When a shadow moved and she realized someone had been leaning against her car, she jumped and let out a squawk.

If only she had pepper spray. But it only took a second to realize that it wasn't Travis. It was Megan. Unlike the very clean, smooth Travis, Megan had streaks of something that looked like rust in her hair, paint-dappled fingers, one of which was wrapped in a sturdy bandage, and an unfamiliar look of sorrow on her face.

She walked forward with her arms open and hugged Cleo, paint, dust, and all.

The hug was exactly what she needed. She tried not to cling, but she didn't rush to let go, either. "Megan. What are you doing here?"

"I'm doing an intervention."

Cleo pulled away and stared. At Megan's serious face, laughter bubbled up, surprising her. "An intervention? From what?"

"There's nothing you can do tonight, and sitting home and moping, worrying that card-carrying a-hole is going to show up is not on the menu. Hence the intervention."

"I appreciate it. I really do. But I'm no company for anyone right now. I want to go home and—"

"Yeah. Are you familiar with the concept of an intervention? This is where you don't make decisions that are bad for you. Somebody else steps in and gets you through the bad time until you're stronger."

She could feel the prickle of unfamiliar and most unwanted tears at the back of her eyelids. She blinked hard. "And how do you propose to get me through this difficult period? Are you going to take me to some cheap bar and get me drunk?" Like that was going to help.

The younger woman shook her head. "Brooke and her husband Kyle have invited us all to their place. You can sleep in the guest suite. In fact, you don't have to socialize if you don't want to. You can hang out in the guest suite if you want. I packed you a bag. Ethan told me where the spare key was to your house. Hope that's okay."

"Ethan's involved in this?" Somehow she wasn't surprised. It was kind of strange to think of Megan packing her a bag, but at least she'd have clean underwear.

"Pretty much everybody in town is doing what they can. If Travis tries to eat at the restaurant, he's going to find his food is very late coming and freezing cold. Anybody who takes in guests is going to discover they have no vacancy. If he even tries to come in the bakery, somebody will head him off at the pass." She smiled her big smile. "Cleo, we've got your back."

This time it was she who did the hugging.

She could see from the woman's determined expression that arguing was pointless. Besides, did she really want to go back to her cottage alone, worrying every minute that Travis would show up at the door? She didn't think he'd force his way in, and she'd changed the locks about two months after he'd left. Her hidden key was in a new spot, so it wasn't like he could break into her place without actually breaking something. Still, even the thought of his face leering at her through her windows made her agree to go to Brooke and Kyle's.

However, she fully intended to take Brooke's offer and lock herself away in the guest suite. Maybe they'd add a bottle of wine and a bag of chips to that intervention and she could curl up in a ball and host a private misery party. It was about all she had in her.

"Come on. I'm not going to pretend it'll be fun, but it'll be less awful than wallowing all by yourself."

Cleo was an independent woman, she wasn't used to being looked after. It really went against the grain with her to accept someone else's hospitality and have all these people organizing her life and her safety around her. And at the same time she was so grateful she didn't even know how to respond to their kindness.

"Do I need to kidnap you or will you get in your car and follow me?"

"I'll follow you. And thanks."

When she arrived at Kyle and Brooke's house she was struck, not for the first time, by the sheer beauty of the place. They hadn't done what far too many rich people who wanted oceanfront houses did, which was to build something huge and ornate that drew attention to the house and celebrated their own wealth and entitlement. This house fit with its surroundings. It was made of cedar and glass, fairly modest from the road, not even trying to compete with the glorious ocean view.

She walked up to the door feeling beaten and sad. Megan knocked and it was Brooke who opened the door. She'd been beautiful in an apron with her hands plunged in dough, but in a cream silk scoop-necked top over wide-legged silk trousers, her hair hanging long and loose, she looked ethereal. Her eyes were the clearest blue, like a glacial lake, her nose perfectly straight, her skin smooth, almost translucent and both wrinkle and blemish free. She was more than six feet tall and standing in front of her, Cleo felt like a dumpy, creased sack of flour.

Brooke reached out and pulled her in for a hug. "I couldn't be more sorry. Come in."

"Got her here," Megan announced, walking past and punching her fist in the air. "Job done."

Even as she tried to thank Brooke, her words were brushed aside. "That's what friends are for."

She realized how true that was. In a very short time she'd become friends with these women.

Brooke said, "Come in. I'll show you your room. Maybe you want to freshen up."

As they walked in, the modest exterior gave way to a luxurious interior. The rich hardwood floors gleamed. Pillars took the place of walls and the front of the house rose, like the prow of a ship, huge, angled windows letting in the spectacular view.

"Your home is amazing," she managed.

"Thanks. We like it."

Brooke led her down a corridor that avoided the noise she could hear coming from some other part of the house. She obviously wasn't the only guest.

It wasn't a room she was led to but a full-on guest wing. A beautiful bedroom contained a king-size bed with linens and pillows that looked so inviting she wanted to throw herself onto the bed and stare out the window at the ocean. As promised, the bathroom was stocked with everything from fluffy towels to hair and beauty products. A fresh toothbrush and unopened toothpaste sat in a jar. There was even a kitchenette. Brooke explained, "We keep that stocked with coffee, tea, snacks. There's wine and water in the fridge. Anything you want, don't hesitate to ask. I completely understand if you don't want to see people right now but, Cleo, we're all here for you."

She nodded once. Her heart was too full to explain how she felt. She ran her finger over the pattern in the bedspread.

"I really appreciate this." It was all she could manage without embarrassing herself by bursting into tears.

"I'm glad I could do something for you. Your class was amazing. It made something click inside me that I can't explain. I'm so grateful to you and Megan and Libby." She looked like she might say more and then left it at that.

She touched Cleo's shoulder, a light, supportive touch. "I took the liberty of putting a few things in the closet you could wear tonight if you feel like changing. None of us care, but if you've been working all day, maybe you feel like something fresh. Up to you."

After Brooke left, she set down her purse and looked around the luxurious room that wasn't hers. She'd run away from her own home because of a bad mistake she'd made years ago. When would her house feel like hers again? When would her life feel like hers again?

From feeling beaten and sorry for herself, she began to embrace the anger and resentment.

Was she really going to sit in bed and sulk when there was a party going on? Was she going to miss her own intervention?

Hell no.

Getting off the bed, she looked at herself in the mirror. She was not dressed for Dinner with the Billionaires. Or anyone. Her shirt sported a smear of ginger and a dusting of flour. Her jeans were okay, but even changing her top would make a big difference. She opened the double wardrobe doors and a light went on inside, revealing a mostly empty closet, but there was a dress and three tops hanging. Cleo smiled, thinking of Brooke going through her wardrobe looking for things to lend a shorter, thicker woman.

Somehow, she'd managed. She pulled out a black and white top with three-quarter-length sleeves. Peeked at the label inside and recognized the designer as one favored by Princess Kate. A simple white floaty dress made her pause, but then the possibility of spilling something on a dress that was probably worth more than all of Cleo's wardrobe put together had her flipping to the next possibility. It was a multicolor, loose-fitting cotton, sleeveless top. She held it up while looking in the mirror and thought the browns and greens flattered her coloring. When she tried it on, the top fit and somehow made her jeans seem stylish. Done.

A quick shower and a bit of makeup made her feel better. Ready to face the world, or at least a small group of friends.

When she appeared upstairs she found everyone gathered outside on a stone patio with heaters and deep, comfortable rattan furniture. "Cleo," Libby said, jumping up. "I'm so glad you felt up to joining the party."

Kyle wandered in looking relaxed and casual in a blue T-shirt and navy shorts. He was about six feet four or five, so taller than his wife. His hair was as dark as hers was fair and when he came up beside her, they were stunning. Truly a golden couple. They had so much, and yet something as seemingly simple as conceiving a child had tripped them up. A shadow of sadness crossed Brooke's face as her husband joined her. The expression was gone as suddenly as it had appeared, and she brought him over to Cleo. She gave a satisfied nod when she spotted the borrowed top but didn't say anything. Cleo felt as though she'd made the right choice, the one Brooke would have chosen for her, and thanked her inner, and previously non-existent, fashionista.

"Great to have you here, Cleo," Kyle Donovan said in a hearty tone, as though he'd no idea there was trouble in her house. Megan walked up at that moment. She'd also changed, into a blue cotton dress that she wore with leather boots. Following behind her was a muscle-bound guy with military-short hair who looked like he bench-pressed tanks for fun. "This is Raoul. We had plans tonight so I brought him along. Hope that's okay."

"Of course. Happy to meet you," Kyle said, shaking the man's hand.

"Cool place," Raoul said, looking around.

"We like it." Seemed like that was their automatic response.

"What can I get you, ladies?" Kyle asked, looking around.

"Dirty martini for me," Megan said. She glanced at Raoul from under her lashes. "And make it extra dirty."

Kyle shook his head at her. "Think I can handle it. Gin or vodka?"

"Gin."

"Right. Libby?"

"I've never had a dirty martini." She sounded like she wanted to try but needed encouragement. She glanced around. "I took a cab here so I could have a drink or two."

Kyle asked, "Want to try one? If you don't like it, I'll make you something else."

Her forehead crinkled. "What makes it dirty?"

"Nothing sinister. Olive brine."

Libby looked very relieved. "I like olives. Yes. I'd like a dirty martini."

He turned to Cleo. She'd had a rotten, lousy day. "Make it three dirty martinis."

Brooke chuckled. "I haven't had one of those in ages. Why not?"

"Four dirty martinis coming up." Then he turned to Megan's guest. "Raoul?"

"A beer if you have it."

"Sure do."

"Why don't we head outside? I've got the barbecue going."

Raoul followed Kyle and Megan sat with Cleo and Libby. Brooke carried in a tray of hors d'oeuvres. This was an impromptu get together. How had she pulled all this together so fast? Did they have staff keeping out of sight? Or had somebody made a quick stop at the store? Maybe they kept the kitchen stocked at all times with pate, cheeses, olives, pickles, smoked salmon, charcuterie, and crackers.

When Kyle returned he bore a tray with four martinis, each with a skewer of three olives. Very professional. He handed out the drinks and Megan raised her glass. "To kicking ass."

She could have been referring to any number of asses, but in this case, Cleo expected she meant Travis. When Cleo sipped, that's whose ass she was hoping to kick. The drink was salty, dry and pretty much pure alcohol. She sighed. Exactly what she felt like.

Libby's eyes widened when she sipped hers. "Oh, my, that has quite a kick," she said, which made them all laugh.

"So, who's made bread since the class?" Megan asked. Libby was able to report that she'd experimented with bread made with her home-grown basil and pecorino cheese. She shook her head. "The children didn't like the green and refused to eat it. I ended up freezing most of it." And somehow, they ended up talking about bread and herbs, gardening and how to keep the deer out of the garden. Travis's name never came up. Which is exactly how important she wanted him to be in her life and conversation.

Slowly, her tense shoulders slid back into place and, amazingly, she began to relax.

She gazed out at a view that was similar to hers, but shifted slightly. There was music playing, laughter, and the feeling that she was among friends.

Ethan walked in, wearing chinos and a short-sleeved white shirt. When she caught sight of him she felt her pulse speed up. Did he feel her staring? He turned and their gazes caught and held for only a moment, but in that moment, she was back in her garden, with the sun warm on her skin, the murmur of bees, and the scent of lilac in the air. And Ethan was kissing her, his lips warm and sure, his body solid against hers. He moved closer and she was almost certain he'd experienced the same surge of lust-memory. He didn't say anything, just came behind her and rested a warm palm on her shoulder, as casual as though he did it every day.

She tilted her head up so she could look at him. "Are you behind this intervention?"

Even upside down his face was beautiful to her. His eyes crinkled at the edges as he smiled. "No. Wish I could take credit, but your baking friends came up with the idea. You okay with it?"

"Yeah. Maybe a night with friends was exactly what I needed."

"How'd it go with the lawyer?"

"I'm getting a crick in my neck. Let's talk somewhere else."

She got up and he took her hand, leading her inside to the empty living room. They sat side by side on a linen and rattan couch and, after taking a breath, she told him about her meeting.

He listened intently, then nodded. "Good. I made some calls but nobody's better connected than Kyle. Especially in Washington State. He got you an appointment tomorrow at eleven with a top divorce attorney."

"Tomorrow?" She put a hand to her chest. "So soon."

"Sooner you get started, the sooner you can get free of that —your husband."

The word husband hung heavily between them like a cement wall blocking her from any hope of happiness.

"I'm not sure I can afford a top attorney."

"Kyle said the first session's free. A get-to-know-you meeting. This won't cost anything but your time. If you like the attorney, I bet Kyle can negotiate a corporate rate."

"A corporate rate." She sighed. "When did I become a woman who needs corporate rates on attorneys?"

He took her hand. "It's been a crazy day." He glanced at her ruefully. "For both of us."

She squeezed his hand. "We should get back."

He followed her back out to the group and walked up to Libby. "I don't believe we've met."

Libby put down her martini glass, only barely managing to get it on the table. Not because she was drunk, but star-struck. "I'm Libby," she said, though she didn't sound too sure.

"Ethan. Great to meet you."

"And this is Megan," Brooke said, assuming hostess duties. "We three took Cleo's baking class last weekend. It's how we met."

"Cleo definitely makes excellent bread," Ethan replied, nodding to Megan.

Kyle returned, wearing a black kitchen apron that said, Kiss the Cook. Raoul followed holding a bottle of beer.

Kyle manned a barbecue that looked like something Cleo had seen on MasterChef. Still, he seemed surprisingly comfortable with the many burners and knobs.

Brooke excused herself to head to the kitchen, refusing offers of help. Ethan settled beside Cleo. Like he belonged there. Their thighs touched and neither of them shifted away.

Raoul settled beside Megan, which left Libby apologizing that her husband was still away. Libby reached for her martini glass. "He's never been away so long before. The kids really miss him. And so do I."

Kyle and Brooke laid out the food on their long dining table. There was steak and salmon, salads and bread. Bread she recognized as coming from her bakery.

She gazed at it. "I would have brought bread. I feel terrible that you had to buy it."

Kyle shook his head at her. "You should. I tried everything. Told that girl I know the owner, but she was adamant. In fact, I think she charged me extra because I knew the owner."

She chuckled. "Well, next time the bread's on me."

"Next time we're doing this at your place. And you can make me a dirty martini."

She felt so much better. The billionaire owner of a media empire was angling for an invite to her cottage. "You're on."

She wouldn't have believed two hours ago that she could end up feeling this good. The food was delicious, the company wonderful, and nobody talked about her problems. Nobody looked at her like she was a sad loser who married a bad man and then couldn't even get rid of him properly. It was nice to have the support of friends. When had she become so reclusive? She always thought she was so outgoing and social, but that was only at work. The minute she finished, she pretty much scampered back to her cottage and slammed the door on the world. Until Ethan had shown up, she hadn't even noticed she was doing it.

There was a whole community of people out here that she liked. People who didn't need advice or bread lessons or a roommate or a lost dog found. These were people who had it together and had something to say that she wanted to listen to. They seemed equally interested in her opinion.

She was smart enough to decline the offer of a second dirty martini, and instead had a glass of excellent wine to go with the excellent meal.

They ate outside, while the sun set and Kyle lit outdoor lamps.

When they'd eaten their fill, Brooke walked out looking both pleased and bashful. "I made dessert," she said, holding a pie in her hands. "Taking your class gave me the confidence to try."

Cleo caught the surprised look on Kyle's face. This was clearly not a common occurrence.

Cleo jumped up and clapped her hands. "I can't believe you did that. It's beautiful."

"It's nothing fancy. Just apple pie."

"Apple pie is my favorite," Kyle said, coming closer to inspect his wife's effort.

"I know," she said softly.

While they were sitting around over coffee and pie, Kyle turned on the outdoor heater so that they could stay comfortable much later than normal for this time of year. He sat back, one ankle crossed over the other, and said, "I was looking at the prospectus for the new project in Atlanta. It's looking good."

Ethan brought his gaze back from where he'd been gazing out at who knew what and said, "No shop talk. This is a pleasant dinner with friends, not a business meeting."

Kyle looked around. "Does anyone mind if I compliment my business partner on a project we're both involved in?"

Cleo certainly didn't. She was dying to know what was going on. Everyone else shook their heads.

Megan said, "Anyway, it's not like we don't all know what you're doing."

Well, not all of them.

Ethan shot her a glance and then seemed to give up. "Fine, but it's boring."

"It's not boring," Kyle scoffed. "What you're doing is changing lives." He turned to Cleo. "The concept is brilliant. It's one of the best charitable endeavors I've ever been involved with, and I've been involved in a lot."

"Charity?" Cleo couldn't help asking the question.

Ethan looked intensely uncomfortable. "I'm not Mother Teresa, I make money on these things. Let's talk about something else."

Now, instead of her feeling awkward, she was happy to pass that baton over to Ethan, who was all but squirming in his chair.

Kyle turned to her as though she were an impartial judge and he could put the case before her. "He buys up old, dilapidated apartment buildings, warehouses, places that would have been bulldozed. And then he hires guys to fix them up, turning them into affordable housing. Not fancy, but clean and livable. Great for families."

That didn't seem particularly outlandish to Cleo, but she could see there was more to the story than that. Kyle seemed to be enjoying Ethan's discomfort. He turned to the former actor. "You should be proud of what you do. I know I am proud to be part of it."

Ethan said, sounding grumpier than she'd ever heard him, "I like to be private, that's all."

In a cool tone, Brooke said, "Maybe you should drop the subject, Kyle."

He was equally cool when he replied, "Sometimes it's good to talk about things, even if they are uncomfortable."

There was a moment of heavy silence and then Kyle turned back to Cleo as though Brooke had never spoken. "The buildings are all renovated using green technology. In fact, some of them have a negative carbon footprint. Plus, he's hiring construction workers who most people won't take a chance on. Former addicts, convicts, people who don't usually get a second chance."

Ethan glanced up at her, his eyes squinted in a glare so she dared not say what was on the tip of her tongue. How awesome it was that he was doing such a good thing for both the world and society.

She'd known she liked him, but now she felt that at least in this man, unlike Travis, she'd shown good taste. Her instincts hadn't led her astray.

Everyone seemed to be waiting for her to say something, so

she just said, "Thanks for letting me know." And to Ethan, she said, "And I'll keep it to myself."

"Appreciate it," he said, sounding as grumpy as he looked.

It was all she could do to bite back her smile. It was endearing that he wanted to keep his good works a secret. Really endearing.

Kyle wasn't finished yet, though. He said, "Of course, he could do a lot more, get a lot more funding if he wasn't so shy about publicity."

Ethan turned to glare at his partner. "Don't you start. I'm not putting my name and my face out there to raise a few bucks. We do fine. Anyway, Brad Pitt has a building charity. If people want to give money to a pretty face and an actor, they should give it to him." He glared at Kyle. "And nobody's stopping you from doing that if being hooked up with a celebrity is so important to you."

Kyle laughed now. "I like my money exactly where it is. And you do good work. It's not a terrible thing to take credit once in a while, you know."

Ethan said, "This is a very boring conversation. I'm going to see if there's any pie left."

She watched him walk away. She didn't want to, she really couldn't help herself. She liked his long, easy gait. Even though he was clearly annoyed by the turn the conversation had taken, he still didn't rush.

Brooke leaned over and said, "His foundation really is amazing. It does great work. Kyle likes to tease, but we're proud to be involved."

Kyle added, "We can take you out on a trip to see his latest building if you like. It's not that far from here."

And she knew how much Ethan would hate that. She suspected Kyle knew it too and was only playing with her. He had a strange sense of humor, that one.

"That's okay. If Ethan ever wants me to see one of his projects, I'm sure he'll invite me."

And if he didn't, that was okay too. It was funny that in all the time they'd spent chatting he'd never bothered to share this part of his life with her. And it must be a big part. Presumably he could have been using his carpentry skills on his own project if he'd wanted to. And yet he'd been all but begging her for a chance to work on her dilapidated potting shed and the rickety fence as though he had no place else to ply those skills.

A horrible sensation washed over her. Did he think she was a charity case?

NINETEEN

Cleo glanced around at the people who were doing their best to make her feel better, especially as she suspected she wasn't the only one here tonight with troubles.

Kyle and Brooke had something going on between them. She wondered if they'd had a fight today and were pretending they hadn't. There was a coolness between them. She could see a yearning look of love that Brooke sent Kyle when he didn't know she was looking, and she caught a glimpse of something that looked like frustrated affection when he glanced back at his wife.

Libby kept checking her phone. She'd been quiet all evening.

Normally she'd weave a few tales around what might have happened, but the urge to gossip, even within the privacy of her own head, seemed a whole lot less enticing when she knew how much she was the subject of town gossip. And she doubted it was staying in people's heads.

They'd be talking about her in the bar and over the dinner tables as people sliced into her hot, fresh bread, cut into one of her pies for dessert. No doubt they'd be discussing how the baker's no-good husband had turned up again. Did they wonder if she was going to take him back?

How many sharp-eyed townies had seen one or both of them visit Oliver Egan today? That was definitely good for some rabid speculation. She didn't blame them. But she felt like one of the clams their town was famous for after it had its shell pried open. Like she was this quivering mass of jelly and vulnerable to everything and everyone from the environment to the beaks looking to make a meal out of her.

Okay, she was being dramatic. She liked the contentment of her simple life. She did not need this drama.

She'd assumed Megan was joking when she'd talked about the easy, disposable nature of relationships, but here she was with Raoul who seemed very new in her life. He was a nice enough guy. Reminded her a little bit of Travis. He had an easy charm and a way of walking with his pelvis slightly forward as though the most interesting thing about him was behind the buckle of his pants.

She had an urge to warn Megan, then realized she didn't need to. Megan knew what she was doing. Nobody was going to get hurt in that relationship.

Libby checked her phone and then put it away. No good news there. She moved over to Libby and said quietly, "Is everything all right?"

Her smile was as sweet as ever but strained. "Oh, yes. Victor talked to the children last night before they went to bed, but he was late for a meeting so he didn't have time to speak to me. He said he'd try tonight."

"At least you know he's fine."

"Yes. He's fine."

"Where is he?"

"Romania, I think." At that moment her phone buzzed and relief bloomed on her face like the first rose of the season. Cleo moved away to give her some privacy.

Unlike Cleo's waterfront property, this one had an easy path to a nice beach. She slipped away, finding the cheerful chatter too loud in her ears. She walked down to a beach that was part sand, part rock. The waves endlessly rolling towards her reminded her that however awful today was it would crash and break on the shore and tomorrow would be another fresh wave. Her small life and her small problems meant so little when she looked at the vast expanse of the ocean and the sky above where the first stars were beginning to shine.

She found a flat spot on a log and sat down. And she let the thoughts and the feelings come through her head the way the waves crashed on the beach, trying not to hang on to any of them, just letting them roll through and hopefully crash and dissipate.

***

Ethan watched Cleo making her way over the rocks towards a patch of sand. A solitary figure, not lonely, simply alone. He knew she was proudly independent and certainly able to fend for herself but still, in that moment, he wondered if she ever got tired of being alone. He thought about following her and then felt movement beside him at the railing edging the terrace and turned to find Kyle leaning on his forearms and looking down at the lone figure on the beach.

"She'll be okay," he said, sounding confident, as though he could possibly know Cleo or what she was going through. "I put a word in with the sheriff, who I'm on pretty good terms with." Then he explained what the sheriff's office had promised.

Ethan was impressed that Kyle had bothered to do a favor for someone he barely knew. As they stood there, an idea came to him for a much bigger favor. "You run a whole media empire, right?"

Kyle looked slightly taken aback at the sudden change of

subject. "Yes," he said cautiously, as though Ethan might have a hidden agenda. Which he clearly did. "But I have other interests too."

Ethan pushed on, not at all interested in any of Kyle's other enterprises. "And in this media empire of yours, I'm guessing you employ any number of investigative journalists."

Now Kyle definitely smelled a rat. "What's this about?"

Ethan's gaze was drawn back to Cleo. She'd reached the patch of sand now and glanced around as though contemplating a swim. He didn't think she was, but he was going to keep his eyes on her anyway. "I'm thinking that Cleo's old friend Travis has come back to Clamshell Bay with a fine story. He was 'taking some time.'" He turned to Kyle. "What if it's not true?"

"I'd hazard a guess it's definitely not true. That guy is a liar and a manipulator of women. He's made a living off his good looks and now they're fading so he thumbs through his little black book wondering who he can hit up for money."

Ethan nodded. He was pleased that their tallies of Travis were so similar. "Here's what I'm thinking. An investigative journalist who did a bit of digging into Travis's background might find something interesting. And if it was a fact that could help Cleo in her divorce case, wouldn't that be a good deed?"

Kyle tapped a loosely curled fist lightly on the top of the balcony railing. "It would. My question is, what would the investigative reporter get out of it? And by that, of course, I mean how would this be useful for my company?"

Ethan was disappointed not to get immediate support, but he'd expected pushback. "I don't know yet. I'm not a reporter, but I know I'd read or listen to or watch an investigative piece about men who use women, even marry them, maybe for money, maybe for a million reasons and then disappear."

"Not exactly a fresh or original story. Unfortunately."

"It doesn't have to be. Isn't there always a new angle?"

Kyle followed his gaze and they both watched Cleo take a

seat on a log. Kyle couldn't possibly miss the lines of tension that radiated from her too erect posture. "Why not hire a private investigator?"

"Thought about it. Cleo probably can't afford it. If I offer to pay for a PI, she'll get all pissy and turn me down flat. But a reporter wouldn't get paid to look into Travis Smith's misdeeds."

"Paid by me, I might remind you." Still, he hadn't said no.

It was a nice night to watch the stars come out, and they stood silent for a minute. "My gut tells me there's a story there. She looked for him after he left and never found him," Ethan pressed.

"Come on. Guy's name is Smith. Must be the most common name in America. He can't help but get lost in a crowd."

Ethan felt as though a finger were tapping on his chest. He wasn't an investigative journalist but he had played a PI on TV. "What if that's not his real name?"

"Whoa, what?"

"Think about it. Man shows up in a small, out-of-the-way town, says his name is Smith, marries a local girl. Maybe he's on the run from something."

Kyle stared at him. "Is that a plot from *Badminton Run*?"

"No." At least he didn't think so. He couldn't remember most of the storylines. It had been twenty-five years and he'd swiftly turned the channel if *Badminton Run* had ever appeared in rerun, so he was pretty fuzzy on most of the show's details.

Kyle said, "Look, I can't promise anything, but I'll float the idea."

Ethan was astonished. "You're the big boss. Don't reporters jump to attention when you bark orders?"

Kyle laughed, sounding genuinely amused. "Are you kidding? They see me as the enemy. A rich guy who made his money too easily and too young, while they work day and night for peanuts exposing the dark truths in society."

He sounded just enough like his feelings had been hurt by this behavior that it took away from the patronizing tone. Ethan got it. He too had suffered from success at a young age that a lot of people, including him, didn't feel he'd earned or deserved.

Besides, Kyle had almost said he'd do it. Ethan wasn't one to let the issue hang in the balance. "So? You'll do it? You'll put an investigative reporter on Travis's tail?"

"Let's just say that I'll bring up the subject with the right editors and producers. If they see merit in the piece, they'll run with it."

Ethan got the feeling that this was as far as Kyle was willing to go and if he pushed him, he might get even less. He nodded. "Could be a great story in the right hands."

"Maybe."

He was about to move away from the railing when Kyle said, "What's your interest there?" He gestured with his chin to where Cleo was sitting.

Maybe this was his payback. So, Ethan quelled his impulse to turn the question off with a joke or a casual comment. Instead, he did something he'd been resisting doing. He tried to work out his feelings for Cleo. He tried to tell the truth, but he wasn't sure if it was the truth. At least not all of it. He gazed down at her sitting on that log, so still, so proud.

"I like her. I admire her. Cleo Duvall has made her own life on her own terms and made a success of it. She has this calmness and sense of certainty that I admire. I'm always looking for the next adventure, and she's happily planting peas and dreaming up new recipes for her bakery." The most extraordinary thing he knew about her popped into his head and so he shared it with Kyle. "Do you know when I talked to her about travel, she said she can't stand to be away from the bakery or the cottage for more than three weeks?"

He was surprised Kyle didn't look as shocked as he'd felt.

"This is a beautiful place. And all her roots are here. She's found her place in the world and loves it."

Ethan thought about all the destinations he'd been fantasizing about, all the trips he wanted to take Cleo on. He wanted to see her face the first time she saw the temples in Vietnam, the first time she saw Machu Picchu, the first time she went snorkeling in the Great Barrier Reef. He'd been thinking of her almost like a sleeping beauty tucked away, and yet what if Kyle was right? What if she was the one who had things to show him?

"I'm going to go see if she needs anything."

"Good luck."

That was such a weird thing to say that he didn't reply. Pretended he hadn't heard the comment. As he headed down the stairs, the music grew softer and the sounds of conversation and laughter diminished. The beat of the ocean grew louder. He breathed in the moist, salt-tinged air. He headed slowly towards Cleo, not sure if he'd receive a welcome when he got to her or whether she'd be annoyed that he was invading her personal space.

Cleo didn't know how long she'd sat there, probably not more than ten minutes, when she saw a dark figure making its slow, easy way towards her.

She hadn't thought anyone had seen her come this way, but here was Ethan.

He stopped a few feet away from her. "Want some company?"

She'd come here to get away from company, but suddenly she wanted his. "Sure."

Only then did he come closer. He sat beside her on the log and gazed out as she'd been doing. "Nice night."

"It is."

He sat in silence for another ten, fifteen seconds. "Makes you think, doesn't it? Looking out on all that? How puny our problems are?"

She turned to stare at him, knowing that he wouldn't see her face in the gloom. "I was just thinking the exact same thing. And on a day when my problems seem bigger than the universe, I come out here and realize they're tinier than the grains of sand on the beach."

"But they hurt all the same."

"Yes. They do."

"I have a plan and I hope you'll approve it."

"Okay," she said hesitantly. There were so many planners around her. For the moment she just wanted to be.

"It's not much of a plan. But I want to get your approval first. Kyle talked to the sheriff's office—"

"He had no right," she exclaimed before she could stop herself.

"Nevertheless. He's that kind of guy. Oversteps sometimes." Somehow the description made her smile and eased her irritation a notch. Kyle wasn't the only one. "But, you can't deny he gets things done. He suggested the sheriff might want to keep an eye on Travis."

"I'm a taxpaying citizen too. I'm sure I would have got action if I called the sheriff's office. Especially as I'm the one Travis Smith is harassing." Harassing was too strong a word. He'd shown up at her house, the bakery, and chatted to her neighbors. His very boldness was an insult. He was letting her know he could get up in her face and make himself at home in her town and there was nothing she could do about it. However, his behavior wasn't illegal, so she wasn't sure what the sheriff could do.

He reached down and picked up a discarded clamshell, a perfect pale shape in the moonlight. "No doubt you would. But you probably wouldn't get as high up the chain as quickly as our friend Kyle can."

She let out a huff of breath. "What's he arranged for me? Round the clock surveillance? A bodyguard?"

He chuckled. It was a low, rusty sound like he didn't use it all that often. "There's not much in the way of law enforcement here. Not much in the way of crime, come to that. He says the sheriff or deputy normally tries to get by a couple of times a week. They're increasing that to three times a week and they'll be sure to drive by your place."

She'd expected she'd be smothered, and this was all Kyle had achieved? "Well, that's not much, is it?"

"No. Travis hasn't threatened you. He hasn't done anything but show up and say he wants to be married to you again. I guess that's not against the law."

"It should be. Where Travis is concerned."

"So, here's what I'm suggesting. I'll moor my boat at your dock tonight. Maybe a few more nights until we figure out where you stand legally. What your options are."

A sound came out of her mouth that was barely her own. It sounded more like one of the gulls that were forever circling the beach looking for tasty morsels. "I don't need a security guard. Or a bodyguard."

"Maybe you do. I didn't like the cut of his jib, that Travis."

Along with a stab of humiliation came recognition that Ethan was a better judge of character than she was. Although, of course, hormones didn't come into it where he was concerned. "How long are you planning to stay?"

"It depends. I'll dock *Vagabond* at your place tonight. Just keep an eye on the place, kind of like a night watchman."

"But that's ridiculous. If you're going to be watching my house, I should be there."

He shook his head. "Until you speak to the lawyer tomorrow, I don't think you should be in the house when he comes by.

You need to know how to handle it, what to say." He turned to her. "Let me do this. Let me be your friend."

There was one of those long, endless moments as she looked at him. She couldn't see his features clearly, but she saw the way the wind ruffled his hair and the moon caught his eyes and made them glitter.

And in her heart, she knew he was right. If Travis knocked on her door, what would she do? She wouldn't let him in. Would she go out and give him a piece of her mind? Say a lot of stupid things that he could then use against her? She didn't know anything about the law. All she knew was she suspected she had to be very careful. And so, she said words that were very hard for her.

"Thank you for helping me."

He must have caught the chagrin in her voice, for his teeth gleamed suddenly in a grin. "Hard for you, isn't it? I've been around here long enough to know that you're the one people come to for advice and help. You don't ask for favors, you give them."

He'd said it in a teasing way, but it made her sound sort of controlling. Like nothing bad ever happened to her when the opposite was true.

She stood and brushed sand off her butt. "We should get back."

"Wait, there's one more thing."

"I'm not sure I can take any more."

He took her hand and they began to walk. It should have been so romantic, with the sound of the waves, the first stars, the scent of sea air, and the warm feel of Ethan's hand wrapped around hers. Instead, she felt tense. Nervous about meeting a fancy lawyer tomorrow and anxious about whatever latest plan Ethan had devised.

"I doubt anything will come of it, but I suggested to Kyle that one of his reporters might have better luck tracking down

Travis's whereabouts after he left you than you had. It seems very strange that you couldn't find him after he left. Who can't be found these days with social media?"

Feelings of outrage warred with gratitude. He was trying to help her, even if his tactics weren't exactly subtle. "Why not hire a PI?"

He took a moment before answering. "Because Kyle's company will pay for it and people love to talk to the media, more than they'll talk to a private investigator."

She had no idea if this was true, but she liked the way he'd managed to land on her side, as though the pair of them had hustled Kyle for a favor. "I doubt there's much of a story in a sleazy character who walked out on his wife."

"Pretty much what Kyle said, but he promised to pitch the idea to an editor. Might come to nothing but I wanted to tell you."

"You could have asked me first."

"I would have if I'd thought of it, but I was talking to Kyle and the idea popped into my head."

They reached the end of the cove and turned back. "If any more ideas pop into your head that involve me, I'd appreciate you running them by me first."

He stopped and turned her to face him. "I should have. I'm sorry."

And that sincere apology nearly undid her. Travis had never once told her he was sorry. There was always an excuse or an argument. And here was Ethan saying he was sorry for trying to help her. She didn't even know why she was comparing the two men. Once again, she was reminded that they were completely different. No, not completely different. The one thing they had in common was a love of adventure and a habit of drifting. However, at least Ethan had been honest from the beginning that he wasn't in her life to stay.

He pulled her slowly to him and kissed her, long and slow. "We'll figure this out," he said.

"Yes. I just want this over with." She blew out a breath. "Okay, I'll call Pepper to make sure she's okay to open alone. See about bringing in one of my part-timers." Her mind already working on the practicalities, which gave her something else to do than worry.

He took her hand once more. His was warm and workman rough and she liked it. Their hands swung easily as they headed back.

TWENTY

The next morning Cleo woke in the unfamiliar bed, much bigger than her own, in the unfamiliar bedroom, also much bigger than her own, and for a moment just stretched, enjoying the luxury. She'd slept deeply and well, against all her expectations.

Then the cold reality of her situation came back to her. She had to see a lawyer about a man she never should have married. A man who'd already caused her a world of trouble and looked ready to cause her a world more.

It was five thirty, her normal start time.

When she'd asked Pepper to run the bakery today with the help of one of the casual part-timers, Pepper had said, "Anything you need. Don't worry about the bakery." Pepper had even offered to call Stacey, their first choice for extra help.

Now that Cleo's life was a mess, Pepper was really stepping up. Still, she phoned to check that her assistant was there already preparing the breads for today. When Pepper answered right away sounding fully alert and with the sound of the Hobart beating behind her, Cleo felt ashamed of herself. Maybe she really was a control freak. She came up with a plausible excuse for calling, reminding Pepper that the pub wanted an extra two loaves of the French today.

"I know, you left a note," Pepper said.

"Right. I did. I'm sorry, my brain's so addled I forgot. Everything okay?"

"Everything's fine, boss. Stacey will be here in an hour. Stop worrying about the bakery and worry about how you're going to keep that grade A asshole from getting any of it."

"I will and that's a promise."

"You've got this."

As she hung up she felt like something cold was squeezing her heart. She'd spent all this time worrying about her house. How had it never occurred to her that a thieving bandit like Travis would go after everything? Including her business. She'd always believed community property was a fair and just way for people to divorce. But in her case, it sucked.

She got out of bed even though it was still early. She was accustomed to early mornings and she knew she wouldn't go back to sleep. She went into the big, beautiful guest bathroom, almost sighing with pleasure when her bare feet hit the heated tile floor. The shower itself was as big as her whole bathroom and had about sixteen showerheads. She stepped in and turned on the jets and pretty much had a full body massage in fifteen minutes. Oddly it helped. She washed her hair and used the fancy salt scrub she found in the basket of goodies that came with the shower. She might be a mess but at least her skin would be polished, also nicely scented with some amazing green soap that looked like seaweed and smelled like jasmine and mint.

And she dried herself on the plushest towels she'd ever touched. She took the time to actually dry and style her hair. Brooke had gifted her all the cosmetics she'd used on her the other day, those eons ago when she'd thought that having dinner with Ethan was the biggest thing she'd have to worry about this week. She took the time to do her face, wondering how Ethan had fared at her dock all night. Had Travis showed up?

The bathrobe hanging on the back of the door was like those in the best hotels. She snuggled into it and went back into the bedroom. She looked out at a slightly shifted version of the same view she saw every day of her life. The sky was just lightening, getting ready for dawn. How many more times would she be able to stand in her own house and watch the dawn? Or the sunset?

She wanted to slap herself for such negative thinking. Ethan and Kyle had helped her hire what was no doubt the best divorce attorney in all the United States of America. She'd be fine.

And if she wasn't, she'd survive.

Travis would never want the bakery. It involved hard work and that was a massive allergen to him. No doubt they could figure something out. She'd managed to pay back the money she borrowed when her mom was sick. Maybe she could get a loan or a mortgage and pay Travis off over time. Her stomach soured at the idea of working harder, longer, so he'd never have to, but she'd rather do that than lose her home.

She dressed and made coffee in the kitchenette. She sat outside on the stone patio in front of her little suite and watched the sunrise. Still, no one was stirring in the main house. She felt twitchy and nervous and couldn't stay here any longer.

After she tidied up after herself, she penned a quick note of thanks and quietly let herself out of the house.

She was accustomed to driving in the wee hours, but normally she was coming towards town, not driving away from the bakery. Naturally, she couldn't help herself. She drove by the bakery and saw the lights were on. Even though she'd already known Pepper was there she was still relieved to see signs of activity. And no sign of Travis.

When she pulled into her drive, she let out a sigh of relief, not seeing another vehicle. She felt incredibly foolish for abandoning her home in case her lowlife ex showed up. Most likely, he hadn't bothered.

She got out of her car and looked out, heart gladdened to see the mast of *Vagabond* bobbing gently beside her dock. Ethan wouldn't have had as comfortable a sleep here as he would have in the marina, but she was grateful to him. So grateful.

The cottage looked perfectly fine and deserted. Just the way she'd left it. That, too, was a relief.

She let herself in and flicked on lights and immediately put on another pot of coffee. It felt like this was a day where a lot of coffee would be drunk.

She couldn't stand here, nervous, in yesterday's clothes. She put the oven on and while it was warming went into her bedroom and dressed in comfy sweatpants and a short-sleeved T-shirt that left her arms free to work. Back in the kitchen she fetched flour, butter, blueberries from the freezer and got to work.

She wasn't very surprised when she got a text from Ethan. "That you?"

He must know it was. He'd no doubt seen her car arrive. Still, she texted back. "Yes. Come up for breakfast." She pulled out her skillet and put on bacon.

He was there within ten minutes, his hair wet from a shower, wearing jeans and one of those endless plaid shirts of his.

He seemed surprised to see her and she misunderstood. "What? Did you think I was too scared to come home?"

"No," he said, taking a step back. "I was noticing how pretty you are this morning."

Right. She'd taken trouble with her hair and makeup. She hoped he didn't think it was for him. But deep inside of herself, she wondered if it was. Still, she could make the excuse that it was for the lawyer, which was also true.

"Something smells good."

"Blueberry breakfast scones, to thank you." And as an outlet for her nervous energy.

"You can thank me any day."

They were just coming out of the oven, and while she let them cool for a minute, she scrambled eggs and added them to the plate of bacon that was warming in the oven. He knew his way around her kitchen well enough to pour himself a coffee and top hers. He even knew the way she liked it. They sat at her table and shared breakfast.

He broke open a scone releasing a puff of steam, then slathered butter on it like a man who never has to watch his weight. And then he bit into it with strong, even, white teeth.

She watched him, somewhat amused. He chewed slowly and swallowed, and then he said, "I know you're the best cook in the world, but every time I taste something you've made, I rediscover that fact all over again."

She chuckled. "I am not the best cook in the world. Not even the best baker. But I'm not half bad."

She'd put off asking as long as she could. "Did Travis come by last night?"

"Not sure. I saw a truck pull in the drive around midnight, but it pulled out again and drove off. Could have been some-body turning around."

But she didn't think it was. His mast was high enough that it could be seen from her driveway.

"Did you get any sleep?"

He looked a little heavy-eyed. "Enough."

They finished their breakfast and he insisted on doing the dishes while she went to get ready for the big day.

Brooke had offered to lend her something, but she'd turned down the offer. She didn't want to look like someone else. She might be going to see a fancy lawyer, but she was going to look like Cleo who ran the bakery in Clamshell Bay. Okay, maybe it was Cleo with a bit of makeup on and nicer hair than usual, but her clothes would at least be her own.

She didn't have anything in her closet that screamed corporate Seattle, but hanging in her closet was a soft jersey wrap dress in a cranberry color that made her feel good. She wore it with the pearls that had been her mother's, and her grandmother's before that. The necklace was her connection to the women who had gone before her, and as she looked in the mirror, she made a silent promise to them that she would fight to keep what they'd built.

When she came out to the living area, Ethan was still there. She picked up her keys. "Well, I guess I'd better go. I'll probably be early, but I don't want to get caught in traffic and be late."

He was leaning back against the kitchen counter that he cleaned as well as she did. "Want some company?"

"You want to come to the lawyer's office with me?" She wanted so much to say yes, but she was starting to lean on Ethan. That couldn't be good.

She could tell he was biting back a smile. His eyes wrinkled up at the corners with the effort. "Nope. Won't even come in. Thought you might like company. I could do the driving and drop you off so you don't have to worry about finding parking. Also, so you don't have to walk far in those heels."

He must see that heels were unfamiliar. She felt like she was tottering. Still, the pumps made her feel taller and more professional.

She was about to refuse, in that reflexive way she had, and then his words from last night came back to her. She was always the one who offered help to others. Maybe it was time for her to accept some help for a change. She smiled and held out her keys. "I would love some company. I don't really want to drive in these heels."

His eyes lit up and she thought he was genuinely pleased that she was letting him come along. She tucked that idea away for later when she had more time to think and wasn't so nervous. "What about Delilah?"

"Delilah's fed and watered and we had an hour of playtime when the rest of the world was sleeping. Janet Beamish sold me a tent thing for cats. She's in there with her toys, extra food and water and a litter box. She'll be fine."

She grabbed the file folder of everything she thought she might need. She didn't own a briefcase, but she did have a canvas shopping bag and that would have to do.

Okay, maybe she spent the first five minutes of the trip making sure he was a good driver, and then when she realized he was perfectly at home in her vehicle, she let herself relax as much as she could on this awful morning.

"What do you think she'll say?"

"Impossible to predict. But Kyle says she's the one you want on your side, and Kyle's usually right about these things."

"I'm sure he is, but I feel bad for Oliver Egan. Maybe our local lawyer can do as good a job."

"Cleo, this is a get-to-know-you meeting. Kyle set it up, but you're in charge. You'll choose this lawyer or you'll choose the one in Clamshell Bay, or maybe you'll hire them both. The point is, you'll have a couple of opinions and a choice in representation."

That was so eminently sensible that she couldn't argue. By the time they got close to Seattle, traffic was clogging up and they slowed and crawled and stopped and crawled a little more.

"I'm so glad I don't live in a big city," she said with relief.

"And I'm glad I don't have to anymore."

They found their way to Fourth Avenue and cruised past the building. It was exactly what she'd expected. Tall and sleek with tinted windows that didn't open and the kind of cool professionalism that had no soul. In her imagination the tower was like a big middle finger flipping the bird to the little people on the streets of Seattle.

They both glanced at the clock. "You're half an hour early. That's good."

"Half an hour more for me to be nervous."

They hit a red light and he turned to her and put his hand over hers where they were clenched in her lap. "Hey. You're the client here."

She felt small and foolish, but she asked anyway. "Would you come in with me?"

He was so surprised he leaned back against the door. "You sure?"

She nodded emphatically. "I'm so rattled I'm afraid I won't remember what she says. You could be like a second pair of ears. Maybe even make some notes."

He seemed to think about it and then nodded. "Sure. I'll be your personal secretary."

She liked the sound of that. "My executive assistant."

"A promotion. Already."

"I think we'd better get parked or we'll go from early to late."

By the time they found parking and walked back, there was still ten minutes to spare. They rode up to the twentieth floor. The office was cool and plush and discreet and everything about it looked expensive, from the well-groomed receptionist who immediately offered them everything from a cappuccino to green tea to the leather club chairs and the magazines fanned perfectly on the glossy hardwood tables.

After a few minutes, when she tried not to fidget and pretend interest in the most recent copy of *Forbes* when she'd have been more soothed by a cooking magazine, a young woman in a navy-blue suit came quietly forward with a big smile on her face.

"I'm Leanna, Bethany's executive assistant. She's ready to see you now."

She didn't dare look at Ethan, her fake executive assistant, certain they'd both start laughing if she did. He might not be wearing a suit, but she was happy to have him at her side, as though she had a cheerleader in her corner. Even though this lawyer was going to be paid to be on her side, she still felt that she needed the support.

They were led down a quiet corridor to a conference room that could seat a dozen, with big windows that gave her an excellent view of downtown Seattle. She chose a seat in the middle of the table and Ethan settled beside her. "Hey," he reminded her softly, once the assistant had left, "you're going to be fine."

She reached out blindly for his hand, glad of the warm comfort.

The woman who walked in, also in a navy blue suit—did they buy them in bulk?—appeared no-nonsense and tough. She was probably a few years older than Cleo with perfectly styled blond hair. Her smile was brief as though it, too, was paid by the hour.

Her eyes flicked to Ethan in surprise, but she held out her hand to Cleo and introduced herself as Bethany Lane.

"I'm Cleo Duvall, obviously, and this is my friend Ethan. He's here for moral support."

The woman glanced at him again, and then Cleo saw the second the penny dropped and she realized who this Ethan was. She was too much of a pro to say anything stupid like, "I used to watch you in *Badminton Run*," but more than ever Cleo was glad she'd brought him. Sure, Kyle the billionaire had made the introduction, but having a sexy former celebrity taking notes didn't hurt either in presenting her as a client to be taken seriously.

Bethany Lane took a seat across from where they were sitting and placed a notepad and recorder in front of her.

The woman wasted no time on pleasantries as she said, "Kyle Donovan told me a little bit about what's going on. But I'd like you to tell me the whole story from the beginning. Take your time."

Cleo drew a breath and haltingly at first and then with more animation told the story of how she'd met Travis, fallen for him, married him. She explained about the bakery and the land and her house, how hard her mother and she had worked, which then sounded like a stupid thing to say. The lawyer didn't care about that. She tried to keep emotion out of her voice, but she felt the anger threaten to choke her. She was aware of Ethan, sitting quietly by her side, hearing the story of how she'd been duped like a naïve spinster.

The attorney glanced up occasionally, and then back to where she was taking notes. Cleo looked at the recorder, a silent witness, and imagined some poor assistant having to type up every foolish thing she said.

"And what did he bring to the marriage?" Bethany asked her.

She'd been such a fool. But it did no good to mention it, they all knew it or she wouldn't be here. "A beaten-up truck and a sense of entitlement."

She didn't get so much as a grin out of Bethany Lane. "And you had no prenup?"

"No." Again, she could have spent half an hour explaining that she'd still been grieving, hadn't been herself, but there was no justification. She'd been a fool and she knew it.

"Children?"

"No." She'd pretty much given up on kids when she met Travis and once she was married, she'd never imagined trying for one. Had she known, deep down, that the marriage wouldn't last? Travis had never brought up the subject either. Maybe because he was too much of a child to ever take responsibility for a baby.

Bethany asked a lot of the same questions the lawyer had yesterday. How long had they been married, what had he contributed, when exactly did he leave and what had she done to find him.

"I did try to find him. Obviously, I was going to divorce him. But he seemed to have disappeared. I thought he was completely out of my life. Until he showed up again."

"So, you didn't file a petition for divorce?"

"No. I didn't plan to marry again so I put him out of my mind, I guess."

The sharp look the woman sent her could almost be pity. Almost.

She told the lawyer about him coming back the day before yesterday, claiming he wanted to move back in with her.

"And you don't want that?"

"No." What she meant was, hell no. "I want a divorce." She swallowed hard. "He left me for another woman, didn't have the guts or courtesy to even tell me. Now he's lying about it, pretending we were just taking some space. I want him out of my life in every possible way." She leaned forward, cut to the chase. "How much is it going to cost me to get rid of him?"

Bethany put down her gold pen and looked at her notes for a minute as though they might talk back to her. Then she took a breath and leaned back in her chair and addressed both of them.

"Division of property isn't straightforward. A judge would look at the length of the marriage, separate property, such as what each of you owned before the marriage, and co-mingled property. He may claim alimony. We can try to negotiate a reasonable settlement, but if it goes to court, a judge will ulti-mately decide."

The injustice burned in her gut. "But it's so unfair. How can he try to get money from me after treating me so badly?"

"It's up to us to fight for you and minimize any settlement you have to make on him."

The burning in her gut grew worse. "What's your best guess?"

The woman shook her head. "Just because you brought property into the marriage doesn't mean that a judge wouldn't award a significant amount of that to your spouse. I would advise you to file a petition for divorce as soon as possible. I will do my best for you, and I am very good at my job."

"This is a nightmare."

Bethany nodded briskly. "Not the first time I've heard those words in this room. And I doubt it will be the last. If you decide to hire me, I'll do everything I can for you."

"I can't believe I'm going to have to pay the man who humiliated and deserted me." She seemed to run out of questions and run out of steam, and with a restrained thank you and goodbye, she shook the woman's hand and she and Ethan left.

They didn't say a word all the way through that opulent lobby and down in the quiet hush of the elevator. Her unfamiliar heels clicked in the marble foyer and then they were out on the noisy street.

"You okay?" Ethan asked quietly beside her.

"I want to hit something. I want to get into a boxing ring and beat people up."

He smiled down at her. "I'm willing. If you want to take a punch at me, I promise not to fight back."

"You're too easy."

"All men aren't like him," he said, turning to her.

She breathed in, deeply, and out again. "I know."

There were good men in the world, she knew that. Men like Ethan. Too bad she hadn't married one of them.

Ethan watched Cleo stomp along as though her fancy heels were army boots. Did she even know how fast she was walking? As though she might be able to speed walk past this difficult period in her life. He thought of her in that pretty cottage, and then imagined the despicable Travis Smith darkening the door-way. "Don't go back there tonight."

She stopped dead in the middle of a busy Seattle sidewalk, causing a couple of millennials to swear and navigate around them, earbuds firmly implanted in their ears. "What?"

He felt a sense of urgency. "What you need is some perspective. Let's stay the night here in Seattle."

"Why would I do that?"

"We could start with lunch. It's after noon. Then, I don't know, go up the Space Needle. Do some shopping."

"You think I want to go shopping?"

"So you wouldn't have to see Travis, and possibly end up in jail for assault, and to take a breather. When's the last time you got away from Clamshell Bay?"

She looked confused. "I don't know. A few months, I guess."

Her face was drawn into tense lines and she looked so sad that he couldn't stop himself. He pulled her closer, leaned down and kissed her.

"Get a room," an irate delivery guy said, veering around them. Her eyes gleamed with sudden humor. He answered her with a grin of his own. "See? Even the FedEx guy agrees with me. How about I book us a swanky hotel for the night. There are some great hotels here in Seattle. Wonderful restaurants. I'll even take you to some bakeries so you can snoop."

She looked as though she were considering it and then shook her head. "Honestly, I'm not in the mood."

He felt as though she'd stabbed him in the chest. "Not in the mood now? Or ever?"

They resumed walking. "Not today. I feel like I need to be in Clamshell Bay so I can protect my home and my bakery from Travis."

He did understand and she hadn't completely turned him down. There was hope. "At least come for dinner on *Vagabond*."

"It's still docked at my place. We'll both spend the whole

time looking over our shoulders for Travis leering through the window or trying to break in."

And there he was again. Travis No Good Smith. Standing between them. About the biggest buzzkill in the world.

"Maybe this isn't meant to be," she wailed.

"Oh no. It's meant to be." He wasn't sure of many things, but of him and Cleo he was certain. "We can sail *Vagabond* back to the marina. We'll have some wine and relax. I don't believe you checked out the master cabin. The bed in there is every bit as big as yours. And very comfortable." If she didn't mind having her hair chewed by a kitten. Probably best not to mention that. "I can sleep in the other cabin if you don't want to pick up where we left off yesterday morning." He wanted to make love to Cleo as much as he wanted to draw his next breath, but he also wanted it to be right. "And when you hear from your lawyer, you'll know how to proceed."

"I haven't even chosen a lawyer yet. That woman was great and everything. Very sharp and professional, but I feel more comfortable with Oliver Egan."

She had a point. "And I'm guessing nobody will fight harder for you than a guy who's been eating your cinnamon buns and dipping your excellent French bread into his stew for decades."

"Exactly."

This wasn't a decision he needed to be part of. He'd given her another option with Kyle's help. He trusted Cleo to know her own business.

"At least let me buy you lunch," he said.

She nodded. "Okay. Lunch would be good."

They didn't go anywhere fancy, he could tell it wasn't right, but they found a bistro where she ate a salad, and he pulled up a few choice stories from his years on *Badminton Run*, show disasters, the time a supposedly trained dog bit a cameraman, anything to ease the look of strain on her face.

When they got back to the car, it was after two and she

chucked off her heels and dug out a pair of running shoes from the back somewhere. She got back into the passenger seat, dipped her head back against the headrest and let out a huge sigh. "I am so glad that is over."

He started the car and maneuvered out of the parking lot.

"Thanks for understanding that I need to get home."

Home. Not a concept that meant a lot to him. As they drove out of Seattle, he said, "You know, I have houses."

She'd been checking her phone, now she glanced over at him. "Okay. You mean the things you build for your charitable foundation?"

"No." He didn't know why he'd brought up his houses. What was he doing? Bragging? He wasn't even certain what he wanted to tell her, but he blundered on anyway, feeling her enquiring gaze on him. "Didn't want you to think I had no solid base."

"Okay," she said again, still sounding puzzled. "We've got the whole drive back to Clamshell Bay. Why don't you tell me about your houses?"

She was right, it would pass the time and maybe he'd figure out what he was trying to say when he started talking. He thought back to the first one. Best to go in chronological order. "The first house was in LA, of course." He chuckled, thinking of how he'd felt when he first walked through the gates as the owner. "Frankie fell in love with it. Very old Hollywood with expansive lawns and a pool big enough for the Olympics." He glanced over. "She got the house in the divorce, which was fine by me. I was done with Hollywood by then." He remembered walking out through the gate that last time as clearly as he remembered first entering the grounds of the place he'd called home for four years. He hadn't so much as glanced behind him for a final look.

"And then you went traveling?"

"Not right away. I wanted a place I could get away to but

far from LA. Oh, and I wanted to be by the ocean. I bought a place in the Caribbean and my first sailboat. I still have Las Brisas. It's not fancy, but it's where I stopped being Nick Badminton and started to figure out who Ethan Crisp was. I learned to sail, got my SCUBA certification, read a million books. Grew a beard."

"Did it work? Did you find yourself?"

He thought about it. "I found out that I didn't want to spend the rest of my life playing. I traveled some more. Bought a house in New Zealand. High on a bluff overlooking the ocean. I thought I might settle there, but after a couple of years my father got sick. I came back. Spent some time with him and my mom." He glanced over at her. "I'm telling you the story of my life."

"And I'm fascinated," she assured him. She glanced at her phone and put it down on her lap.

He never droned on like this about himself. What was wrong with him? Well, she seemed like she wanted to hear it and maybe he needed to tell his story. With houses acting like chapters. "Now that Dad was gone, Mom wanted to live in Maine. She had a sister there. My aunt Betsy. They lived together in a house in Portsmouth and I bought a place on the coast. I spent a lot of time there until Mom passed a couple of years back. Then I bought *Vagabond*."

"Which of those houses is home?" she asked. Excellent question.

"I don't know. Whichever one I'm living in, I guess." Even saying that made him feel twitchy, like he was missing something everybody else knew.

They kept driving and Cleo kept checking her phone until finally he put his hand over hers. "Turn it off."

She glanced up at him looking startled. "Excuse me?"

"I know what you're doing. You're either worried that your assistant can't handle the bakery, when we both know she can, or you're wondering if either lawyer has come back to you with a plan yet. It's too early."

She went from rigid annoyance to unwilling understanding. "I hate having my fate in other people's hands."

His lips twitched in spite of himself. "Hadn't noticed."

"Fine," she said, making a dramatic production out of turning her phone off and shoving it in her bag.

"That's better."

They listened to music, chatted when they felt like it, were quiet when they didn't and the miles rolled by.

They were almost back at Clamshell Bay when Cleo suddenly stiffened. "I was having such a good time I forgot to turn my phone on."

He turned and looked at her. "And I'm guessing the world didn't end."

"We won't know until I get my phone back on and get some reception, now will we?" But she was smiling when she said it.

Cell reception came and went as they got closer to Clamshell Bay. And then he heard a few electronic tones that suggested she had messages. She looked down at it and punched a few buttons, and then frowned. "That's weird. There's a message from Kyle. He wants us to come over tonight." She glanced up. "He must have got my number from Brooke."

"Kyle needs to get a life. Doesn't he have anybody else he can cook steak for and entertain at his fancy beach house?"

She shook her head looking puzzled. "I don't think it's a party."

"What does it say?"

She read aloud, "Come over tonight at seven. Got something to show you. Bring Ethan."

"For a guy with a communications company, he could work on his communication skills."

"What do you think it is? What do you think he wants?"

"I don't know. Maybe he's bought a new boat he wants to show off."

"Do we have to go? I feel so tired."

"We'll go at seven, stay ten minutes, congratulate him on whatever new toy he's showing us, and then we'll be on our way."

He realized he was using the word *we* as though they were a couple, but at least she didn't call him on it. She nodded and put her head back again against the headrest. He liked her face. Even in profile while she was looking worried, he liked her face.

Even though Cleo and Ethan had stuck with the idea that Kyle wanted to show them some new purchase, she didn't believe that for a second. She didn't think Ethan did either. But what would Kyle want with her? She barely knew the man. Was his wife in some kind of crisis? But then why hadn't Brooke called her? She'd tried to call Brooke and got voicemail, which puzzled her even more.

Had he found an editor who was interested in her sob story? Maybe they wanted to interview her about what a dupe she'd been. She couldn't imagine putting herself through that, even if it might help other women.

She insisted on going back to her place and changing into clothes she felt more comfortable in. There was no sign that Travis had been by but that didn't mean anything. She was going to have to buy a surveillance camera, something she'd never wanted to own or thought she'd need.

Once she'd changed into comfy jeans, sandals, and a soft cotton T-shirt, she felt better. Even though there'd been no messages from Pepper, she called to check in before the bakery closed.

"How did it go?" her assistant asked.

"Fine, I guess." Though she felt hollowed out inside from the trip to the attorney who hadn't delivered any better news than Oliver Egan had. "How are things at the bakery?"

"Not too busy." She didn't want to ask about Travis but luckily Pepper wasn't shy about mentioning his name. "Travis walked past this morning but he didn't come inside. I haven't seen him since. I don't think anyone has."

Was that good news or bad? She didn't even know anymore. "Great, I'll see you tomorrow."

"Boss, I think you need to take a couple days off. Me and Stacey can handle things fine." Before Cleo could protest, Pepper lowered her voice. "Seriously, I think Stacey really needs the money. Her husband's out of work again and they have medical bills."

"Oh, no. I'm sorry to hear that." She thought about it for a minute and then decided she did need a few days off. She had to prepare for a legal battle. "Okay." Stacey wouldn't want charity any more than Cleo would. "Tell her I called and sounded super stressed and asked if she could work for two or three more days."

"You're a good person, Cleo," Pepper said.

Her heart lightened a little. "So are you."

Once she got off the phone, she realized that Stacey was doing her a favor. She did need a few days off. And, if she could put Travis out of her mind for a few hours, maybe she could enjoy time with the most interesting man she'd met in forever.

"Everything okay?" he asked when she caught up with him outside, checking that the potting shed remained a skunk-free zone.

"Yep. I even scored myself a couple of days off."

His eyes turned warm and sexy. He came closer, looped his arms around her. "That is most excellent news. Any ideas how you might like to spend them?"

She tilted her face up to his. "A few."

When he put his mouth on hers, she felt a rush of passion stronger than any she ever remembered. When they finally pulled apart, she was breathless. As much as she wanted to take Ethan to her bedroom, she didn't want to be distracted thinking Travis might show up at any moment. For all she knew he'd been lurking somewhere waiting for her to return. "Let's go to your boat," she said. "And sail away from here."

Naturally, the minute they were aboard, Delilah let them know in loud and piteous tones that she had not appreciated being left alone. Ethan had added a cat tent to his supply of feline necessities, but the kitten bounced out as soon as the door was open and leaped onto Ethan's feet. "She doesn't like solitary confinement," Cleo said.

"Who does?" Ethan fussed over the cat while Cleo went into the galley to put on coffee.

Ethan came up behind her and kissed the nape of her neck. "I'll get the engine going and we'll dock at the marina. As soon as we're finished at Kyle's, I am going to show you my state-room." He put his lips against her ear. "I give a very thorough tour."

"Must be quite the stateroom," she replied, feeling like they'd been toying with each other for days.

"You'd be amazed. The tour could take hours. Days."

She shivered, her whole body aching for him. "I have a few days off," she told him, trying to sound cool even as her voice came out husky with passion. "And I can take a few more if I need to." And instead of feeling guilty about taking a break, she could feel good about herself for doing Stacey a favor.

"Good," said the man behind her. "I have plans for you." Then, he said, "Come on, Delilah. Let's get the engine going."

"Wait, how will we get to Kyle's? My car's here. I should pick you up later."

He shook his head. "Come with me. We'll cab back together

and get your car. Trust me, an ocean cruise is exactly what you need."

"Oh, all right."

It wasn't a long journey, but Cleo settled back lengthwise on the padded bench which had been designed so it was like a lounger. She put her feet up, leaned back and closed her eyes. The late afternoon sun was warm, the boat engine puttered along to its own rhythm. Delilah, robbed of her hero, deigned to step daintily onto Cleo's lap and then climbed up her midriff to sprawl across her chest and fall noisily asleep, her purring harmonizing with the boat's engine.

Cleo wouldn't have believed she could find peace in the midst of chaos, but somehow, she did. When she felt herself drifting to sleep, she didn't try to fight it.

She woke when Ethan slowed the engine. They were approaching the marina. She shifted the sleeping kitten, then got up to tie the fenders in place and grabbed a dock line as Ethan pulled up alongside the dock. She jumped lightly down and secured the aft line, while he cut the engine and joined her, tying the stern line.

"Nice work," he said to her. "If you ever want to crew on as a deckhand..."

She laughed. "I'll keep that in mind." Sun was dancing on the water's surface but it was nothing to the expression dancing in Ethan's eyes.

"We're here," he said, glancing at his watch. "With an hour to spare. Lots of time to cab back, get your car and head to Kyle's."

"I hope it's good news," she said.

"Kyle's not one to waste anybody's time, least of all his own. Come on. I'll get Delilah settled and we'll head out."

Not being able to bear the sad, beseeching, kitten eyes that stared out of the tent, making her feel remorseful, she said to Ethan, "Okay. Ten minutes at Kyle's and then we come back here. You cook dinner while I fuss over that poor cat."

"You know, I'm starting to think adopting that kitten was the best thing I ever did."

A warmth bloomed inside her somewhere around her chest. It was the first time he'd admitted that he and that kitten had bonded.

Even in the midst of all her misery she felt like good things were still happening in the world.

TWENTY-ONE

When they got to Brooke and Kyle's place, Ethan took her hand. She thought about pulling hers away and then thought, ah, what the hell. Everyone in town must know by now she was crazy about the guy.

And she was, she realized. In spite of her terrible history, she was crazy about the guy.

As though he'd realized the direction of her thoughts, he turned around and, before the door was even opened, leaned down and kissed her. It was a kiss full of promise and acceptance.

It was Kyle who threw open the door saying, "Good. Come in, come in." There was a sense of suppressed excitement about him.

Ethan said, "This better be good."

Kyle merely said, "You can decide for yourselves." And then he led them, not into the living room where they'd been before, but downstairs to a home movie theatre with a big screen and leather viewing seats.

Ethan shot him a suspicious glance. "You're taking us to the movies? Can I get popcorn?"

"Sit down and shut up."

Brooke came floating in looking elegant and fragile. "I'm so sorry I didn't get your messages. I was at the doctor." She didn't say any more, but Cleo had to wonder if she'd gone for another fertility treatment. She was so wrapped up with her own troubles she forgot other people had them too. She wished she'd stopped to bring some bread or something nourishing for Brooke. Instead of glowing with life, she seemed to be getting thinner.

Kyle ushered them into seats and then said, "This is raw footage of an investigative piece one of our news teams is working on."

She settled beside Ethan, and to her surprise he took her hand again. Maybe he knew she needed the comfort. She felt jangled and nervous.

And then the screen sprang to life. It looked like TV news, one of those reports where somebody's being hounded by the press and doesn't want to talk to them. To her surprise, she saw Travis on screen. He was clearly in Clamshell Bay. He was standing in front of the bakery. *Slimeball.* She hoped he hadn't gone in and bothered anybody.

While all these thoughts were tumbling in her head, a reporter's voice off-camera said, "Travis Smith?"

Her no-good husband turned and with an easy grin, said, "Yeah. Who wants to know?" She could see his gaze shift and a puzzled frown replace the grin. He must have spotted the camera. "What's going on?"

The guy identified himself as Timothy Zussman, Washington Shore News. "We're doing a feature on bigamy. Wondering how it feels to be married to two women at the same time." The words were so easy, as though he were giving a weather report. *Bigamy?* What? She felt as though she couldn't breathe.

Travis looked like he was having the same problem. The

easy grin faded into a look of cold fury. "Don't know what you're talking about," and he turned his back on the reporter.

"Bigamy, Mr. Smith. It's when the same person is married more than once without getting divorced." As though Travis might be unfamiliar with the term.

She turned to Kyle who sent her a thumbs up. Oh, he looked pleased with himself.

The reporter followed and yelled to Travis's back, "I have here a marriage certificate for a Travis Smith, married to Delores Esposito in New York. But there's no record of divorce. And then the same Travis marries Cleo Duvall four years later. Do you have a comment?"

Travis took a step away and then turned back. He looked angry but also a little frightened. "Lots of guys have the same name. I was only ever married once to Cleo Duvall and we're still husband and wife."

"Don't think so. My colleague showed Delores Esposito your photograph and she identified you as her husband. She gave me a message that you should call her. Your wife misses you."

The footage changed now to Delores Esposito, a woman about the same age as Cleo, with big brown eyes and dark curly hair. As she told the story of meeting and marrying Travis Smith, an entrepreneur, she went from tearful to angry. Her story was amazingly similar to Cleo's. He'd wooed her fast, promised her a bright future, even taken her to look at fancy houses they'd buy. She showed off a sizeable engagement ring and her marriage certificate. "The ring turned out to be cubic zirconia," she told the camera. "And we never bought a house. After we got married, he lived off my earnings. And then he left one day, leaving me with a pile of debt."

Now back to Travis. Kyle paused the recording and said, "This will all be smoothed out for broadcast, just wanted you to see the raw footage. The team moved fast. I can't believe how quickly they figured out Travis Smith was a bigamist. Lucky break when they found Ms. Esposito. This is going to be great."

Great? Finding out she'd married a bigamist wasn't exactly comforting news.

Kyle pushed play and she watched as the reporter in Clamshell Bay laid out the facts. Travis tried to walk away and the guy jumped in front of him, pushing a big microphone at him repeating, "What do you have to say for yourself? What would you like the women of America to know? Do you have anything to say to your wives?" And he really emphasized that word *wives* so that the s on the end slithered across the airwaves like a snake.

"Get out of my way."

It was fascinating watching Travis look so unsure of himself. The reporter tried one more time and then Travis roared, "Will you get out of my goddamn way?" And he walked forward. The camera quickly veered to him pushing a young reporter in the chest. The guy tripped on the curb and fell backwards. Travis didn't even pause, he kept walking.

The report went on for several more minutes, but she barely took any of it in. Bigamy. Felony. County Sheriff's Office. Words and phrases swirled in her head but they seemed to all say the same thing to Cleo. *How could you have been so stupid?*

Finally, when there was no more, they all sat there. She felt the three of them looking at her, waiting for a response. Finally, she said, her voice sounding wispy, "Is it true?"

"Timothy Zussman's the best investigative reporter we've got in Washington and the New York reporter's won awards. Oh, yeah. It's true. The team's doing a full feature on bigamists."

One bright thought poked through the rubble of ugliness. "So, if he was already married..." She couldn't finish the sentence in case she jinxed herself.

Kyle finished it for her. "Then you two were never legally

married. You're a free woman and Travis Smith could end up in jail."

She'd felt as though she were suffocating as Travis had stalked her and done his best to destroy all her peace and contentment. It would be a while before she found that calmness again, but the relief she felt almost made her nauseous. "You're sure? I mean, Travis was right, there are lots of people who have the same name."

"Trust me, it was him. There's more digging to be done, but after the i's are dotted and the t's are crossed, you're a free woman."

Kyle looked as pleased with himself as though he'd just made another billion dollars. Although he probably did that every day. He said, "You owe it all to Ethan, you know. He told me to put one of our best guys on Travis and investigate him. I figured we might turn up something, but bigamy? I owe you one, man. It's a win for both of us."

And yet why did it feel like a loss?

Ethan kept casting glances of understanding, but Kyle didn't seem to be clueing in. "I'm going to fetch champagne. And let's celebrate."

She shook her head, unable to even speak. It was Ethan who spoke up. "Can we take a raincheck? I've got a headache. I did a lot of driving today."

She was so grateful to him for taking the heat on himself.

Kyle glanced at both of them in surprise and then nodded, slowly, some of his satisfaction ebbing. "Sure. I'll keep the champagne on ice. We'll do it another time."

"Thanks." He stood up and she followed. "If you don't mind, I need to get some painkillers and lie down."

"Yeah. Sure. You all right to drive?"

"I can drive him," Cleo said quickly, before they found themselves being chauffeured by the all too happy Kyle.

They were about to leave when Kyle's cell phone rang. He

stopped them with a finger in the air. "I think you're going to want to hear this."

And then he answered the phone. Cleo looked at Ethan as though he might know what was going on and he only shrugged. Kyle nodded, looking very satisfied. He ended the call with, "No. Follow it up. Stay on the story. And thanks. Great job."

He threw a fist in the air, did an almost soft shoe dance. "I had my reporter waylay your ex one more time at the hotel where he was staying. But he was already gone."

Her heart lightened even more. "You're sure?"

"Oh yeah. There's some question as to whether he paid the bill before he left, but it's pretty clear he's not coming back. I've told the team to stay on top of him. The sheriff will want to talk to you."

"I understand." Maybe she'd reach out to Delores Esposito, another woman—one of how many?—who'd been duped by Travis Smith. "I don't need him to go to jail, only to leave me alone and stop using women."

"I'll keep you posted," Kyle said, "but I'm pretty sure your ex-not husband won't be bothering you again." He raised his hands. "You might want to get an annulment just for your peace of mind."

Her smile was grim. "Oh, I will."

She hugged Brooke on her way out and then they got in the car. The wind was whipping the waves into a frenzy, which pretty much matched her mood. Beside her, Ethan was quiet for a minute and then said, "He means well, you know."

How could he read her thoughts so accurately? She turned to look at him and saw such understanding in his eyes it almost undid her.

"I know. And he did such a good thing."

He nodded. Reached for her hand. "It's just that you had to face the fact that you married a bigamist."

She banged her fist against the steering wheel. "How is my judgment so off?"

"It isn't always off," he said softly.

"I have the worst taste in men!" she wailed.

There was a silence. "Again, maybe not all the time."

She turned to glance at him and wondered if he was even telling the truth. And then she let herself see beyond her own humiliation and anger. She squeezed his hand. "I'm sorry. You are one of the good guys."

"Not perfect. But I can show you my divorce decree if that helps."

She smiled in spite of herself. "Not necessary."

"As tactless as Kyle can be, he got one thing right. You're a free woman."

"Turns out I always was. Even when I thought I was married."

"Will you still come back to my boat?"

She thought about it and then shook her head. "Will you come back with me? To my cottage?"

"I will go with you anywhere."

She felt as though she'd been waiting for Ethan for a really long time. Her body might be out of practice, but she had a feeling they'd be good together, even if she knew it could only be for a little while.

"We should pick up the cat. She'll go crazy being left alone all this time."

So they drove to the marina and she waited in the car while he fetched the cat carrier. It seemed so domestic as they drove back out to her place. Ethan, her, and a one-eared pet kitten.

As the shock wore off, the relief finally sank in. Travis was out of her life forever, or very soon would be.

When they got back to her cottage, she didn't have to worry about a greedy ex waiting to pounce. She touched the pearls at her throat that she hadn't taken off. She hadn't let down her mother and grandmother after all. Would they approve of Ethan?

She watched him as he unzipped the cat carrier and let Delilah out. The cat raced around the room, then jumped up on the couch and leapt on a throw cushion as though it were a dangerous enemy.

Ethan stood there looking at her. "You okay?" She felt he was holding back, waiting to see how she wanted to spend the evening.

"Yes." She walked up to him, threw her arms around him and kissed him. And then she just let herself go. Not caring that her body was middle-aged and imperfect. Not caring that she had the hands and feet of a baker and the scars that went along with her profession. Ethan didn't seem to mind.

He undressed her slowly, like a man who had all the time in the world, pausing to kiss each part of her that he revealed until she was worried they'd be making love on the floor in her living room, and she wasn't quite ready for that. She took his hand and led him into her bedroom.

She put on only one of her bedside lamps so the light was dim. She'd have gone for complete darkness but she found she wanted to see him. As he had, she took her time undressing him. Her hands fumbled a bit when she got to his jeans and he ended up taking over and shucking them off himself. She felt that his patience was coming to an end and that lit a fire in her.

When they were naked, he touched her everywhere, and when they made love, it wasn't with the mad passion of youth but with the knowledge that this was something special.

Something real.

TWENTY-TWO

Cleo woke up the next morning almost startled to find a man in her bed. Then the night came back to her and she smiled and moved over, wrapping her arm around his warm torso and placing her head on his chest. He was still half asleep when he brought his arm around and pulled her even closer.

She lay there for a while, letting her head rise and fall on his chest in the rhythm of his breathing, like a boat bobbing on the ocean, but after a time she grew restless and got out of bed. She was such an early riser it was nearly impossible to sleep in. Besides, she was filled with energy. She closed the bedroom door quietly behind her and went into the kitchen. Delilah roused and came to investigate, rubbing against her ankles. She hadn't been pleased to be shut out of the bedroom last night but she seemed to be in a forgiving mood. Cleo gave Delilah some food and water and then put muffins on to bake and a pot of coffee on.

Some time later, Ethan came out of her bedroom in nothing but boxer shorts. He was still a very nice looking man. Long and lean like a runner. He stretched, "A man could get used to waking up to the smell of coffee and fresh baking," he said.

She made a light reply, but deep down she thought he probably wouldn't. And that was okay. It was okay for things not to be forever. He'd given her so much joy. She had to be prepared that it would end, and it would end soon. He'd been nothing but honest with her from the beginning. This wasn't a forever kind of guy.

And she was a forever kind of woman.

The sun was shining and so they took their coffee and muffins out to the gazebo. The cat chased a butterfly and then, trying to jump and catch it, fell and sneezed, which made them both laugh.

After breakfast, she got calls from Megan and Libby, both calling to check in to see how she was feeling and to congratulate her on being free. Libby understood best what she was going through. "No one wants to be lied to by the man they trust with their heart," she said, sounding sad.

"Exactly. And it's made me trust myself and my judgment."

"I think you are older and wiser now and your judgment is just fine." Libby, who was so often tentative about giving her opinion, sounded very firm. Ethan's name wasn't mentioned but the message was clear. In choosing him, she wasn't making a mistake.

She settled against Ethan and he put an arm around her. "This is a beautiful spot," he said. "No wonder you love it."

"I do."

He gazed at her and said, "Cleo Duvall." And then he looked at her curiously. "For Cleopatra? You certainly are regal and like a queen."

She laughed. "Don't forget my mom was a hippy. Cleo was from Cleodora. I think she was a Greek goddess or a river god or something. My mother always said Cleo was for glory and Dora was her gift."

"So a gift of glory. That's nice." He said, "Cleodora, come with me."

She wasn't even sure what he was asking, but her heart rate sped up anyway. "Come with you where?"

"On my boat. You, me, and Delilah. We can go anywhere we want. Do anything we like."

"What about the bakery?"

"Don't you think Pepper could manage?"

"Probably." In fact, Pepper was getting better every day and she'd really stepped up when Cleo had been troubled by Travis. Maybe giving her a try on her own wasn't such a bad idea. It would be nice not to be quite so tied to that bakery. Stacey would be delighted to have some extra work.

"But what about your charity projects?"

"I have a staff of people who run them much better than I could."

"Don't you ever get bored?"

His eyes were intense when he turned to her. "I'm not saying we'll spend the whole time onboard *Vagabond*. Yeah, I get bored. Then I do something else. Cleo, I want to show you all the places in the world that are beautiful and amazing. I want to feed you croissants in Paris and baklava in Greece and dumplings in Vietnam."

She felt like he was offering her the whole world on a platter. But after fifty-two years, she knew herself.

She glanced up and said, "I would be delighted to travel with you on your boat, or anywhere you like." She reached for his hand and held it between both of hers. "For three weeks."

His smile was bittersweet. "You did warn me."

"I'm too old to change."

"Three weeks, huh?"

He looked out at the dancing waves and then back at her. "Cleo, a lot can happen in three weeks."

A LETTER FROM THE AUTHOR

Dear Reader,

Thanks for reading *The Bakery at Clamshell Bay*. While the Clamshell Bay stories are fiction, they are inspired by my experiences and those of my friends. As women, we bond and support each other by sharing our stories with laughter and sometimes a few tears. I wouldn't have made it through some of the tough times without my friends, my Cleo and Libby and Megan and Brooke. I really love hearing from readers like you. You're welcome to drop me a line at Sara@SaraJaneBailey.com.

If you'd like to join other readers in keeping in touch, here are two options. Stay in the loop with my new releases by clicking on the link below. Or sign up to my personal email newsletter on the link at the bottom of this note. I'd be delighted if you choose to sign up to either – or both!

www.stormpublishing.co/sara-jane-bailey

If you enjoyed reading *The Bakery at Clamshell Bay* and could spare a few moments to leave a review, that would be hugely appreciated. Even a short review can make all the difference in encouraging a reader to discover my books for the first time. Thank you so much!

Join other readers in hearing about my writing (and life) experiences, and other bonus content.

www.sarajanebailey.com/newsletter

I hope to see you in Clamshell Bay again soon,

Sara Jane

Made in United States
North Haven, CT
24 September 2023

41912545R00145